free fall

Jenefer Shute is the author of *Life-Size* and *Sex Crimes*. She lives in New York, where she teaches at Hunter College of the City University of New York.

By the same author

Life-Size
Sex Crimes

free fall

JENEFER SHUTE

Secker & Warburg

LONDON

Published by Secker & Warburg 2002

2 4 6 8 10 9 7 5 3 1

Copyright © Jenefer Shute 2002

Jenefer Shute has asserted her right under the Copyright, Designs
and Patents Act 1988 to be identified as the author of this work

Passages from *The Black Box*, ed. Malcolm MacPherson, are reprinted by
kind permission of HarperCollins Publishers Inc., New York.

First published in Great Britain in 2002 by
Secker & Warburg
Random House, 20 Vauxhall Bridge Road,
London SW1V 2SA

Random House Australia (Pty) Limited
20 Alfred Street, Milsons Point, Sydney,
New South Wales 2061, Australia

Random House New Zealand Limited
18 Poland Road, Glenfield,
Auckland 10, New Zealand

Random House (Pty) Limited
Endulini, 5A Jubilee Road, Parktown 2193, South Africa

The Random House Group Limited Reg. No. 954009
www.randomhouse.co.uk

A CIP catalogue record for this book
is available from the British Library

ISBN 0-436-20586-6

Papers used by Random House are natural,
recyclable products made from wood grown in sustainable forests;
the manufacturing processes conform to the environmental
regulations of the country of origin

Typeset by Palimpsest Book Production Limited,
Polmont, Stirlingshire
Printed and bound in Great Britain by
Mackays of Chatham PLC, Chatham, Kent

The simulator is one of a range of training devices which can supplement airborne experience. Every effort must be made to select and use the appropriate device.

We can produce only a very limited subset of the information available in the real world but this subset, while potentially useful to some individuals, may not be appropriate to others. Fortunately the human being is very adaptable, and the world is full of redundant information.

—*Flight Simulation*,
eds J.M. Rolfe and K.J. Staples

1

Wednesday, July 19

———

This story begins in an undignified position.

I was doing the Downward Facing Dog when I heard the news, trying, in that inverted stance, to find relief from the G-forces of the day. Remaining upright, my body had begun to remind me, was a belated aspiration in our species, a constant, subliminal source of strain. The Dog was supposed to undo all this, undo gravity itself. But as I strove, on the living-room rug, to achieve serenity, I was distracted by a twinge of tendonitis in my left Achilles and by the cat who, wanting attention, began butting my outstretched arms, threatening to bring the whole Dog down.

Through the open window came the usual, muted roar of the city, soundtrack of my summer nights. Then—or at least this is how I recall it—a succession of car doors slammed in the street below, people shouted their noisy goodbyes, the traffic lights changed on Amsterdam Ave, and, in the relative hush that followed, I could hear the quiet, chatty voice of the kitchen radio. It had, I realized, been prattling all along. In tonight's top story, it said, the Coast Guard and other emergency services are still searching the waters off Long Island, where Flight FIN 770, bound for London, crashed at 8:32 this evening, apparently after exploding in mid-air.

Shit, I thought, scrambling in a graceless, amphibian manner to my feet, London. I wish I knew, I wish she'd told me, which flight she was leaving on. It probably wasn't that one, I reasoned—what were the odds, given the number of flights from JFK to London every day?—but still, I wished I knew for sure. My mother, I did know, insisted on flying FIN whenever she traveled, which wasn't often these days. She'd racked up a stash of frequent-flier miles on a European trip years ago, before my father died, and had remained loyal ever since, not understanding that the miles too were mortal, that, unused, they expired.

Anna would know, I thought, shuffling into the bedroom and glancing at the clock, but it was, what, 5 a.m. in Johannesburg, too early to call, barring an actual emergency. Well, this might be one, I thought, and then immediately quashed the idea. Of course it wasn't. The odds were against it. Reason was against it. And since when had my life been a disaster movie, featuring fiery crashes into the Atlantic? The disasters so far had been small and private, disasters of the heart.

Anyway, if I called Anna now, that would, in itself, constitute high drama. In the normal course of events, my sister and I spoke on the telephone precisely four times a year: her birthday, my birthday, Christmas, and New Year. On these occasions, we exchanged stilted greetings, benign disinformation about our health and our careers, polite queries about, on the one hand, her daughters, and, on the other, my cat. We'd usually compare the weather, too, as this was a reliable topic: whatever it was in New York, it would be the exact opposite in the southern hemisphere; wow, each of us would say, we could really use some of that [snow/sunshine] here right now!

I went back to the living room and thought about resuming the Dog, but found I now lacked patience for yoga practice, lacked patience even for Ella, who'd collapsed coquettishly on the rug, presenting her soft white belly for petting. Ignoring the cat, who flipped irritably to her feet and stalked off, I walked back into the kitchen and began fiddling with the radio, feeling, superstitiously, that the news would be true only if it came from the same source.

In tonight's air tragedy, the announcer said—sounding incongruously smug—rescue workers are still searching an area fifteen miles off the coast of Long Island, in water 120 feet deep, for survivors of the crash of Flight FIN 770. Some two hundred passengers and seventeen crew members are believed to have been aboard the Boeing 747, bound for London, which plunged into the ocean at 8:30 this evening. No survivors have yet been found, the Coast Guard commander reported, adding that rescue units were "hopeful," though fire and darkness were hampering their efforts. Eyewitnesses reported a mid-air explosion, a fireball . . .

I switched the radio off. It was getting on for 11:30, late for a weeknight. I should just go to sleep, call my sister in the morning, and confirm that it had indeed been a false alarm, that my mother, Eleanor Lilian Roth, had been on another flight, had arrived safely in London, and had made it, through perilous hordes of pickpockets and white-slave traders, to her hotel, where the room, sadly, had not been up to snuff—unclean in some way—and she'd had to request another.

Yes, that was clearly the logical thing to do. So, mechanically, I flossed and brushed my teeth, smoothed on the moisturizer that smelled like peach parfait, and did some kind of facial exercise that Lauren had showed me (a death's-head grimace, repeated sixty times, that was supposed to prevent the jaw from sagging, though it seemed to be anyway). I pulled on my silk boxers and Lucky Strike T-shirt, relic of some boyfriend long gone, checked that the front door was indeed bolted, and slipped beneath the sheets. Ella leapt up, with a chirp, and settled herself on the pillow, appropriating most of it. Next to the bed were the collected stories of Chekhov, which I was finding rather dull, and a thriller about genetic engineering, which I was finding rather dumb. I'd picked it up last week at O'Hare, waiting for a connection to Bloomington, Indiana, to conduct a focus group on hairspray. I caught airplanes like buses, I realized, never thinking (or allowing myself to think) that they might crash. Well, a bus might crash too, I thought; a brick might fall off a building and smash my skull.

Just go to sleep, I thought, clicking off the lamp. Tomorrow you have the meeting with the team from Gillette. I clicked the lamp on again, checked, neurotically, that the alarm was indeed set for seven, and let the room lapse back into darkness. Ella, disgruntled by all this moving around, resettled herself on the pillow, plopping her haunches on my hair, as if to prevent me from lifting my head again. Feeling the warmth and vibration of the cat's body through my skull, the comforting and proprietary tangle of her paws in my curls, I closed my eyes and tried to breathe—something, according to my yoga teacher, I didn't do very well. My breath came short and shallow, and, in the thin, watery night behind my eyelids, I saw flashes of light. Flares. Pinwheels. Fiery pinwheels, plummeting, in pieces, into the deep.

This is ridiculous, I thought, bolting upright and reaching for the light switch again. I'm not going to be able to sleep until I get this idiotic idea out of my mind. I tried to think of some way, other than calling my sister, that I could find out what I needed to know. TV? Internet? Too soon for names to show up there, surely, and names were what I needed. Calling the airline wasn't really an option, under the circumstances: I'd never get through, and, if I did, what would I say? Excuse me, my mother was scheduled to fly to London some time around now, I'm not sure when, on some airline, I'm not sure which, and I was just wondering . . . So—it was by now almost midnight, 6 a.m. in Johannesburg—I got out of bed, went to the desk and, chilled by the air-conditioning, picked up the phone and speed-dialed the thirteen digits, a brief chattering song.

My sister answered on the third ring, her voice wary, furry with sleep, her South African accent turning the second syllable of "Hall-o?" into a rising diphthong.

"Anna?" I said. "It's Kim. Did I wake you?"

"No. I mean yes, but the alarm's about to go off, at six. I have to get the girls up."

"Sorry to call so early but . . ."

"Oh, that's okay. Is everything all right?" Anxious now, alarmed.

"Everything's fine. But, listen, I just have a stupid question."

"Yeah?"

"It's about Mom. Do you know what flight she was on to London?"

"Um, yes, I have it written down somewhere. Do you want me to look?"

"Please. You know, we haven't spoken since . . ."

"Yes, I know . . ."

"And I *thought* she was leaving today, on FIN. I'm not sure, I might be misremembering."

"No, that sounds about right. We're meeting her at the airport on Saturday and I remember she only had two nights in London on the way back, I booked the hotel."

"Well, could you do me a favor and check the flight number."

"Okay, Kim, but why?"

"Well, I know this is really stupid, but I heard on the radio that a plane crashed, a FIN flight, so I'm not going to be able to sleep until I know it wasn't hers. My imagination's going wild over here, I guess because of what happened between us and everything—"

"A flight to London?" My sister's voice rose sharply, and I immediately felt guilty, protective. I should have kept my fears to myself, should have obtained this information some other way. Should have shielded Anna from distress. I remembered a time in our early adolescence, when I was about thirteen, Anna twelve, and I'd somehow developed the secret conviction—part wish, I could see now—that my mother, who complained constantly of stomach pains, was dying of cancer. I'd kept this secret to myself for a few days, until, bursting with it, I'd unburdened myself to Anna; that night, I'd heard her tossing and sighing in our shared bedroom, unable to sleep, imagining a motherless life.

"Yes, but, Ann, do you know how many flights there are to London from JFK every day?"

"Just hold on, okay, I'm going to look."

I heard her footsteps pad away from the phone, I heard the roaring, expensive silence between New York and Johannesburg, a kind of cosmic crackle; I imagined my sister rifling through some bureau drawer cluttered with bills and pot-pourri. I heard a man's questioning voice, Angus's, then footsteps back to the phone and the hollow, clumsy clatter of the receiver being picked up.

"Kim? Okay, I have it. Depart JFK, 19/7, that's yesterday . . ." For a second, I felt relief, until I remembered that "yesterday" in Johannesburg was still "today" in New York, that 19/7 was 7/19, July nineteenth, which had just— I glanced at the clock—come to a close.

". . . FIN 770, 18:10, arrive London Heathrow at 5:23. So she should be there by now, just getting in. Kim? Kim? Are you still there?"

Nothing. Numbness. A deep pool of nothing at the core of my being. Then two quick thoughts: one, that Anna had given the wrong answer, as if in an exam—I'd called to get reassurance, not to have my irrational fears confirmed— and two, that it couldn't be true. Anna had made a mistake. The travel agent had made a mistake. The airline had made a mistake. Or Eleanor, unknown to Anna, had changed her flight. Had missed her flight. This, I knew even as I thought it, was even less likely than the absurd possibility that my mother had been aboard a plane that had crashed. Eleanor always arrived at the airport at least three hours before takeoff, waiting vigilantly in the departure lounge with her hand luggage on her lap to prevent someone, some Arab, from sneaking an explosive in there. She was infamous for overestimating, by a factor of two, the amount of time it would take to get to any airport. There was no way, barring a sudden blizzard or a highway pile-up, that Eleanor would miss a plane.

"Kim? Are you there?"

"Yeah, I'm here. You said 770?"

"Yeah, seven-seventy, seven-seven-oh."

"Well, this is crazy but that's the one."

"That crashed?" My sister's voice swerved up, high and panicky, and again I felt the pall of guilt: I should have handled this alone, should have behaved like a grown-up, called the airline, obtained information, weighed, by myself, what to do.

"Yes, but listen, Anna, I'm sure it's a mistake. I'll call the airline and check. We don't know if she really was on that plane, so there's no need to start worrying yet. I'm sure it's just a mix-up."

"What do you mean, mix-up?"

"I don't know," I said, and realized that I hadn't meant anything by it, that it was just a word. "A change of plans?"

"Yes but, God, Kim . . ." Anna was now close to tears, her voice trailing off, helpless and choked. I heard Angus's voice again, closer, more querulous.

"Listen, Ann, here's what we do. I call the airline here and you call the hotel in London, see if she's checked in yet, and we take it from there. Okay? Okay, Ann? Can you do that for me."

"'Kay," she whispered.

"I'll call you back in ten, fifteen minutes, however long it takes me to get through. And, Anna, don't worry, okay? I'm sure this is just a false alarm."

"Okay, Kim. Okay then, bye."

"Bye."

I imagined her, in her long flannel nightie, turning toward Angus, who would be hovering anxiously by, having gleaned, from her side of the conversation, what was amiss. I imagined Anna burying her head in his bony Scots shoulder. I imagined his gentle embrace, his troubled face as he stared, over her head, into the darkness of the arriving hours.

On the other hand, Angus was an alcoholic, presumably not at his best at 6 a.m., so perhaps none of this was happening. Perhaps he was complaining about having been woken up so early, demanding an aspirin, a cup of tea. I'd noticed that I tended to imagine married life as either idyllic or hellish, depending on how lonely I felt at any given moment. At that moment, 12:03 a.m., I felt utterly alone, but in a familiar way, like an astronaut in a space capsule, facing, with grim, belted-in competence, the difficult tasks ahead.

Right, I thought. Call the airline. Call FIN. I reached for the directories, stacked neatly beneath the phone, but, unsure whether to look under "FIN" or "Flight Incorporated," I dialed Information instead, noting, as I did so, that my hand was shaking. I checked again to see what I was feeling: nothing; the same reservoir of nothing beneath my ribs. A sense of calm deliberation, of purpose. Information, I thought, that's what I need.

The 800 number for FIN was busy on the first several

tries, as I knew it would be. I hit redial, anticipating a long wait and wondering if I should instead call the main number for the airport—airport security, the police department, something like that. I leaned back in the chair and put my bare feet on the desktop, noting that they looked strange, alien and scaly in the harsh light; just as I'd begun idly checking the balance in my checkbook—it was closest to hand, top right-hand drawer—I heard a man's voice, "FIN, how may I help you?"

The mundane greeting comforted me, the soft Southern drawl. Clearly, nothing was wrong. Would they be answering the phones that way if the situation were dire, if people's mothers were dying in plane crashes? Would they be answering the phones at all?

"Oh, hi, I need some information please," I said, swinging my feet off the desk and sitting straight in the chair. "About Flight 770?"

His voice changed immediately, becoming flat and brisk. "I'm sorry, ma'am, we cannot give out information on that flight."

"No, you don't understand," I said, "I need to find out if someone I know was on that flight. My mother."

"I'm sorry, ma'am," he repeated, "we cannot give out information about that flight."

"What do you mean, you 'cannot give out information on that flight'? I know it crashed, it's on the news already."

"I'm sorry, ma'am."

A strong emotion surged in my throat, a bird trapped in a flue. "Look, don't give me that, I just need a simple piece of information. I just need to know whether she was on that flight or not."

"I'm sorry, ma'am, I'm not able to answer that question. Any inquiries about Flight 770," he responded, sounding as if he were reading from a script of some kind, "should be addressed to the following number. Do you have a pen handy?"

"Ah, yes," I said, scrambling for one.

"1-800-555-7700. That's 1-800 . . ."

"Thank you," I said, slamming down the phone. I was panting, I wasn't sure why. The existence of this other 800 number made everything seem more grave. I had a sudden flash of my mother's face, from the week before, in the bedroom of the beach cottage, scrunched with rage, screaming.

I can't do this, I thought, then *You have to.*

I had a strong urge to call Anna back, but suppressed it, remembering the cracked panic in my sister's voice. The 800 number was busy, of course. With each beep of the busy signal, I felt a rising helplessness, a mounting urge to cry. What am I supposed to do? I thought, I don't know what to do. I picked up the phone and walked back into the bedroom, where Ella lay curled on the pillow with one ear cocked, one eye slit open. I felt an urge to push my face into the cat's warm fur, which I did, just for a moment, until my nose tickled. Ella tolerated this but looked ready to spring away if any further liberties were taken.

"This number is exclusively for inquiries about FIN Flight 770," the recorded voice informed me when it clicked on at last. "All other customers should call FIN's regular customer service number, 1-800-FLY-FINN. Media calls should be directed to Flight Incorporated's main office in White Plains, New York. Repeat, this number is for

inquiries about FIN Flight 770 ONLY. If you need assistance, please stay on the line and a FIN representative will
be with you shortly." Even in a crisis, even in matters of
life and death, I thought, access to information seems to
involve being subjected to Vivaldi over a telephone line for
an indefinite chunk of time.

"I need some information," I said, when a tired-sounding
woman's voice finally came on. I took, this time, a brusque,
assertive tone, more like my usual manner of doing business, a tone that said, I'm being pleasant and polite right
now, but that may not last if I don't get what I need. I felt,
all of a sudden, enormously fatigued and lay flat on the
bed. "I need to find out if someone was on that flight. My
mother. She was supposed to be on it. I don't know if she
was or not, but my sister said . . ."

"I'm sorry, miss," the woman said, in a dull, mechanical
voice, "but we are not permitted to give out that information until it has been verified and formally released
by Flight Incorporated. The list is still being reconciled
at headquarters."

"You're kidding me," I said, feeling all my energy, all
my combativeness, drain away in an instant. "Please, you
can't do this," I whined. "I have to know. I know she was
scheduled to be on that flight, I have the itinerary—"

"I'm afraid I can't confirm any passengers at this time,
miss."

"Please," I repeated, helplessly. "Please. Please. I have
to know. It's my mother . . . My sister's waiting, in South
Africa . . . I don't know what to do, who to call. Please.
Please, you have to help me."

Something in my voice must have affected the woman

because, after a second's hesitation, she switched to a softer, more conspiratorial, tone. "All right, then," she said, exhaling, "go ahead, give me your name."

"Roth, that's R-O-T-H, Kim Roth."

"The passenger's name please?"

"Roth, Eleanor. Eleanor Lilian."

Silence. A tapping of keys. A final double tap.

"Miss? Miss Roth? I'm very sorry but for further information you'll have to come to the airport."

Tiny flashes of lightning went off before my eyes, my own private weather. This was it then. This was really happening. A funnel of dread opened up inside me, from sternum to gut, and I felt that, if I wasn't careful, my heart might drop through it. Something bad had happened, something irreparable. Some kind of immunity had been lost. My mother had been on that plane, transformed instantly by that fact from a word—*plane*—or a number—*770*—to a brutal, actual machine, a pod that had shattered apart, raining down aluminum, fire, and human flesh. My mother's flesh. I couldn't think about that right now.

My voice, I heard, had become very quiet. "What do you mean, I have to come to the airport? It's"—I checked the clock—"12.46. It's the middle of the night. I have to work tomorrow."

"Miss . . . Roth," the woman said, "we don't have an accurate passenger manifest at this time. We only have preliminary information, information that hasn't been verified yet. And based on that preliminary information, I'm recommending that you go to the airport, to our crisis center, at the FIN terminal, where you will be able to get updated information and counseling. Do you have a family member or friend who can go with you?"

"So you're telling me," I whispered, my throat constricting, "that she *was* on the plane?"

"Miss, as I said, we don't have a confirmed manifest at this point, but right now, I'm so sorry, please don't take this as official, we do have an E. Roth on the list from the gate."

I didn't hear anything else the woman said. I was alone, tumbling through space. The world was black and very loud. Ella, when I next looked, had leapt off the pillow and run away.

I began, numbly, to dress. I have to cancel my nine o'clock with Gillette, I thought, as I pulled on a pair of khakis and a white T-shirt. I have to call Anna. I have to feed Ella, because I don't know what time I'll be back. I brushed my teeth again and then, out of habit, dabbed on some powder and lipstick. What am I doing, I thought, putting on makeup at a time like this? I had another sudden flash of my mother's face, blue-white, subaquatic, lips swollen and agape like a fish's. Enough, I told myself. You don't know anything yet. There may be survivors. Surely not *everyone* can have died. You need information, that's what you need. You need to (a) go outside, (b) get a cab, (c) find the FIN terminal, (d) get some information. That is what you need to do.

But first I had to call Anna. I imagined her crouched by the bedside phone, tearful, waiting, gnawing her fingers, while Angus got the girls out of bed, administered their morning routines, kept them distracted and at bay. I rehearsed what I would say. Anna, I would say, it appears, but at this point, only *appears*, that Eleanor was on that flight, so we have to prepare ourselves for some very bad news. On the other hand, all the information isn't in yet—there might well be survivors, for all we know. I'm going to the airport now to get more information.

"Anna," I blurted, as soon as I heard my sister's quavering voice, "she was on that plane. It's all my fault." Then I heard a dry bark of a sob, my own.

2

Thursday, July 20

The ballroom at the Ramada Inn was still decorated for some function—sales conference or pharmaceutical convention, who knew what—with massive floral arrangements everywhere, dominated by tall, open-throated orange lilies, which looked as if they should be perfumed, but weren't, I knew. I thought about how the pollen could stain your curtains, stain your fingers saffron if you didn't watch out. Stain even, once, Ella's little white nose.

That's what I was thinking about, pollen, in the ballroom of the Ramada Inn, sometime after 2 a.m. Everything surrounding me seemed surreal, supersaturated—the brilliant light from the chandeliers; the dazzling table linens, rich as whipped cream; the tigerish yellows and oranges of the lilies—and I inhabited this vivid space as if it were a dream or a movie set, in which, at any moment, my role would be made clear. There were people around me—about a hundred, I estimated—clustered in groups around the tables, as if awaiting a banquet, except that many were weeping. Some embraced. I had chosen a table alone, off to one side, near the service entrance, and while

I waited—for what, I wasn't sure—I stared into a lily's throat and thought about pollen. I thought about a poem I'd memorized in high school, something about perfect grief and what the poet had learned from it—namely, that the something-or-other has a cup of three. Some kind of flower. Wood something. Woodsplurge? Could that be right? The literature I'd studied growing up in Africa was filled with the names of things I'd never seen—robins, bluebells, nightingales. Holly. Hedgehogs. Lilac. Gorse.

I was sitting in the ballroom of the Ramada Inn at Kennedy Airport at 2 a.m. with a throng of traumatized people, more arriving all the time, waiting to find out if my mother, Eleanor Lilian Roth, had died in a plane crash, and none of it was real. The FIN official had promised a briefing within the half-hour, some kind of counselor—greeting me solicitously at the door—had counseled me to prepare for the worst, and I was thinking about gorse. It was a kind of prickly stuff, right? I felt hollow inside, tender—as if the inside of my body had been exposed to a mild toxin—but otherwise calm, with a blank, suspended sensation as if, any moment now, real life would resume.

I was sitting in this ballroom because there were too many people, too many stunned and disbelieving people, more stumbling in all the time, and so the crisis center, or whatever it was called, had been relocated from the FIN terminal to the airport Ramada. Just from the language I'd heard the FIN people use—"crisis center," "trauma team"—I'd expected something else altogether, something more like an emergency room on TV: a teeming, hyperkinetic site where information was shouted on the trot. Instead, I thought, I'm in a ballroom, I'm having a ball. I imagined saying that to Anna and my eyes stung with tears.

When I'd jumped out of the cab, after a fast blank trip through the spangled night, everything at the FIN terminal had looked, at first, bewilderingly normal. I could see, through the glass doors, the curved white counter with its bright red logo (an abstract empennage); the winding, roped-in line of passengers shuffling their baggage forward a foot at a time; the ticket agents in their red uniforms and striped ties, tagging bags. I was seized by a hallucinatory sense of unreality, as if I were losing my mind: could people still really be getting on planes, FIN planes? I'd expected a scene of chaos and desolation, all flights canceled, the whole operation shut down. As I'd hesitated, wondering if I were in the wrong place or whether I was indeed losing my mind, a small mob of men had rushed out, shouldering cameras like automatic weapons. The sight had chilled me, filled me with dread.

Then I'd noticed that the place was crawling with police. Dogs, too, German shepherds on tight leashes. With a somnambulist's obscure intent, I'd made for the terminal door but was blocked by a young cop who'd told me, in the unlikely lilt of the islands, that no one was allowed in, ma'am, unless they were ticketed for a flight. Could he see my ticket, my ID, please?

"A flight?" I'd said. "You mean this fucking airline is still allowed to fly?" I heard my voice begin to crack, tried to collect myself, tried to explain why I was there. "The woman *told* me to come here," I kept repeating, like a child. "The FIN terminal. Isn't this the FIN terminal?" He took my driver's license, then, half turning his back, muttered something into his walkie-talkie and waited for a long staticky while until something came back, some kind of crackling confirmation. I couldn't understand anything, it was like a secret code. The world around me had become indecipherable, some kind of obscure charade conducted over my head and behind my back. I stared mutely at the pavement, noting how the mica glittered in the neon light.

Then, turning toward me, taking my arm, which I didn't appreciate but felt too anesthetized to resist, the young cop guided me down a hallway to a first-class lounge, which had been cordoned off, nightclub-style, with velvet ropes. The ropes added an incongruous fillip of glamour: I half expected to see a bouncer, complete with guest list. Instead, two more cops were stationed there and a tall, thin woman in a tomato-red suit, with a name tag, a clipboard, a French twist that was coming undone, and—you didn't notice this until you were up close—a tear-stained face.

As I waited, behind an older couple in Broncos windbreakers and a large glazed man reeking of booze, I was aware of nothing but a kind of numb impatience. Hurry up, can't you, I kept thinking, the way I might at a Starbucks counter, waiting to pay for my espresso and get back to the office. My attention—which surged and dispersed unpredictably—kept returning to the clipboard, the ragged-edged, many-paged printout through which the woman flipped constantly, while constantly also consulting a—what was that—a walkie-talkie? a cellphone? I heard two thoughts formulate themselves with great clarity inside my head, as if likewise transmitted from a distant source: one, *this is actually happening*; two, *I'll believe it when I see the body*. This latter thought shocked me, sent a brief white flash of nausea across my brain.

The woman seemed to be sending people away, pointing them back down the hallway—perhaps sending them home, I thought, with a quick pulse of hope. Perhaps it all really was a giant mistake, a hoax of some kind; perhaps nothing had happened, no one had died.

But when my turn came and the woman, avoiding eye contact, had flipped once more through her printout, to the Rs—pausing there, holding her place with a long pearly nail—she'd directed me to a FIN courtesy van, down the hallway and out the double glass doors, this gentleman will escort you, ma'am, where I'd waited with some Iranian people, the boozy man, and the older couple, who didn't speak. I stared out of the window, at the sickly yellow lights of the parking lot, at the endless stream of hotel vans and car-rental vans and airline vans, the drivers hopping out to sling luggage and then hopping back in again, hopping out, hopping in. After a while, the white-haired woman began to sob against her husband's chest. He patted her rhythmically, reassuringly, but his face, staring over the top of her head, had sagged into an expression of grave puzzlement. When, finally, the van arrived at the Ramada, I hurried away, seating myself as far away as possible from them in the cavernous room, as if to quarantine myself from their grief. Now, thinking about the woman's face crushed into her husband's chest, I wanted to let loose a howl of loneliness, an animal cry.

"If I may intrude for a moment?" said a voice at my elbow. "Are you by yourself here?" I looked up, my eyes failing at first to focus. A woman with a notepad, a chin-length bob haircut, and an expression of practiced empathy was standing over me, inclining towards me as if I were a patient in a bed. She looked about my age, late thirties, and somehow this irritated me all the more: if I was to have grief therapists, or whoever they were, dispensing their unsolicited comfort, like the shower of sparkles from a fairy godmother's wand in a Disney cartoon, then I wanted a wise old woman, a grandmother, a Holocaust survivor, goddamnit, someone seamed and seasoned by sorrow, not some perky Ph.D.

"Yes," I answered, since some answer was required of me. "I just came straight out here . . ."

"And who—do you mind if I sit for a moment?—is the Loved One?"

"My mother," I replied. Even in this moment of extremity, when I felt cored, scoured, in body and soul, my mind snagged on the woman's words. Loved one? Was that accurate? A question, I knew, you weren't supposed to ask about your family. Your mother. Especially if she was dead. Especially if she had been blown to bits, and her flesh, blackened and bloody, had fallen, like so much meat, into the deep.

"Your mother," the woman echoed, compassionately, her expression, both radiant and pained, encouraging me to continue.

"Eleanor Roth," I continued curtly, trying to cut this short. "From South Africa."

"South *Africa*?" said the woman. "How interesting. What's it like there?"

Oh, I wanted to say, there are lions and giraffes walking

around the streets, it's quite hard to maneuver your car. That, I'd learned, was the mental image most Americans had of South Africa, if they had one at all. Instead, I just said, "Please . . ."

"I just want you to know," the woman said, reaching out and giving me a gentle squeeze on my left deltoid, "I just want you to know that I'm here, right here in this room, if you need to talk, or just need a hug, okay? It's hard to be alone at a time like this."

"Yes, thank you," I said, tensing my arm to withdraw it, "but what I really need is some information. I'm waiting for the briefing, do you know when it will be? They haven't told us anything yet, not one word, what are we supposed to do, just sit here all night with a bunch of strangers?" My voice, I noticed, was beginning to rise. With indignation. With fatigue. With a vague, inexplicable sense of injustice.

"Soon," the woman said, "very soon. The briefing will be very soon." Her tone was soothing, hypnotic. "In the meanwhile, I'll let you be alone, if that's what you want. Just remember that I'm here if you need me. My name's Christina Barnes. And try to think positive thoughts while you're waiting, I know it's hard. Try to focus on all the good times with your mom."

The last time I had seen my mother, five days earlier, she had been screaming. Eleanor had been screaming as, it seemed, only Eleanor could scream, the way, I imagined, a drunk might yield to the luxury of the binge, of the blackout: with shame, with relief, with the voluptuous gratification of letting go. The bedroom of the beach cottage had become too small to contain her, contain the two of us and our rage, and we were stumbling, tripping, knocking things over in the dark, among the faded wicker furniture and fussy fabrics, as if we were indeed both drunk, drunk on the fermented rage of forty years.

Why, I wondered, had I expected it to be any different? Because—the answer was—I always expected it to be different, even while knowing it would always be the same. I always hoped that *this* time—whichever time it was, the occasions becoming fewer and farther between—I would find the right words to use. The right words to avoid. The right, neutral-to-benign expression for my face. And if I failed, which I inevitably did—Eleanor would always blow up, would blame, would attack, in an ecstasy of uncontrol— it was less painful, somehow, to tell myself that it had been my fault, my failure, than to acknowledge that I had no control whatsoever over Eleanor's rage and that it would never end.

This most recent episode, at the beach, had been the first time I'd seen her in three years. It was also the first time Eleanor had been to New York, which she had resolutely avoided, picturing it as a hellhole of rapists and muggers and dark-skinned people, a sinister Boschian throng of monstrous and perverted semi-humans, thriving on filth and crack, whatever that was, all the while scheming to commit unspeakable crimes against Eleanor Roth the moment she set foot there.

"But, Mom," I'd said, "it's really nothing like that, you watch too much TV."

"I don't know why you always have to criticize me, Kim," she'd replied.

Though I'd lived in the US for some fifteen years—using a graduate fellowship from Berkeley as my ticket out of South

Africa and its, to me, insoluble contradictions—my mother
had never visited me, had never seen any of the places I
had lived, from the incense-scented crash pad in Oakland
to the condo on the Upper West Side. My father, traveling
on business, had visited me occasionally over the years,
stopping off in San Francisco or Chicago or New York
to take me out to dinner and meet whatever boyfriend
happened to be around. But Eleanor, never. We'd talked
about the distance, the discomfort, the expense, knowing
all along we were talking about another kind of distance,
another kind of cost.

But this summer Eleanor was traveling anyway—traveling, reluctantly, to London to visit a cousin who was dying of
bone cancer. And I, with my fortieth birthday approaching,
with the same lines that time had etched on Eleanor's
skin appearing on my own, with a quite concrete sense,
since my father's death, of what "too late" might mean,
with the apparently indestructible fantasy that *this* time I
could make things turn out right, had persuaded Eleanor
to accept a ticket to New York. I'm a grown woman, I'd told
myself, I can handle this. This time it *will* be different.

"It's just too far," Eleanor had argued, "too expensive,
with the rand the way it is. And the trip to London is bad
enough—twelve hours, you know, Kim, crammed like a
sardine into that thing, climbing over people to get to the
toilet. And the toilets, oh my God, after a few hours . . ."

"But, Eleanor," I'd insisted, "please. I want you to see
my place, my things. My office. My cat. I want you to see
how I live. So you can, you know, imagine me better."

"I've seen the photos," Eleanor said. "It's a nice little
flat."

"Also," I said, "you can catch up with your friend Maude—how long has it been?"

"Oh, I don't know, eight, nine years, perhaps . . . But the airfare, Kim, it's so much money, it's outrageous what they charge these days, the crooks. You don't need to go spending that much on me, you know, you should be saving it instead. Investing it. For your old age, because who's going to take care of you then?"

"For God's sake, Mom. I want you to come. I have the money. It's much less in dollars."

"I don't know, Kim. It's such a long trip. My legs swell."

Eleanor hated to fly. She hated to get on planes, to entrust her life to a machine that she herself wasn't steering and that, moreover, flouted the laws of gravity every time it took off. Also, the details of travel, of reservations, baggage retrieval, currency and cabs, overwhelmed her, incapacitated her—Roger had handled these matters when he was alive, reveling in a certain sense of savoir faire. So Anna was overseeing the arrangements in Johannesburg, the cousin, Marcelle, was responsible, from her sickbed, for ensuring that Eleanor survived London, and I, it seemed, was answerable for New York. Answerable for a tetchy, terrified sixty-four-year-old, who had no desire whatsoever to be there.

Somehow, through sheer doggedness, I had persuaded her to come to New York, to spend a week or so taking in the sights of the city, to stay, at my expense, in a quiet little hotel on the Upper East Side. (We both knew that cohabitation was out of the question: my apartment was too small, I told her, and she gratefully agreed.)

With an odd dissociative logic, the lucidity of someone doing something she suspects is insane, I had gone on to plan Eleanor's visit as I imagined any daughter might, as if we had tacitly agreed to impersonate a mother and daughter spending "quality time" together: a few days in Manhattan for shopping, sightseeing, and theater, a few days' relaxation at a friend's house on Long Island, and so on. But all along I had been numb with foreboding, undone by the prospect of spending ten days in Eleanor's exclusive company, something I recognized now—and should have recognized then—as a mistake. More than a mistake: an impossibility. An act of desperate, misguided longing which, I now saw, had killed my mother. I had killed my mother. As I thought this, a thought as crystalline as the chandeliers in the Ramada ballroom, something twisted inside me, like a blade, and I let out a small moan.

The trouble had begun on the drive out to Sag Harbor, four days into Eleanor's visit. For the first few days, from the moment she'd emerged crumpled and bewildered from customs at Kennedy, she'd been strained and polite, hyperpolite, in a way that tore at my heart. Like courtly strangers, paralyzingly solicitous of the other's needs, like a comedy duo unable to get through the door for their "No, after you"s, we'd shopped at Saks, we'd seen *Miss Saigon*, we'd had tea at the Plaza. But many of my plans had quietly been abandoned—the trip to the World Trade Center, the outing to Ellis Island, the walk in Central Park—because, jetlagged and heat-exhausted, fearful in crowds, Eleanor had wanted to rest much of the day and was much happier in her air-conditioned hotel room with a magazine and a cup of tea than on the soupy streets of the city. "The humidity,"

she'd say, shaking her head. "We don't get that at home. I
don't know how you survive."

In retrospect, I saw, we should have abandoned the trip
to Long Island as well. But I'd thought it might be restful,
refreshing, had made sure to reserve a huge, tank-like rental
car with potent air-conditioning—hoping, perhaps, to put
Eleanor into a cryonic state for the duration. Eleanor was
a notoriously nervous, fretful passenger. She was a nervous
driver, too, creeping along with the spasmodic, freeze-
frame motion of a frightened squirrel, braking abruptly in
response to perceived threats in her peripheral vision. But
as a passenger, she was worse, constantly bracing against
anticipated impact, constantly gasping out urgent, startling
warnings, constantly accusing the driver of reckless disregard. To drive with Eleanor was to have an agonized
mime show ongoing in the passenger's seat. (Remembering
this now, in the Ramada ballroom, I wondered, and then
instantly tried to erase the thought, how my mother had
reacted in a plane that was really about to crash, whether
she'd had time to flinch, to gasp, to exclaim, or whether,
after all those years of bracing for the smash that never
came, she'd died silent, surprised, her mouth stretched into
a mute O.)

Why, Eleanor had wanted to know, did we have to go
so far? It wasn't even a three-hour drive, I assured her,
it would be over in no time. We would stop often along
the way, for lunch, tea, and nice clean restrooms. Why,
Eleanor had wanted to know, was there so much traffic?
There really wasn't, I'd said, this was nothing, you should
see it on Fridays. Why, Eleanor had wanted to know,
was I driving so fast? I was well under the speed limit,

I replied, look, not even fifty miles per hour. "You know I don't understand miles," replied Eleanor, who lived with the metric system. "I just know you're going too fast."

By the time we uncrumpled ourselves from the car, we were both frazzled and frayed, a condition heightened by my futile search for the house keys which were not, as my friend Lauren had promised, in the large clay urn next to the front door. Nor were they under the doormat, in the mailbox, in the dog kennel, or any other place I could think of. While I searched, with mounting irritation, peering helplessly through the windows of the white clapboard cottage, Eleanor stood off to one side, next to the car, face pursed into an expression of forbearance, hairdo whipped by the salty wind. Finally, I thought to look in the urn again, and there the keys were, under some loose soil at the bottom, with a cheery note. I couldn't understand how I had missed them the first time.

"Let's have a cup of tea," I said, as I struggled with the swollen front door, giving it a smart kick, "and then think about dinner." The cottage, as we entered it, smelled musty and damp, like old, foxed books; it looked desolate in the declining light, with a half-completed jigsaw puzzle (Turner's *Fire at Sea*) laid out on a listing wicker table. A large window overlooked a crotchety strip of sea.

"Look," I said, pointing, "that's the beach. We can check it out tomorrow."

"It looks very unsafe," Eleanor said, peering through the grimy pane. "With all those rocks. Do you have sharks here? A shark attacked a man in Durban, well, Salt Rock, actually, last month, just before I left. A colored man. Bit off his leg and he bled to death."

After dinner—wild mushroom lasagna and a mesclun salad, which I'd transported from Balducci's to forestall the inevitable conflict about cooking and food, and which Eleanor adjudged, respectively, "too oily" and "too bitter"—there was a lull, during which, it being too early to retire but too late to embark on any kind of activity, my mother began to poke around the cottage, examining its contents with frank voyeurism. The TV was on, as background noise, but neither of us felt much like sitting after our long drive, so, while I changed into my running shorts, she puttered and prowled. As she opened drawers, squinted into the blackened oven, examined the inscriptions in Lauren's books, I hoped, with a guilty pang, that my friend hadn't left anything too revealing lying around— her St. John's Wort, her vibrator, her unpaid bills. When I came out of the bathroom, having given the cabinet a hasty check, Eleanor was in the master bedroom, unpacking, arraying her pill bottles on the bedside table.

"This them?" she asked, picking up a photograph in a seashell-encrusted frame. It showed Lauren and her family—her parents, her brother Ben, and Einstein the dog—leaning against the railing of the deck, arms about each other's shoulders, looking windblown, happy, and brown.

"Yup," I said, taking the picture from Eleanor, examining it with a half-smile, "that's them. That's Lauren, on the end there."

"Jewish?" Eleanor asked. "They look Jewish."

A slight coolness, the precursor to heat, ran through my veins. "Yes," I said. "They are. And . . . ?"

"And nothing," Eleanor said. "I was just asking." She

took the picture back from me and examined it more closely.

Though in the States "Roth" is a common Jewish name, I had been raised as an Anglican: in Eleanor's version of the universe, Roth was a venerable Anglo-Saxon appellation that could be traced back, through Roger's family tree, to a small Cotswold village in the thirteenth century. There was some document, from some genealogical service that advertised in the back of magazines, to prove this. There was, however, no document diagramming Eleanor's own family tree: the dour Afrikaners on her mother's side, the immigrant diamond-peddler from Wales on her father's. No pictures of them in the family album, either.

I felt a familiar, vigilant coolness, which I experienced as an actual physical chill on my skin, a familiar tensing of shoulders and jaw, a familiar slowing-down of time. I could also feel Eleanor sensing my sensations: despite all the time and distance between us, we still knew each other's bodies like lovers, like predators and prey. Whatever she says, I told myself, don't react. Just stay calm.

Eleanor replaced the photograph on the nightstand. "Well," she said, "they look pretty pleased with themselves."

And then, suddenly, in a sequence I was never able to reconstruct, we were fighting, screaming, lashing out, spitting invective in the manner each of us had perfected over a lifetime, inflicting flesh wounds on the heart. I had said something to trigger it, I was sure, I always did, but afterwards, and now, as I sat head in hands in the merciless light, I could not, literally could not, if my life depended on it—and somehow I felt that it might—

remember what. Something that Eleanor had construed as criticism, as an attack, that much I knew. Something about Lauren's family? But what? Or something else altogether, in an attempt to change the subject—some ill-judged joke about our snooping? About the cottage? About our plans for the next day? You never knew, and this was the true horror of it, you could never know what would set Eleanor off, so profound, so cryptic, so vigilant, was her rage, and, even after you had, you might still not know why. I had said something, that was all—what? what? I battered the closed doors of my memory—and then Eleanor was screaming, we were both screaming, screeching, escalating into a well-practiced frenzy, spitting and spewing words, a lifetime's worth of words, words like "crazy," "bitch," "you always," "you never," "you think you're so . . .", then, caged in the cluttered, airless room, shoving and pushing at each other, Eleanor's fingernails digging into my forearms, I shoving, with brutal repulsion, the weak, doughy flesh of my mother, shoving my own mother away, this crazy woman, this banshee, who hated me, who wanted, I knew in my heart, to kill me.

It was like a fugue state, an alcoholic blackout, these fights of ours, which had begun in my early adolescence. No memory ever remained to me of the moment-to-moment interaction, the escalating violence; all that remained was the sense of having been overpowered, engulfed by something savage and shaming, something that poured over me, seized me and pounded me like a tsunami. How, I wondered, would you explain that to the grief counselor? What would you say: unfortunately, we had a slight tiff, my mother and I, we drove back to the city the next morning in silence, I dropped her at her hotel, tacitly entrusting her to the care of her old friend Maude (a former Johannesburg suburbanite, now a widow on the Upper East Side), and I never saw her again?

There was a sudden screech of feedback, and I looked up, startled, to see, at the front of the room, a small, rabbity man with a ginger moustache doing a modified foxtrot to disengage the microphone cord from his feet. "Ladies and gentlemen," he said, experimentally—loud, derisive screech from the mike, which he shook and then tapped—"if I could have your attention please." He waited, as if anticipating further electronic heckling, then continued. "My name is Bruce Baumer, and I'm the director of corporate communications for FIN. We're now ready, on this tragic occasion, to give you an update on the status of Flight 770."

3

Thursday, July 20

"The history of aviation accidents," he said, by way of introduction, "is a history of things that have never happened before." The people in the room, myself included, seemed baffled by this pronouncement, cowed. We trained our ravaged faces on him, trying to translate. We wanted to know who was alive, who was dead.

"At this moment in time," he continued, consulting a yellow legal pad, then an extra-large, black plastic, deep-sea diver's watch, "2:48 a.m., I regret to say, we have very limited information at our disposal regarding the cause of the accident, the tragic accident, if it was indeed an accident. Or, um, the number of survivors. A massive rescue effort is currently underway, involving the US Coast Guard, the US Navy, the Air National Guard . . ." At that moment I heard only the word "rescue," picturing Eleanor clinging stalwartly to a piece of flotsam in an icy, littered sea, like a survivor from the *Titanic*. "What took you so long?" I imagined her rebuking the handsome young rookie from the Coast Guard as he roared up in his cutter.

But there had been a fireball, an explosion, bodies falling

broken and burning out of the sky. What could there be to rescue, what could remain?

". . . what we do know," the gingery man, what was his name, Baumer, was saying when I tuned him in again, "is this." A piercing shriek, as if of outrage, from the amp. "Um," he said, experimentally, "this: a Boeing 747 designated as Flight Incorporated flight number 770, bound for London Heathrow, took off this evening at 8:19 from runway twenty-two at JFK, two hours late due to," and here he consulted the yellow pad again, "late arrival of incoming aircraft. From, I believe, Athens, Greece. The temperature was seventy-one degrees, winds were light from the southwest, visibility was twenty-five miles." Yes, I remembered the soft air, like a tender hand to the cheek, as I'd walked home from the gym, though I hadn't been thinking about it then, the tenderness of the dusk: I'd been making a to-do list in my mind. (Bananas, body lotion, cat treats, check Gillette stats for southwest, return Lauren's call.)

"By 20:30 hours, Flight 770 had reached an altitude of about 10,000 feet," he continued, reading from the pad. "It then received clearance from Boston Air Route Traffic Control Center to climb to 15,000 feet." A mile, I rummaged in my memory, that was, what, five thousand and some feet, why didn't I know these things, I'd known them as a child, then the metric system, then back to miles, okay, so call it three miles, three miles in the air, nobody could survive that, plummeting to meet the hard slap of the sea. "At 20:31, that's 8:31 p.m.," he announced somberly, "Flight 770 disappeared from the radar screen."

A babble of questioning voices, a rumble and shriek,

like the din of an approaching subway train, but I wasn't listening, I was picturing, instead, something I'd once seen on TV, a movie about air traffic control, men peering tight-lipped at a bank of screens, trying, by their glacial light, to avert catastrophe. All I remembered now was what a plane looked like on a radar screen: a tiny green cross in a box. Contained in that box, not even an eighth of an inch square, were the lives of 230 people. When it disappeared, so did they—Eleanor among them, gone, crossed out. Was that possible? It all seemed so abstract, so remote, like a video game I'd once played, where the goal was to hit pedestrians with your car. When you did, the scurrying little stick figure was replaced instantly by a "ping" and a cross, a miniature grave marker. So Eleanor had disappeared, exiting the car on East 86th without a word or a wave, dropping out of the sky, pinging off the radar screen.

I searched my heart for the appropriate feeling, the abysm of loss that would make me shriek and wring my hands like the woman across the room, who was performing a gesture that until then I had supposed to be a literary device, not something a person would actually do with her hands, wring and twist them, tear at them, as if to pull them apart. Instead, all I felt was a blank mute rage. Eleanor can't die now, I thought, I'm not done with her. She's not done with me. I have a few questions to ask her, a lifetime's worth, beginning, and perhaps ending, with the hardest one: why did you become a mother? The question sat like a stone in my mouth, a stone in my heart. A pointless question, an unanswerable question, a tautology: why did you become a mother and create me, who could then ask you that?

Two FIN employees, a man and a woman, each in the shoddy red blazer of the airline, were escorting the hand-wringing woman out of the room as her shrieks began to escalate. Feeling in my own body the risk of contagion, the risk of craziness and keening, I was grateful to see her go.

Baumer was talking about a bomb. "Airplanes don't just drop out of the sky," he was saying, "they don't just explode in mid-air, so naturally, yes, we are taking very seriously the possibility that there was an explosive on board. There's nothing a crew member can do to make a plane explode like that. The FBI is on site; there will be, naturally, a very thorough investigation. But at this moment"—he consulted his oversized watch again, some kind of tic, I realized—"I have to emphasize that we just don't know. All we have right now are eyewitness reports—an explosion, a, a fire, a fireball, then the aircraft broke up." He looked desperate, utterly unqualified for his job. "And that, um, concludes this briefing, though of course we will continue to provide information as it becomes available."

As he stepped aside, gratefully but guiltily, offering empty palms to the questions that pursued him, I felt myself descend, like a space creature, from the strange bright bubble I'd been inhabiting, a bubble of light and silence, where my thoughts, like mannequins on a runway, had turned and flashed themselves for my inspection. A bubble where Eleanor floated among the wrack of the *Titanic*, where a fireball blossomed like a giant peony against the dusk, where a plane had split apart, the way a mother's body splits apart, dropping the child's body a long way into a strange sea.

The ballroom was abuzz with people, in groups and pairs, weeping and clinging to each other. One woman had fallen to her knees, praying or sobbing, I couldn't tell, her face pressed into the unyielding lap of a chair. An angry contingent, led by a bald-headed man with the rosacea of a drinker, was badgering anyone with airline ID, demanding names, a passenger list, which, I realized, hadn't been released yet. There were over seven hundred names on the manifest, I heard someone say, the names of everyone who'd ever made a reservation for the flight, whether they paid for it or not, whether they ever showed up. Seven hundred: so many who had changed their minds, who, through their vacillation, had saved their skins. This idea offended me somehow, this ghostly cargo of the indecisive. I would have been killed, I thought, because I rarely changed my plans. That didn't seem fair. Nothing seemed fair. I scanned the room around me: I seemed to be the only person who had arrived alone, who was sitting alone. How could that be? Surely others had been alone too, in the middle of the night, when they'd heard the news?

I felt a dark, draining fatigue set in, like a suction pump to the brain.

Anna, I thought, I need to talk to Anna. I staggered to my feet, which were numb and tingly, big snowboots of ischemia. I hadn't thought to bring the cellphone: why not, what was the matter with me? Okay, I thought, this is a hotel, big bank of phones in the lobby. Fumbling in my pocket for change, I made my way to the gilded double doors through which people had been coming all night, each time pausing in a stutter of hesitation before entering the sparkling, clamorous space of the ballroom. I became aware, peripherally, of a red-jacketed figure hastening up on my left with some kind of admonitory gesture, before I opened the doors and was blinded. Soft explosions, like popcorn popping, loud whirring (the sound of a certain bird from the African bush), a cacophony of voices, a syncopated starburst, stabbing the eye. In a panic, I pushed the doors shut. I was shaking, my body pulsing with shock.

"I'm so sorry," said the FIN representative, a sun-dried man with a golden pompadour. He placed a soft but insistent hand on my upper arm to restrain me. "We're having them removed, they're going. We've tried to keep them out but the hotel hasn't cooperated, it's just a madhouse out there . . ." He looked exhausted, close to tears. "You'd think, wouldn't you, at a time like this . . . We're getting a police barrier set up around the whole area. In the meanwhile, though, it's better not to go out there. I can let you out through the kitchen if you want to leave."

"No," I said. "Not now. I don't want to leave. I just want a phone. I forgot mine."

"This way, then," he said, turning me about. He steered me around and through the chaos, ushering me gently as if I were blind, which was how I felt, dazzled, impaired, my body limp, as if about to accordion inward. So many people, all of a sudden, such clots and clusters of them, so much noise. At the back of the room, behind some folding screens I hadn't noticed before, was a tangle of equipment and wires, a patched-together jumble of phones, computers, fax machines, a beeping, flashing Medusa terminating in an inelegant array of adapters.

"Watch your step," he said, indicating a treacherous snarl of cords at my feet, "and, please, if you'll take a

seat here"—a metal folding chair—"I'll find you a phone."
I acquiesced, I obeyed, I'd never be able to make another
independent decision in my life.

He reappeared within seconds, handing me a risibly tiny
phone, pushing the "on" button with his thumb as he did
so. I had a moment of panic, blanking on Anna's number,
which was programmed into my phone at home so I never
had to dial it. Then, miraculously, the near-palindromic
sequence of numbers, bracketed by two curvy 9s, presented
itself to my brain. I had no idea what time it was—time had
become an abstraction, an irrelevance—but I knew Anna
would be at home, near the phone, not presiding, kindly and
briskly, over her second-grade classroom. Sure enough, she
picked up after half a ring.

"Anna?"

"Oh, Kim, thank God. I've been trying and trying you."

"I'm at the airport. Well, in some hotel. At the airport."

"And . . . ? I've been watching CNN, Kim, oh God, it's
so terrible, the fire . . ." Her voice dwindled, choked off.

"I know," I said, though, at that moment I realized I did
not. Did not know anything. Fire was an abstraction to me,
merely a word, as was water, drowning. Crash. Explosion.
All words. I hadn't yet seen a single image, sequestered here
in this ballroom with a phalanx of corporate minders. A
sudden rage seized me, a sense of having been massively
ripped off.

"She hasn't checked in to the hotel in London. Maude
doesn't know anything. No messages here. Was she—?"
Anna asked, tremulously.

"I don't know. Yes. Probably. They haven't given out
any names yet. Officially."

"But was she—?"

"Well—yes. It seems so. No official list, though. No survivors, either. Yet."

"Oh God," Anna whispered. "Oh no." I felt, again, a surge of helplessness, of guilt. I had failed in some way, failed, as the elder sister, to make everything all right, to take the situation in hand, to sweep off to the airport and return with Anna's mother, soaked, complaining, reeking of jet fuel, but alive. Anna's mother, I realized: a different person from my own. A person with whom it was possible to have a close, sustaining, if not uncomplicated relationship. A person to whom, and I closed my eyes with a pang, you might turn for comfort.

"Anna," I said, "sweetie." I realized I had no idea what to do next, what to say. This wasn't like a normal death, if there were such a thing, an old-fashioned death, a death in a hospital, where the conversation would be determined to a large extent by what had to be done next—paperwork, hiring professionals to remove the corpse, picking up a plastic bagful of possessions. I wasn't even sure if there would be a body. A whole body. Even a piece. At this thought, my stomach seized and I gagged silently, violently. My eyes burned with tears and I thought, perhaps this is the only way I can weep for her.

"Anna?" I asked. "You still there?"

A stifled "Yes." Then a tiny, tremulous voice. "What are they telling you there? What happened?"

"Not a whole lot, they're not telling us a whole lot." And again, a jolt of undefined rage. "Just that . . ." I tried, and failed, to recall some specific piece of information that Baumer had imparted. "Three miles. That's all I

remember, three miles. In the air." I let my eyes rove
around the screened-in area, an enclave which, with its
chaotic tangle of equipment, its ant-like clusterings and
dispersals of people, and its high level of noise, human
and otherwise, accorded more with my notion of a "crisis
center" than the chilly opulence of the ballroom.

"It says on CNN," Anna began, and then I realized there
were TV monitors too, four of them, right in front of me,
"that there was a bomb. Terrorists. Something to do with
the Olympics."

I felt a dark irony rise, like a bloated corpse, from the
night waters of my emotions, an ugliness that I let surface
and sink, something I couldn't afford to fish out and
examine right then. Eleanor had lived her whole life in
fear of "them," the poor, the darker pigmented, the people
with unpronounceable names, lived with the conviction that
"they" were out to get her, that, at any moment, "they"
would rob, murder, rape, destroy. And now, perhaps,
"they" had. It was too much to think about, too much
to confront. I turned my attention back to the telephone,
a tainted taste on my tongue, like spoiled meat.

"I don't know," I said. "I don't know anything. You
probably know more than I do. I'm just not getting any
info here. I don't know what to do, Anna." I felt perilously
close to tears. "Whether to stay here or go home. What
should I do?"

"I don't know. Stay there? Because if you go home, you'll
just have to come back, won't you?"

"I suppose. But it's so awful here, so . . . unreal. In this
ballroom, you know . . ."

"Oh, Kimmie. Oh, God. But at least they'll tell you what's

going on, won't they? As soon as they know? So perhaps you should stay there. And I'll stay by the phone here. I don't know what else to do."

"Okay. And I'll call as soon as I hear anything. Anything . . . you know. Definite."

"Oh God, Kim. Can you believe this is really happening?"

"No. No, Anna, I really can't. I'm just, kind of numb. Just trying, you know, to deal . . . I'll call you as soon as I can, okay?"

"Okay, Kimmie, bye."

"Bye, Ann." I wanted to say something more at that moment, something like "I love you," but in my family we never used those words. I couldn't imagine saying them, even then. I tried to imagine something else I could say that would convey the same intent. She had, without thinking, called me Kimmie, a diminutive from childhood, infusing it with all the tenderness and helplessness of her childhood self.

I stood frozen for a while, then my gaze focused and I realized I was staring at something, at the array of TVs in front of me, like an installation in a museum, each tuned to a different station, each flashing and flickering out of phase with the next. If I watch long enough, I thought, I might have some kind of seizure. At first I couldn't decipher what I was seeing on each screen: a field of darkness spattered with bursts and whorls of orange light, like the birth of a universe, or the death of a star. Then something shifted in my brain and I understood what I was looking at. It was the ocean, the Atlantic Ocean, some fifty miles from where I sat, littered with the burning wreck of a Boeing 747.

One of the cameras pulled back and up, high, for an

aerial view, and the splashes of fire resolved themselves into a long, narrow slice on a dark ground. A snake of fire, I thought, eating, eating, with its flickering tongue. Fire on water: it seemed counter-intuitive, perverse.

If Eleanor is dead, I thought, something in me will never be set right. Something that's wrong, broken, will never be fixed.

But how could Eleanor be dead, how could she have ended up there, in that messy expanse of sea, jammed with boats, strewn with debris? My mind balked at the idea, failed to accommodate it. I stared blankly at the next screen. Technicolor flares and roving searchlights swept the sky, evoking, bizarrely, the blazoned nights of Hollywood. It's a movie, I thought: that's what it is, Eleanor's in a movie. She's not in the Atlantic, she's on TV. That thought made sense for about three seconds, provided an odd kind of comfort.

Then another image appeared, indecipherable: a flat dark space traversed by a mobile necklace of lights. There was too much noise around me, too much talking and beeping; how was I supposed to know what I was looking at?

"Here on the eastern edge of Long Island," I heard a voice say, above the hubbub, then I lost it again. Cut to a colorful map of the area, with a moving red arrow showing the trajectory of the plane. A small orange star, like a punctuation mark, showed where it had blown up, against an ocean tinted a mild baby blue, a coastline the creamy ecru of perfect beach sand, the color of picnics and honeymoons, shades so sweet you almost wouldn't mind being vaporized there.

Cut back to the crawling lights. Those were ambulances, I understood at last, a convoy of ambulances, moving slowly, nose to tail, down Route 27. They were empty, the voice said, their services had not been required. A temporary morgue had been established at East Griffiths—cut back to the map, iris in—the town nearest the orange star. That's what I was looking at: a cortège of empty ambulances.

Enough, I thought, enough. I had, at that moment, a strong, precise craving to black out, to lie down on the floor and lose consciousness. To be absent, just for a while, from the grotesque narrative in which I had suddenly become enmeshed. Stumbling out of the screened-off area, where no one had paid me the slightest attention, I saw that a buffet had been set up at the opposite end of the ballroom—coffee and sandwiches, piles of shiny fruit, and, what was that, scrambled eggs. I contemplated the idea of food, drink, caffeine. A valve in my throat revolted. All I wanted, was this too much to ask, was a little oblivion.

There were, I estimated, at least five hundred people in the room by now, many weeping, others sitting stunned, everything happening at a great distance from me, an inexplicable series of gestures performed by strangers under a blinding light. With the over-deliberate movements of a drunk, I wove my way to a quieter place near the wall, aiming for an abandoned cluster of chairs, littered with trash. Why couldn't people pick up their sodden tissues, their empty wrappers? Why couldn't they all just go away? There was an odd pressure behind my eyes, as if fingers were pushing and squeezing on the nerves, trying to dislodge the eyeballs. If I don't lie down, I thought, I might faint. I knew this though I'd never fainted before. I'd come close a few times while having blood drawn, each time shocked to see, outside my body, the rich festive red of my life.

The chairs were fake Louis something or other, an oval seat and back, upholstered in a green-and-beige-striped fabric that had been so sprayed with stain guard that it looked like plastic. I imagined trying to curl up on one and sliding right off, like a cat pushed off a lap. Then I thought of pulling two chairs together, face to face, and inserting myself into that scant space, rolling myself into a ball, nose almost to knees, hands tucked neatly under my chin. It might work, I thought, like two airline seats on the long haul to Africa, but without the insoluble problem of the seat-belt attachment, which, sooner or later, sticks into your bones. I wondered, briefly, if Eleanor had had her seatbelt fastened. Of course she would have: the sign would still have been lit, the aircraft would still have been climbing, and my mother would still have been rigid in her seat, vigilant, as ever, for the least shift in the engine's tone. For the least lurch of turbulence, the least agitation in the attendant's demeanor. Then, boom.

I wasn't sure how much longer I could stand up. My head felt like a helium balloon rising away from my feet, which, in turn, had relinquished their relationship to the floor. Fainting, I remembered reading somewhere, is self-correcting, because, by falling down, you automatically lower your head. I didn't want to put this theory to the test. So I made for the wall, for a corner formed by a huge fluted pilaster, and backing into it, wedging myself into the angle, slid, semi-voluntarily, to the floor, clasping my knees and resting my head on my arms.

I closed, at last, my eyes.

Instantly, a horror show. Smoke and flames, I pictured; fumes, screams, a hellish, plummeting prison, a gut-emptying plunge. The stench of fuel and burning flesh. The roar of wind. I opened my eyes, then shut them again. The shock of decompression, lungs seared and spasming for air, brain scrambling desperately in its cage, the terrible rushing, sucking fact of gravity. I opened my eyes again. How long, I wondered, do you get? How long do you get to understand what is happening to you?

PUERTO PLATA,
DOMINICAN REPUBLIC, 1996

CAPTAIN: After-takeoff checklist.

COPILOT: After-takeoff checklist: landing gear up and off, flaps are up, checked up, altimeters later, after-takeoff completed.

CAPTAIN: Okay. Center autopilot on, please.

COPILOT: Center autopilot is on command.

CAPTAIN: Thank you. One zero one three. Rudder ratio, Mach airspeed trim.

COPILOT: Yes, trim.

CAPTAIN: There is something wrong. There are some problems. OK, there is something crazy. Do you see it?

COPILOT: There is something crazy there at this moment. Two hundred [mph] only on mine and decreasing, sir.

CAPTAIN: Both of [the speedometers] are wrong. What can we do? Let's check their circuit breaker.

COPILOT: Yes.

CAPTAIN: Alternate is correct.

COPILOT: The alternate one is correct.

CAPTAIN: As aircraft was not flying and on ground, something happening . . . We don't believe [the speedometers].

FLIGHT ENGINEER: Shall I reset its circuit breaker?

CAPTAIN: Yes, reset it.

FLIGHT ENGINEER: To understand the reason?

CAPTAIN: Yeah.

Cabin: Sound of aircraft-overspeed warning.

CAPTAIN: Okay, it's no matter. Pull the airspeed [back]. We will see.

Cabin: Overspeed warning stops.

COPILOT: Now it is three hundred and fifty [mph], yes.

CAPTAIN: Let's take that like this . . .

Cabin: Sound of four warning-alert tones; sound of stick shaker starts, indicating a stalling aircraft, and continues to end of recording; sound of four warning-alert tones.

COPILOT: Sir . . . nose down

FLIGHT ENGINEER: Now . . .

COPILOT: Thrust . . .

CAPTAIN: Disconnect the autopilot. Is autopilot disconnected?

COPILOT: Already disconnected, disconnected, sir.

CAPTAIN: [It will] not climb? What am I to do?

COPILOT: You may level off. Altitude okay. I am selecting the altitude hold, sir.

CAPTAIN: Select, select.

COPILOT: Altitude hold. Okay, five thousand feet.

CAPTAIN: Thrust levers, thrust, thrust, thrust, thrust.

COPILOT: Retard.

CAPTAIN: Thrust. Don't pull back, don't pull back, don't pull back, don't pull back.

COPILOT: Okay, open [the throttles], open . . .

CAPTAIN: Don't pull back. Please don't pull back.

COPILOT: Open, sir, open . . .

FLIGHT ENGINEER: Sir, pull up.

CAPTAIN: What's happening?

COPILOT: Oh, what's happening?

Cabin: Ground-proximity warning system alarm, "Whoop, whoop, pull up, pull up," continues until end of recording.

COPILOT: Let's do like this . . .

End of tape.

4

Thursday, July 20

———

"Honey," I heard a voice say, "you okay? Need something, some water or something? Need the medics? Red Cross is here."

Still curled, nose to knees, on the floor against the pilaster, I felt absurd, self-dramatizing, as if succumbing to a fit of the vapors. But at the same time I balked at standing up, at opening my eyes. If I don't stand up, I thought, if I don't open my eyes, I won't have to deal. I'll deal when I have to, when I hear an official voice informing me that a Mrs. Eleanor Lilian Roth has been positively identified as one of the victims, identification having been accomplished by means of the well-stocked handbag still clutched within her grasp. The image made me want to giggle, Eleanor laid out on the coroner's table with her ostrich-skin handbag (her "good" bag) gripped in both hands, then, just as suddenly, made me want to weep.

I remembered what a source of fascination my mother's handbag had been to me as a child, how satisfying the snap when it opened or closed, how secret and feminine the objects within, everything cohabiting in a grubby,

scented jumble, everything dusted with the orangey face
powder she favored. On a good day, she'd let you dig her
keys out for her—a solemn, adult responsibility—or fish
around for the loose, jewel-colored candies that tended to
accumulate at the bottom.

No, I thought, I'm not going to open my eyes. I wanted
someone to sew them shut, as if I were dead.

"Honey?" The voice repeated. "Need some help?"

I could pretend to be unconscious, I thought, but then
they'd really call the medics. So, like Ella when she didn't
want to be disturbed, I cracked my eyelids open a sliver
without otherwise stirring. A shiny chrome object stood
in front of me, like a towel rack, with a woman leaning
on it, a man hovering behind. Why, I wondered, is this
woman, this not-so-old black woman, leaning on a towel
rack? Everything was so crazy, I yearned to get back
to reality, a state that seemed to be located physically,
concretely, somewhere else, a place I could reach by
taxicab. I continued to stare, without moving, at the
quadruped thing. I know what that is, I thought: it's
a walker. The shock has made this poor woman need a
walker.

"You feeling faint?" she asked. "Need a hand?"

"I was," I said, sliding myself gingerly back up the wall
to a standing position, leaning into the angle, light-headed
again, "a bit, but it's all right now. More like, you know,
wiped out. From all this . . . waiting."

"Yes," she said. "I know." She paused. "I'm Bernice,"
she said, then, swiveling slightly at the waist to indicate
the man behind her, "this is Harold. We're from Utica."
He nodded, though his gaze was glazed, unseeing. He had

a kind, crumpled face, shiny bald spot, thick glasses. He looked as if he had just been thawed from a centuries-long deep-freeze and had no idea where he was.

"Kim," I replied, looking closely, for the first time, at the woman's face. It was distorted, ashy, puffy, a relief map of grief. That's what I should look like, I thought, except I've barely shed a tear.

I didn't know how to say the next thing, so I just said, "And, ah, who—?"

"Our daughter, Louise. Twenty-six." As she uttered the name, Bernice's eyes flooded again. They looked inflamed, as if her tears were caustic, causing her pain. She proffered, without yielding it, a passport-sized picture. I craned my neck to see it: a pleasant-looking young woman with a puff of straightened hair, a striped scarf draped artfully around her neck. She looked as if she might work in a bank or car-rental agency, as if she would smile easily, remember your name. I shook my head, indicating, I hoped, empathy. What I felt was despair.

"And you—?" she asked.

"My mother," I said. "I don't have a picture. I don't know why I don't have a picture." I felt that this failure, this omission, would tell Bernice everything she needed to know about me. I wanted to confess everything to her right there—confess how I had failed as a daughter, failed to love, failed to forgive. I wanted to tell her this before she wasted any more of her compassion on me, any of her tears.

But before I could say anything, a loud commotion broke out in the front of the room. A man with a Brooklyn accent was yelling, fists wheeling blindly, spit spraying from his mouth. He was threatening to sue. He was threatening to punch somebody out. He was threatening to talk right now, you hear me, right this fucking minute, to the press. He wanted information, that was all, he wanted names. A man in a suit and a woman in a Red Cross jerkin converged upon him, talking in low tones, laying on hands, but their intervention only incensed him further. They should take their fucking hands off him right now, he said, and tell him one thing: why was it taking so long for them to release a list? Why couldn't they get their fucking act together? This wasn't right, he repeated, this just wasn't right, then, forearm over face, he sobbed.

Bernice shook her head then, with some effort, lowered herself into a chair that Harold had pulled up. He pulled another one closer for me, then sat down himself. I noticed that he was vigilant, utterly attentive to his wife's movements at all times without conveying the slightest unease. I wondered what was wrong with her, what illness she had.

"I have MS," she said, in a matter-of-fact way, pointing to the walker. "Multiple sclerosis." I nodded. I was transparent to her, it seemed. I wanted to tell her about Eleanor, how hard I had tried, how it wasn't my fault, but I didn't know whether or not that would be a lie.

Instead, I said, "Still no list, right? No update? What's the matter with these people?"

"No, honey," Bernice said, with a deep, collapsing sigh. "We just have to keep on hoping, keep on praying. I heard one of those Red Cross people say that, with the water temperature at sixty-five degrees, they could survive for

eight hours. Up to eight hours. Though, the Lord knows,
you always hear of miracles. Remember that little boy
down the well there in Texas? Or that little Cuban boy,
what was his name?"

There was a silence while I, and, doubtless, the others,
performed a mute calculation: the plane had crashed at
8:30, 8:30 plus eight, 6:30, no, 4:30 a.m. I looked at my
watch, an odd appurtenance, something I hadn't consulted
in what seemed like days, something that belonged to
another life, a life of meetings and presentations, of fretting
on subway platforms, of gulping half a sandwich in three
minutes flat, of rushing madly down eleven flights of stairs
because the elevator was too slow. I wasn't sure if my watch
had stopped working, or whether I had lost the ability to
decipher Roman numerals, because the configuration of
its face conveyed nothing to me.

"Um, do you know what time it is?" I asked Harold, as
if timekeeping were somehow a masculine domain.

"It is," he said reluctantly, "just after five. Ten after."
He looked at his watch again, then at the broad, squat
back of his hand. "Honey," he said, addressing Bernice,
"we have to be strong." His voice was thin, depleted, as
if strained through a sieve. "When I spoke to the man at,
I don't know, 3:30, he told me there were no survivors.
That all the ambulances were coming back empty. That
all the boats were full. Of, of . . . bodies." And parts of
bodies, he didn't add, but I did, to myself, out of some
stoic notion that naming things would make them easier
to bear.

"Harold spoke to the man from the Post out there,"
Bernice told me before turning towards her husband and

taking his hand. She stared stubbornly at the floor, at the
glossy circuitry of parquet squares. "Maybe that's what
he said, hon. But how does he know? He can't know
everything. *Someone's* got to survive, it stands to reason.
And if anyone's going to survive, it's going to be Louise. I
just know it. She's a tough one, that girl. She's a survivor."
Her eyes filled with tears again, and, as she scrubbed them
away, she became conscious of me again. "No offense, Kim,
sweetheart. I'm sure your mom is a survivor too."

Was Eleanor a survivor, I wondered? What did it mean
to be "a survivor," anyway? That you weren't dead yet?
That you had endured your life? Well, that she had done,
conveying by her every action that it was something to be
endured, something from which every prospect of joy had
long since been drained.

She had endured a difficult childhood, that much I
knew. She seldom spoke of it—there were many things
of which she seldom spoke, including sex, love, her three
brothers, and what, if anything, she'd ever hoped for from
life—but, filling in the blanks, working from things half
remembered, overheard, I'd constructed a childhood for
her that was poor, precarious, full of privation.

This was the story I'd put together: Eleanor's mother,
an adventurous young woman from Durban, had married
a Welshman, from Swansea, an immigrant connected somehow with the diamond business. I'd never seen a picture
of him, but someone, my grandma perhaps, had told me
he was handsome, with a toothbrush moustache. Setting
up house in one of the seedier suburbs of Johannesburg,
the couple had produced, in short order, four children.
Then—and here the story became murky again—World

War II intervened, Leonard went off to fight, husband
and wife were separated for five years, his health was
ruined (his lungs, I think, or am I thinking of mustard
gas, trenches, the wrong war altogether?), the marriage
foundered, and they separated for good. Exit the Welshman, leaving, I gathered, a makeshift family, ill provided
for, hanging on to the lower-middle class by its fingernails.
Eleanor, as the eldest, had been responsible for raising
her three brothers, while her mother worked at a florist
shop in a fancy hotel, sometimes coming home at night,
sometimes not.

Searching my mind, I could remember only two anec-
dotes Eleanor had ever told me about her schooldays. One
was that she had been promoted two grades because she
was so bright. And the other, that for a whole term she'd
had to leave school early, walking the daily gauntlet of her
classmates on the tennis courts, because her fees hadn't
been paid. She'd told me that once, in anger, when I was
about twelve, grousing about the rules at my fancy private
school (we had to call the teachers "Madam," something I
refused point-blank to do).

After school, Eleanor had found work as a bookkeeper
at a Sunday newspaper, decent pay, with a cafeteria
lunch thrown in, she always said, so she could subsist on
beans on toast for dinner. There had, of course, been no
money for college, no sense of entitlement either—hence, I
always thought, much of her lingering bitterness and class
resentment, her fear of falling. After marrying Roger, who
came from an educated but impecunious English family—
and who had strolled into Eleanor's office one day, selling
advertising—Eleanor had tried, as far as possible, to erase

all traces of her past, all ties. No one had a camera, she
said, when I asked to see childhood photos, we were too
poor, people didn't have cameras then. I knew this was
a lie: I'd seen some myself, as a small child, at my
grandmother's flat, before Eleanor stopped taking us
there. Pictures of Eleanor and her three brothers, skinny
and wet, at the public pool. Pictures of Grandma Belle
with dark lipstick and a camellia behind one ear.

Nowadays, I supposed, it would be called "passing."
Except Eleanor hadn't passed, she'd failed. She'd created
a cage for herself, a cramped and airless cage, then
railed against it, flailed against it, as if someone else
had put her there. She'd endured a lifetime's worth of
imaginary illnesses and imaginary enemies, of loneliness,
lovelessness, and, I was sure, self-loathing, while creating
more enemies and more loneliness with each lashing out.
My heart ached, literally ached: oh, Eleanor, I thought,
why did you have to die like this, among 229 strangers,
just to prove yourself right?

"Yes," I said, so belatedly that Bernice looked up,
startled, "I'm sure she is."

"She's . . . ?"

"A survivor. My mother, Eleanor. She's had a tough
life. She's from South Africa, you know," I added, just
to get that out of the way.

"And you?" Bernice asked. "Do you—?"

"No, no, I live in New York. Don't really want to go
back there, South Africa, you know—to live." I didn't
know how to explain this to people, so I usually didn't
try. How to explain that you lacked a sense of place, a
sense of home—any feeling for mother country, father

land? That you preferred to be anonymous, that you didn't, in fact, want to be known? That you wanted— as if this were possible—to leave it all behind you, to shed your past like a skin?

This produced an awkward pause. We exchanged demographic information to fill it: Harold ran the computer lab at Utica College, Bernice worked for an interfaith ministry, administering a social services agency in the rougher parts of town, I was in market research. No, not advertising—analysis, focus groups, test marketing, that kind of thing.

Another pause.

"You know," Harold said, leaning closer and lowering his voice, "what they're saying, they're saying it was a missile."

"A missile?" I asked, bewildered, associating missiles with, if anything, intercontinental nuclear war. "A *missile*?"

"Yep. It's on the radar, apparently, clear as day. A blip, heading toward the plane. Eyewitnesses saw something too, like a streak of light."

"My God, but how—?"

"One of those shoulder-launched jobs, it could be," he said with a shrug. "From a boat."

"Shoulder-launched?" I said. "God. I've never even heard of that. How do you know all this, Harold? I haven't heard anything, I've just been sitting here. Waiting."

"Harold couldn't just sit," Bernice said, as if it were an endearing quality (and somehow, because she presented it that way, it was), "he had to go scrounging for information, see what he could find out."

"Information, and a whole bunch of rumors," he agreed.

"Well, what else have you heard?" I asked.

He hesitated. "Bunch of rumors, that's all. Nothing you need to think about right now. Right now, you got to think about getting your mom out of there, pray for her."

I nodded. Praying wasn't an option, as far as I was concerned, though I did find myself, at times, bargaining with the universe. This didn't appear to be one of those times. I was pretty sure that Eleanor was dead; I practiced saying the words in my mind, as a form of pre-emptive magic, *Eleanor is dead, my mother is dead, my mother died in a plane crash.*

I thought about asking Bernice and Harold about their daughter, what she did, where she was going, what her plans were, her hopes, but, remembering Bernice's face, her awful wince of grief at Louise's name, I faltered. Some other time, I thought, later. There'll be plenty of time, plenty of later; we'll be here for ever, in a kind of limbo, right here at the Ramada, as if we too have died.

Bernice, I realized, glancing across at her, was in fact praying, lips moving silently, hands clasped in her lap, tears coursing from under closed lids. She wore a green blouse, a string of painted wooden beads, and an ankle-length canary-yellow skirt, which, in their cheeriness, clashed horribly with her face. I looked away, feeling that my very glance was a trespass. Harold scanned the room with a blank, restless gaze. Acting on some odd impulse, which had nothing to do with vanity, I opened my slim Kate Spade shoulder bag and took out my compact, consulting the mirror to find out . . . what? I wasn't exactly sure. Whether I still existed, what I had become? I was shocked to see how old I looked, with blue-black hollows under my eyes and deep creases between my brows. My cheeks were pale and mottled, my nose pinched. Something had happened to my lips. I could make no sense of what I was looking at. It was like staring into the eyes, the vacant grey eyes, of a stranger.

Out of nowhere, the words of the old spiritual floated through my brain, *sometimes I feel like a motherless child.* I closed the shiny black compact with a snap.

"See that?" Harold said, gesturing to the front of the room where two large men in suits and earpieces were conferring amid a faint crackle of walkie-talkies. "Something's happening. At last, man."

A tingle of attention traveled through the room as people began to register the agitation around the door and the podium, a convoy of big suited men, FIN officials, and hotel security guards in green polyester blazers, who cordoned off the front of the room. The unruly clamor quieted to a buzz, as people sat down or straightened in their chairs, their faces vigilant and strained. Bernice opened her eyes and intertwined her fingers, crushing the knuckles of each hand in a rhythmic, alternating squeeze. I felt an illogical leap of hope, which made me think, oddly, of Ella's ever-optimistic arrival at the sound of the refrigerator door. Something was happening, eternity had been interrupted, something might be dispensed.

From an official-looking cluster nearest the door, I saw someone detach himself and make his way to the podium, a small man who looked vaguely familiar, as if I'd seen him once on the subway or in a dream. "Uh, good morning, ladies and gentlemen," he said into the mike, and I recognized him, the tentative voice and the glance at his watch; it was Baumer, but, was this possible, at least ten years older, his eyes deeply pouched, his skin creased and papery. He looked as if, without the lectern to lean on, he might fall over.

"At this very sad time," he began, then cleared his throat, "I'm honored to present to you a special visitor, a very special visitor, who is here to update you on the rescue operation and to share with you his grief, well, your grief, to share his thoughts and feelings with you and to let you know that the hearts and prayers of the entire state are with you. The entire country, I mean, of course, the entire world." He sipped from a plastic cup. "Ladies and gentlemen, the governor of the state of New York, Governor Galanis."

Galanis made his way, head bowed, to the podium, shook hands with Baumer, who scrambled aside, and then, with a practiced politician's square-and-drop of the shoulders, lifted his face to the crowd. There was a second of intent, ravenous silence. I wouldn't have been able to pick him out of a line-up, I realized, so nondescript was he, so studiously bland, so thin-faced, thin-lipped, and thin-haired. This was the governor? Who had voted for him? I wondered for a moment, crazily, if he might be an impostor.

As soon as he began speaking, in a thin, nasal voice, I realized that he had nothing to say. It was the usual boilerplate about tragedy, about thoughts and prayers, about acts of God. About terrorism not going unpunished. Then, responding to the taut stillness in the room, he shifted to a more purposeful tone. He had just come from East Griffiths, from the Incident Command Post, he said, where he had been fully briefed by the Incident Commander and had committed the full support of all state agencies to the recovery effort. Thirty-five state and federal agencies were responding, as he spoke, some 2,500 people, right now, out there at the Coast Guard station. He mentioned cutters, helicopters, Falcon jets, names and acronyms I didn't understand, C130 this, HH-60J that. He said the FBI was treating the accident area as a potential crime scene. I pictured a quadrant of the Atlantic, sapphire blue, marked off with black-and-yellow tape.

Then his voice, surprisingly, began to fail.

"I know you're all here because you had loved ones on that flight," he said, "and I want to pledge to you that we'll do everything in our power to bring them, their uh, bring their remains back to you. When I was out there, near the crash site, and I saw the, the devastation, all I could think of was my own family, my son, my eleven-year-old son—" He choked, stopped, swallowed, then added, "George." I'd seen the son on television, a hyperactive brat who'd mugged and misbehaved throughout the inauguration, at one point actually climbing under his chair, grimacing and capering like a creature in its cave. "So I can only imagine," Galanis continued, in a broken whisper, "what you must be going through right now, what pain." His smooth, pink, camera-friendly skin had flushed a hectic mauve; tears glistened in his eyes.

I felt more alarmed than gratified by this display: I wanted someone, the grown-ups of the world, whose ranks I had temporarily deserted, to take charge, to be in control.

I wanted the bland, phlegmatic governor to stay bland and
phlegmatic.

"I'm going to walk around now, talk with you individ-
ually," he concluded, taking a deep, ragged breath, "but I
do want to remind you that the state Office of Mental Health
has established a family assistance center here, with, uh,
I believe, six crisis counselors and"—he gestured vaguely
out into the crowd—"fifteen more on standby, so please
remember they're here to help you in any way they can.
The Red Cross is here, with supplies. We all want to do
everything we can to help. And," he concluded, again with
a catch in his throat, "God be with you."

His tears, unexpectedly, transmitted themselves to me, in
a sudden, stinging upsurge of self-pity. Something terrible
has happened to me, I thought, I've become part of a huge
tragedy, a public event. My life has exploded, crashed
and burned; I'm on a lifeboat that I can't leave. These
people—I looked around the room—these strangers will
be tied to me for ever. A family of some kind, kin.
I felt lost among them, helpless and baffled and full
of grief.

At that moment, Bernice, following some inner train of
thought to its conclusion, said, to no one in particular,
"You know, it's true, how many times do you get up in
the morning and see something on TV and think, 'Oh
that's terrible, those poor people,' and drive to work and
forget about it. But then one day the phone rings and it's
for you."

"Why, who called you?" I asked, jealously, and, I
realized, over-literally. "I had to call the airline myself."

"Louise's boyfriend. He'd taken her to the airport, seen

her on to the plane. Then he was driving home, back to Syracuse where he lives, and he heard it on the radio. Swerved right off the road."

I pictured the dark road, the dark, nauseating skid. "Where is he now?" I asked.

"At home," Bernice said, shaking her head, "the poor boy. His mama and sister are with him, I think. He wanted to come right back, but he had to talk to his boss this morning, get some time off."

I thought of all the phone calls I had to make, all the cancellations, all the meetings and appointments that had seemed so crucial just a few hours ago, on another planet, Planet Life. I thought about the presentation I'd been scheduled to make to Gillette, how I'd almost torn my hair out trying to get the graphics just right, fixing glitch after glitch through the long, headachy afternoon. How the colors on one pie chart had remained, to my chagrin, a little off—a washed-out cerise, a watery teal, how they'd nagged at me on the subway home and on the treadmill at the gym. I'd been worrying about the colors on a pie chart when two hundred people, my mother among them, had been blasted, without warning, into space. Blasted to bits, dropped, in a flaming rain of metal and flesh, three miles through the air. Meeting the surface of the sea with an impact that, I imagined, would shatter every bone in the body, drive the femur through the pelvis, the spine through the skull.

Eleanor, who was fat in the manner of short, multi-parous Mediterranean women, had always referred to me as a "bag of bones." You're too thin, she'd say, you're nothing but a bag of bones. Now it's you, Eleanor, I thought, you who are the bag of bones. I pictured bones laid out, like an incomplete jigsaw puzzle, on a metal lab bench. Pieces of my mother scattered, fragmented, missing: a forensic puzzle, a problem of rememberment.

MECHANISMS OF INJURY:
THE KINETICS OF TRAUMA

With any trauma victim, determining the extent of injury is important for determining treatment and decision-making. The obvious injuries are usually the ones treated, but the hidden injuries are usually not. Hidden injuries that are not recognized—and thus not treated—may be fatal. In trauma, it is not sufficient merely to have good patient-assessment skills; one must also develop a high index of suspicion.

Mechanism of injury

This refers to *how* a person was injured. The mechanism may be a fall, motor vehicle accident, gunshot wound, or so on. The science of analyzing the mechanism of injury, sometimes called "kinetics of trauma" or "kinetics of injury," helps the EMT determine the most likely injuries sustained as well as develop a "high index of suspicion" for probable injury.

The process of analyzing the mechanism of injury is based on physical laws. Basically, the laws state that:

- A mass in motion contains energy.
- Energy is influenced by the interaction of velocity and mass.
- Energy travels in a straight line.
- Energy is neither created nor destroyed, only changed in form.

Effects of Energy

Energy travels in a straight line. If energy, transmitted to a human body, continues to travel in a straight line without interruption, injury may not occur. However, energy traveling through the human body is frequently interrupted. The interruption may be because there is a curve in the bone, or an organ or tissue is caught between two hard surfaces (crushing or compression force) or pulled against a fixed point (shearing or deceleration force). In both instances, energy is forced to change form because it can no longer travel in a straight line. This results in injury. The injury is either blunt or penetrating.

Falls

A feet-first landing causes energy to travel up the skeletal system. Energy will be transmitted up through the femurs to the hips and pelvis. Because the femur has a natural curve at mid-thigh, fractured femurs may also occur. The next energy dissipation points are the hips. Energy may dissipate at the socket, forcing the ball of the femur up through the acetabulum, fracturing the hip socket. If energy remains, the spine will absorb the force at every curve.

In falls of fifteen feet or greater, the internal organs are more likely to be subjected to the same deceleration forces. The liver may be forced against the *ligamentum teres* and be literally sliced in two. The spleen may be torn from its stalk-like attachment. The heart may be torn from the aorta, and the ligament attaching the aorta at its arch may be ripped, causing traumatic aortic tears.

5

Thursday, July 20

——————

It was the phrase "refrigerated trucks" that was haunting me now, a phrase that wouldn't mean much unless you were picturing a particular person, particular flesh. Picturing why, like meat, flesh might need refrigeration. Picturing how, as in a power cut, meat might present a storage problem, how it might need to be dry-iced until someone could deal with it.

Also the word "remains," which, for me, evoked the dinner table. Leftovers. Something that might end up in the dog's dish.

Refrigerated trucks, lent by the Ride'n'Haul company, were queued up outside the coroner's office, holding bodies and "remains" for "processing," the TV news said.

I tried, but failed, to imagine Eleanor's flesh as anything but whole. I always pictured her body as huge, much bigger than it really was, ballooning into sight, in perpetual, agitated motion. A child's-eye view, I supposed. Nor could I, for some reason, imagine it sinking. They must have found it by now, I decided, floating peacefully, almost contemplatively, on the lap of the sea, facedown as if to observe the fish.

On a local TV station, a reporter, wind-buffeted on an anonymous strip of sand, brows solemnly knit, had signed off by saying: "And, folks, if anyone should find a body part on shore, call 911." I wanted to break through the screen, leap right into the box and strangle him. Was no one paying attention, I wondered, was no one thinking how the word "body part" might affect someone waiting in torment, holed up in a hotel room, waiting for word?

After the governor's briefing, after waiting around for another empty, anguished hour or so with Harold and Bernice, I had begun, vaguely, to realize I had to do something, go somewhere, before I collapsed. My body hurt all over, tender and achy to the touch, and there was, I didn't know how else to describe it, a pressure, a dry black puff, behind my eyes. If I could just lie down, just close my eyes, for an hour, I thought, I'd be fine. Just close my eyes.

Christina Barnes, no longer quite so perky-looking, was making the rounds again—I understood, for the first time, that she was my personal "grief counselor," assigned by FIN—and, after a long, scrutinizing look at me, had repeated FIN's offer of a room at the Ramada. "For all the families," she had said, "for as long as they need them. It's very important to get some rest, some quiet time, at a time like this."

"But I live in the city . . ." I'd said, helplessly, "the Upper West Side. It's not that far."

"Well, it's up to you, of course. You might want to be closer, though, close to the other families and to the briefings, when they occur."

"My cat—"

"Up to you," Barnes had repeated, briskly. "I can
organize someone to take care of the cat, if you can get
me a key."

"No," I said, feeling able, at least, to make one decision.
"She hates strangers. I'll call Lauren."

As I waited, blankly, in a chaotic line at the registration
desk, clutching, like a talisman, the pink voucher Barnes
had given me; as I was escorted, by an oversolicitous
bellboy, down a mirrored corridor that perpetuated to
infinity the red-and-green checkerboard of the carpet; and
as, at last, I slid the safety chain into its cradle on the door
of my room, all I could think about was dropping on to the
bed. My body lusted for rest, my brain for blackout.

But instead, driven by a numb compulsion, I reached
for the remote on top of the TV. News of the crash was
on every channel—it was, after all, a local story—except
for one, where squeaky-voiced cartoon characters gibbered
at each other, blithely unaware, in their brightly colored
world, that something terrible had happened, that humans
had died. Most people, I realized, would only now be waking
up to the news, which would be just that to them, news,
not the alternative universe to which, like a convict, I'd
been sentenced and shipped overnight, with no possibility
of appeal and no hope of escape.

I need to turn this off, I thought, I need to call Lauren,
break the news to her, I need to call Miles, have him go
through my schedule and my messages with me, decide
what to cancel, postpone, reassign. Miles was my assistant,
an ambitious, superefficient twenty-something who wore
whimsical bow ties to work, had an encyclopedic knowledge

of jazz, and whose perfectionism, luckily for both of us, was
on a par with my own. Miles will handle it, I thought, Miles
will explain, people will understand; at the thought of their
compassion, self-pity stabbed me. I felt that I might cry
soon. I felt I might implode. I felt that if I continued to
stare at the screen, I'd see something terrible, something
I'd never be able to scour out of my brain.

Okay, I thought, turn off the TV. Make some calls—
Lauren, Miles, maybe Anna again—then lie down. Rest.
But, sinking to the edge of the bed, remote in hand, I
continued to stare, as if my brain itself awaited instructions
from a giant channel-changer somewhere, orbiting the earth
perhaps.

I was mesmerized by the debris. The surface of the ocean
was strewn with trash, which, when you looked closely, was
not trash at all but the objects that had defined people's
lives, things you would pack in a suitcase for an overseas
trip. I thought of the suitcases hurled three miles through
the air and split open, like so many piñatas, by a whack
from the sea. I saw, among hunks of wreckage, shampoo
bottles floating by, shoes, a bright orange backpack. I saw,
what was that, a big stuffed Garfield, baring its demented
teeth to the sky. Tears smarted in my eyes, in my throat,
for the child who had carried that on board. I felt that
to show these objects like this, orphaned and adrift, was
a violation—what if, oh God, what if I saw something of
Eleanor's, her handbag perhaps, or her flowery blouse—
but as long as the cameras panned, I continued to stare.

I saw a stack of Styrofoam cups go bobbing by. Some long
green canisters, oxygen perhaps. Items I couldn't identify: a
yellow sleevelike thing in the foreground, a white starburst

that might once have been a book. And then, a sight that wrenched me, an upside-down seat, bouncing on the swells like a rodeo pony that, having bucked off its rider, is feeling its oats.

I clicked at once to another channel, where grim-faced Coast Guard workers in white moon suits and blue gloves were unloading body bags. The bags were shiny and black, I noted, like the big, heavy-duty ones for household trash. The bodies were a biohazard, the announcer said, rescuers had to scrub down with bleach. Click away from that. A panoramic view of the crash site from last night, a messy, tattered tongue of fire on a trash-filled sea. The *debris field*, it was called, and I could see why: so much refuse, so much waste, the detritus of a gigantic, shattered machine and of 230 lives.

Why aren't I feeling more, I wondered? Why aren't I racked with grief?

I couldn't remember Lauren's number, so I looked it up. The bedside clock said 8:10; I assumed that meant a.m. I couldn't remember what day of the week it was— Wednesday? Thursday?—but I knew Lauren would still be home, in her cluttered East Village studio, finishing up the newspaper or attacking, with exhortations and a purple pen, a pile of student compositions. None of the classes she taught at City College met before noon.

"What's up?" Lauren asked immediately, on hearing my "Hi." "You got a cold or something?"

"No, why?"

"You just sound weird, kind of croaky."

"Well, something's happened."

"Yeah? What?" Lauren's voice became vigilant, alert.

I could hear her putting something down, a coffee cup perhaps.

"Did you see the paper this morning?"

"Uh-huh, got it right here."

"The plane crash?"

"Yeah, saw that. Oh God." There was a pause, a tiny whirr of comprehension. "Don't say . . . Who?"

Suddenly, I couldn't speak. No air was available, a fist was pushing into my windpipe, right at the base of my throat, where the collarbones meet.

"Kim?" Lauren's voice had risen.

"My . . ." I said, and stopped. "El . . ." I tried, "Eleanor." And then I began to sob, for the first time, real sobs, spasms, heaving wrenching sobs that wouldn't stop.

"What?" Lauren asked, uncomprehending. "Wait, wait, wait, honey. Eleanor? Your mother?"

A sob of assent.

"But I thought she left already, last week, after you . . ." Lauren's voice trailed off, trying to make sense.

"No. No, she stayed," I managed to say, "she was here."

"She was here in New York?"

"Mmm."

"And she left yesterday, on that FIN flight?"

"Mmm."

"My God. Are you sure? Kim, are you sure?"

The sobs were beginning to subside. "As sure as I can be, right now. They haven't given us a list yet, but—"

"Wait, where are you? Where are you calling from?"

I managed, piecemeal, to explain. Lauren was having a hard time putting all the information together—Eleanor, plane crash, Ramada Inn—but once she did, once her brain had cleared a space for the unthinkable, her practical side kicked in. I could picture her running a hand through her dark frizzy hair, leaving it awry, on end, as if charged with excess energy from the circuitry within. I could imagine her scribbling a list, big loopy script embellished with arrows and underlinings.

"Okay, honey, so what do you need? Do you need me to bring you some stuff out there, toothbrush, clothes, things like that?"

No, I said, the hotel had provided a toiletries kit. I'd be going home soon, anyway, and I didn't care what I looked like. What I smelled like. I sniffed the armpit of my T-shirt. It stank, a rank adrenal stink.

Okay then, Lauren said, she'd get a cab out to the Ramada right away, to be there with me, fuck her classes, they'd do just fine without her. No way should I be alone at a time like this. I was tempted, for a moment, by the thought of Lauren's presence—her strong, enveloping hug, her copious tears, her formidable common sense. I imagined the comfort of her warm, plump body to weep against. But then, almost immediately, I felt overwhelmed by exhaustion, by the need, like a sick cat, to be left alone. I tried to explain this to Lauren. I used the sick-cat analogy, Ella at the back of the closet, behind the shoes.

"Okay," Lauren said eventually, "I know you well enough to know that if that's what you say, then that's what you mean. But, honey, if you change your mind, at ANY TIME, for God's sake, just call. I can't bear to think of you sitting alone out there, in some crummy motel, waiting . . . Just tell me what I can do from this end. Phone calls? Do you need me to call people for you, cancel things, I don't know, take care of things?"

No, I told her, I was about to call Miles. He could do that.

"I just wish there was something I could do," she repeated. "I can't believe this is happening. You see it on the news, you know, and it just seems so . . . unreal."

"I know," I said. "I don't think I really believe it yet either. I'm on another planet here, it's hard to explain. Just . . . you know."

"If you need me, if you need anything at all, you just call, okay? Any time, anywhere. I'll be at City from about 11:30. Get me out of class if you need to—those lazy bums will thank you." Lauren always referred to her students, mostly the hard-working sons and daughters of immigrants, as lazy bums, pieces of shit, and so on, but in fact she loved them fiercely and taught them with ferocious dedication. "And," Lauren continued, "I'll do Ella, of course." She had a set of keys to my apartment for this purpose, co-parenting, she called it. "Poor little punkin."

I wasn't sure if she meant Ella or me. After a slew of "Love you"s and "Look after yourself"s from Lauren, I hung up, feeling lonelier than before. I glanced around me. The stale, chilly air mumbling out of a metal box, the enormous bed with its cheap staticky spread, the two water glasses with their white paper hats—what the hell was I doing here? I was stricken with a sudden fear that right then, that very minute, crucial information was being dispensed somewhere, in the ballroom perhaps, and I was missing it. I almost ran out, down to the ballroom again, but remembered that, before I did anything else, I had to

(a) call Miles, and (b) rest. I kept repeating this in my mind, over and over, (a) and (b).

Just in case, though—with the same urgent sense that I might miss something—I clicked on the TV. New footage, this time: eyewitness reports, a sequence of random people (fishermen and partygoers and amateur videographers) looking self-important and grim. "We saw what looked like fireworks in the sky," one couple said, "a big white flash." They had been eating corn on the cob at the time, enjoying their new deck. An orange fireball, a man in a boat reported, then a "waterfall of flames." "We looked up," said two teenage girls, on the beach in the dark for some unspecified purpose, and there was this, like, "giant ball," then "you just saw pieces drop out of it."

One man, an engineer by training, was almost pedantically precise. I had the sense he'd been fantasizing about this moment all his life, the moment when he would be called upon, on national television, to describe a bankrobber or a UFO. There was a glint, he said, quick and sharp, as abrupt as a camera flash but not as bright. Then a ball of brilliant orange light that expanded for a moment—he moved two cupped hands apart—and then fell—pointy, downward gesture with the right hand—leaving behind a column of fire that, instead of following the first one, unfurled upwards (fingers opening from a loosely closed fist). He used the words "column" and "unfurled," also the word "plummeting." The plummeting streak of fire, he said, then split in two, forming an "inverted Y," which he described in the air with steepled hands.

I was having trouble visualizing what he was describing. It seemed overly complicated, abstract. A plane had blown up, that was all. Who cared about column A and column B, about unfurling balls of fire? I wanted him to shut up, I wanted his fifteen minutes to be over.

On CNN, they were playing tapes from air traffic control, distorted, disembodied voices, almost robotic. There were subtitles along the bottom of the screen so you could understand what they said. The last communication from FIN 770 had been "FIN heavy, out of one-three for one-five," referring, apparently, to 13,000 and 15,000 feet. I didn't know what "heavy" meant. Then another plane in the area, USAir, crackled in: "We just saw an explosion up ahead of us here, somewhere's about 16,000 feet or something like that, it just went down— in the water." Boston air traffic control tried for several minutes to rouse Flight 770. Back to USAir, what exactly had he seen? "It just blew up in the air and then we saw two fireballs go down to the water." Then the delayed, robotic realization: "I think that was him."

"I think so."

"God bless him."

Her, I thought, not him, *her*.

Then, at last, footage, grainy and small. The fireball blossoming against the deep blue dusk. A heartbeat, an in-breath, and then the forked cascade, the forked tongue of fire. Once more, in slow motion. The dark smoke coiling from the sea, the white haze suspended in the air. It was beautiful, I thought, silent, surreal. It seemed to have nothing to do with death.

I wanted to lie down, close my eyes. I could feel an immense ache of grief gathering somewhere in my body. I felt, at that moment, not the grief itself but its imminence, a tidal wave gathering somewhere out at sea. I needed, very badly, to lie down. But that was (b). What was (a) again? Miles.

"Kim Roth's office," he answered, at once. He was surprised I wasn't in yet, surprised to hear my voice on the phone. "What happened?" he asked. "Subway hell?"

I was getting better at saying it, I noticed, more adept at stringing the words together. They still sounded like a lie, an outrageous fabrication, something a person with Munchausen's would say, but I was able, at least, to utter them. Miles was stunned into silence for a few seconds, and I sensed that, beyond the immediate shock of the news, he was having difficulty imagining me, his boss, with a flesh-and-blood mother. I thought I'd mentioned Eleanor to him when she was in town, but then again, maybe I hadn't. Or perhaps Miles needed to see me as self-created, not bound by blood or class, so that he, an NYU graduate from Muncie, Indiana, could create himself. More likely, I concluded, I just seem so old to him that he can't believe my mother is alive. Was.

Once he regained speech—"Oh my God, Kim, that's unbelievable, I'm so, so, so sorry"—Miles became, as I'd known he would, solicitous, mindful, hyperefficient. I could almost hear his brain booting up to full power, whirring and clucking like a diligent hard drive, almost see him scrolling through my schedule, pausing briefly to ask about certain items, saving the rest to deal with later, cut, paste, delete. "Gillette we'll reschedule for Monday," he said, "and Tammy can handle it. Don't even give it a thought. Aloe Shaving Gel? I mean, really. I think you have more important things to deal with right now."

Along with his solicitousness, and his genuine concern, I sensed something else in his tone, a shimmer of titillation, a slight, ignoble thrill. I could imagine—and why not, he was human, he was twenty-five—his illicit sense of self-importance at being the bearer of such news, at being the one, as soon as I hung up, to disseminate it to the group. I could imagine the phone calls, the e-mails, the hallway consultations. I could imagine the puzzlement: "Kim? Roth? I didn't even know she had family. In this country, anyway."

Again, the idea of other people's compassion proved contagious. Something terrible has happened, I thought, tears springing again to my eyes, my mother has died. I need to get her body and get out of here. Then what? Anna and Angus and the girls will never be able to afford to fly here for a funeral, so I'll have to fly to Johannesburg. With a corpse. Or part of a corpse. On a plane. I don't think I can do that, I thought, and lay flat on the bed.

The telephone shrilled next to the bed, so loudly that I leapt, heart pounding, to my feet.

"Mrs. Bender?" a man's voice asked.

"No," I said, all that adrenalin instantly re-allocated to a spike of irritation, "you have the wrong room."

"Oh, I'm sorry, are you, ah," he paused, "Mrs. Roth, then? Room 310?"

"Ms. Roth." Mrs. Roth is dead. Mrs. Roth is floating, face down, in the debris field; Mrs. Roth has sunk, hair streaming behind her, to the bottom of the sea; Mrs. Roth is cooling her heels in a refrigerated truck.

"Ms. Roth, then, this is Blah-blah-blah from FIN," he gabbled in a monotone. "Just wanted to inform you that there will be a briefing for the families at 9:30 in the Rococo Room."

"The Rococo Room?"

"The ballroom. Where you were."

"Oh, okay."

"You're welcome, goodbye."

Information, then, at last. Facts. Details. I suddenly wasn't sure if I could handle facts and details. What if, I thought, I just can't deal, I start to crack up? What if there are certain kinds of information that the mind can't contain, that split it open and empty as a seed pod?

I glanced at the clock radio next to the bed: 8:40 a.m. I could rest for a while, I thought, just close my eyes, shut down my brain. But what if, I thought, something is happening, right now? What if, at this very minute, they're fishing Eleanor from the drink? Jolting upright, I reached once more for the remote.

The wreckage, I saw, was being transported to a giant military hangar—footage of flatbed trucks moving solemnly through suburban streets—where experts would try to piece it together, like an enormous shattered egg.

On CBS, a couple of talking heads were speculating about plastic explosives, PETN, Semtex, whatever they were, I didn't care. An obscure Afghan organization had threatened to "respond in an extreme way" to statements by "the stupid American President, the butcher of the world." Another organization, calling itself the Commando of God, had threatened to disrupt air traffic in the US as a protest against the Olympics. A man in Queens claimed to have brought the plane down with his secret ray gun.

No shortage of enemies, ever—in that, Eleanor, you may have been right.

Did it matter, I wondered, how Eleanor had died, who was responsible, or simply, starkly, that she was dead? I couldn't decide. I just wanted her body, needed to know where it was. The Air National Guard was aiding the search, helicopters dropping sea dye into the water to mark the dead.

My mother, sea-dyed, shrouded in an inky swirl. What color would that be, I wondered, the dye for the dead, and how, I wondered, would it stay in place? I pictured blood in bathwater, unfurling from the body like red smoke.

At my father's funeral, I'd felt oddly reassured by the solidity of the coffin, the heft of its brass handles, though the thought of his body boxed in there had torn at my heart. Why hadn't he chosen to be cremated, I wondered, given that he'd made such a good start by smoking himself to death? He'd died by fire, Eleanor by water (though perhaps, too, by fire, perhaps by what the coroner, on CNN, had called "multiple anatomical separations." He'd meant, of course, dismemberment, but to me the phrase had sounded, for a second, like a description of life, of the whole long sad sequence of cleaving to other bodies and being cloven from them).

Sitting, that day, in the small, sleepy Anglican church where my parents had been married and my father was being eulogized, drowsy, despite myself, in the stifling, lily-scented afternoon, I had wept bitterly, grievously, not so much for his death—which had been, after all, a foregone conclusion once the coughing and spitting began—as for his unlived life. For the slow process of attrition that had transformed him from the eager, debonair young man in the wedding photographs to the skinny, stooped, and defeated one, old at sixty, whose last breath in the oxygen tent, I couldn't help imagining, had been an exhalation of relief. A blue-eyed, dark-haired Gregory Peck lookalike who'd grown stringy and psoriatic with age, he'd dreamed of being an actor and, though he'd left school at fifteen, was able, all his life, to recite the major soliloquies from Shakespeare. "*The Raven himself is hoarse*," he'd declaim, driving me to school on chill, dark Highveld mornings, when we'd hear, in the distance, the desolate caw of a crow, scratchy and dry as the winter grass.

I glanced again at the bedside clock: 9:15, already, somehow. Time to get going. Time to head to the, what was it, Barocco Room.

I climbed off the bed and straightened my T-shirt, smoothed down the crumpled legs of my pants. I combed my hair and buckled on my sandals, watching myself perform these actions with numb deliberation, as if demonstrating them. As if, I thought, miming safety protocols—seat belt, oxygen mask, flotation device—to a planeload of passengers before takeoff. In the unlikely event of depressurization, I told them, please put the oxygen mask over your nose and mouth, and breathe normally.

TOKYO-HANEDA AIRPORT, JAPAN, 1985

Cabin (Public-address system): Put on oxygen mask. Fasten seat belt. We are making an emergency descent.

FLIGHT ATTENDANT (*on public-address system to the passengers*): May we ask you passengers with infants . . . nearby passengers . . . please be ready.

CAPTAIN: Right turn. Right turn.

COPILOT: I did it.

CAPTAIN: Yes. Do not bank so steeply.

COPILOT: Yes, sir.

CAPTAIN: Do not bank so steeply.

COPILOT: Yes, sir.

CAPTAIN: Recover it.

COPILOT: It does not recover.

CAPTAIN: Pull up.

Thirteen seconds go by while the crew tries to regain control of the aircraft.

CAPTAIN: All hydraulics failed.

COPILOT: Yes, sir.

CAPTAIN: Descend.

COPILOT: Yes, sir.

Another fifteen seconds go by.

CAPTAIN: Hydro pressure is lost.

COPILOT: All lost?

CAPTAIN: All lost.

Two and a half minutes go by.

FLIGHT ENGINEER: How about cabin pressure? Have cabin masks dropped? So? Well, cabin pressure, please.

Slightly more than a minute passes.

FLIGHT ENGINEER: Cabin pressure dropped. What? More aft . . . ah. What was damaged? Where? Coat room? Ah, coatroom . . . general . . . it dropped in baggage space. It would be better to land. All persons inhale [into] masks. Captain?

CAPTAIN: Yes?

FLIGHT ENGINEER: Do we put on masks?

CAPTAIN: Yes, it would be better.

FLIGHT ENGINEER: I think it would be better to inhale emergency mask.

CAPTAIN: Yes.

For another three minutes the Boeing 747 flounders.

CAPTAIN: Nose down. Lower nose.

COPILOT: Yes, sir.

CAPTAIN: Lower nose.

COPILOT: Yes, sir.

CAPTAIN: Lower nose.

COPILOT: Yes, sir.

CAPTAIN: Stop saying that. Do it with both hands, with both hands.

COPILOT: Yes, sir.

FLIGHT ENGINEER: Do we [put landing] gear down?

COPILOT: Gear down?

CAPTAIN: Speed does not drop.

COPILOT: Speed does not drop.

CAPTAIN: Lower nose.

COPILOT: Yes, sir.

For the next ten minutes, the crew wrestles with the controls and the throttles.

CAPTAIN: Power, power, lower nose. It is heavy. Lower nose slightly more. It is heavy. It is heavy. Oh, it is heavy.

. . .

FLIGHT ATTENDANT (*on public-address system to the passengers*): Those passengers who accompany babies, please keep your heads on seat backs and hold your babies firmly. Did you fasten seat belt? All tables are retracted. Please check it . . . Sometimes we land without notice . . . We keep contact with ground . . .

CAPTAIN: Lower nose. It may be hopeless. It is a mountain? Raise nose.

COPILOT: Yes, sir.

CAPTAIN: Control to right. Right turn. Raise nose. We may hit the mountain.

COPILOT: Yes, sir.

CAPTAIN: Right turn.

Cabin: Sound of ground-proximity warning system.

CAPTAIN: Max power.

COPILOT: Max power.

CAPTAIN: Hold out.

CAPTAIN: Left turn.

COPILOT: Yes, sir.

FLIGHT ENGINEER: Hold out.

CAPTAIN: Left turn, now . . . Left turn.

COPILOT: Decrease power slightly.

CAPTAIN: Right, right . . . Lower nose.

COPILOT: Fully controlled now.

Cabin: warning sounds stop.

COPILOT: It is totally ineffective.

CAPTAIN: Lower nose.

COPILOT: Good.

CAPTAIN: Here we go.

COPILOT: Yes, sir.

FLIGHT ENGINEER: Do I increase power?

CAPTAIN: Power, power.

Cabin: Warning sounds.

CAPTAIN: Power. Let's increase power, power . . .

Cabin: Stall warning sounds: "Pull up, pull up!"

CAPTAIN: Ah, it is hopeless. Max power.

COPILOT *or* FLIGHT ENGINEER: Max power.

CAPTAIN: Stall. Let's hang tough. Hold out.

COPILOT: Yes, sir.

CAPTAIN: Lower nose. Hold out, hold out.

COPILOT: Fully controlled.

. . .

CAPTAIN: Do not lower nose. It increases speed.

COPILOT: Yes, sir.

CAPTAIN: It's going down.

COPILOT: Yes, sir. Raise nose, raise.

Five minutes go by, while the crew struggles with the controls.

CAPTAIN: Raise nose, raise nose, raise nose. Stop flap. Do not extend flap so deeply. Flap up, flap up, flap up, flap up, flap up.

COPILOT: Yes, sir.

CAPTAIN: Power, power. Flap.

COPILOT: I am retracting.

CAPTAIN: Raise nose, raise nose, power.

Cabin: Ground-proximity warning: "Sink rate. Pull up, pull up, pull up, pull up!"

Cabin: Sound of collision with the first peak.

Three seconds go by.

Cabin: Sound of collision with the second peak.

End of tape.

6

Thursday July 20

One hundred and three bodies had been "recovered" overnight, the medical examiner had said. Odd choice of words, I thought, when none of them would ever recover from their passage, Icarus-like, through air and water and fire. Then, perhaps, to earth: the bed of the sea.

Blunt-force trauma, the examiner called it. The body of a person killed by a bomb has a different "signature," he'd explained, the flesh is shredded and may be singed. Not to get too technical, but, so far, he hadn't seen much sign of that. Some burns, yes, but those appeared to be mostly from the superficial fire, the snaking jet-fuel spill. You'd had, of course, various "insults" to the body: the blast, the blaze, the long drop into the dark sea, the inhalation of water into the lungs, otherwise known as drowning. So . . . Of the 103 recovered, only two had been identified; for the rest, he'd said, passing a hand over his balding pate, his staff would need the families' help. Medical records, dental records, DNA. And so on.

I can get all that FedEx'd from Johannesburg, I'd thought, the annals of Eleanor's body, the two Caesareans, the hysterectomy, the gall bladder operation, the herniated disc, the high blood pressure, the broken thumb last year from falling off a kitchen chair while attempting to feather-dust the light fixture. Portraits of her bones, her lungs, her digestive tract, even, perhaps, of her brain. The annual ghostly, grinning apparition of her teeth. Her abscesses, her crowns, the incisor she chipped that time in Durban, biting into a fresh lychee, forgetting that, unlike the canned ones, it contained a stone.

"What about clothes, jewelry?" someone had asked. "Can't you use those?"

Um, the official had replied, well, no, in the vast majority of cases, there was, unfortunately, no, uh, no clothing. No jewelry, either, to be quite frank. Either lost in the initial blast, or on impact. In some cases, of course, the fire . . . But a few, he brightened, a few do have clothes.

"All I want to know," a man had wept, interrupting, "is how much they suffered, my wife and boys, how much time they had, to know, to feel—" He couldn't continue; a grief therapist, hovering nearby, swooped in for the hug.

"Well," the medical examiner had responded, shifty-eyed. "Naturally that's something we can never know for sure. But all the evidence suggests, and I want you to believe this, that whatever happened up there happened, and that, uh, consciousness was lost by virtually everybody very, very quickly." He surveyed the packed ballroom, his audience suddenly, breathtakingly, silent. Perhaps they were praying, I thought, or performing calculations. As for me, I was parsing out his sentence, the "virtually" and the "very, very."

He'd assured us, again with that weary swipe at his head, that his office was working at full capacity, around the clock. He didn't describe precisely what that involved, but having talked to Harold before the briefing, I'd gleaned a vague and gruesome sense. Harold had described the county morgue, a two-story cinderblock bunker with dark-tinted windows, where, he said, all the autopsy tables were full, each surrounded at all times by three more bodies awaiting their turn. How he knew this I didn't ask. He'd described the FBI agents standing by with plastic cups for shrapnel from the victims' flesh, the bank of fans running non-stop to clear the air. I imagined, or tried to—having seen, on TV, how those arriving at the crash site had instantly covered their noses and mouths—the acrid reek of fuel, the stench of burned flesh, salt water, decay. The fumes of disinfectant in the morgue. I pictured the corpses, in quiescent rows, their skin leached a chalky white, eyes washed grey by the sea. Then, I couldn't help it, I pictured Eleanor's face, matte and blanched as no amount of powder could ever make it in life, staring at me with blind, sea-marbled eyes, as if to ask why, why did you do this to me?

Pearls, I thought, those are pearls that were her eyes. The vitreous of the eyeball, Harold had told me, is used in toxicological tests because it resists deterioration for up to three days.

"I think I'm going to be sick," I'd whispered to Bernice, who'd pushed my head gently down into my lap and, after a minute or so, offered me a sip from her Evian bottle. The sickness passed but not the vertigo, the sense of an unstable, emptying world, as when, a child ankle-deep in the ocean, I'd felt the suck and slide of the undertow when the tide raced out, the very sand, it seemed, coursing beneath my feet.

"Picture the busiest day of your life," the medical examiner had concluded, "then double, no, triple that. Then project that into the weeks ahead, with no end in sight. That's us, that's the county medical examiner's office right now. That's how hard we're working to identify your loved ones and get their remains right out to you." He didn't seem to realize how bizarre, how cavalier, it sounded, comparing his grisly chore to a killer day at the office, although, I supposed, that was exactly what it was to him: long days, long nights, a shitload of work.

"It hasn't even been twenty-four hours, not even a whole day," Bernice muttered in a stubborn monotone, "so what are they talking about? How can they know anything for sure? There have to be survivors, I just know that in my heart, and if there are, then I know Louise is one." Harold made no response; he stared into his lap, at his intertwined hands. I had heard Bernice's theories already, her hopes, obsessively repeated: an air pocket in a section of the cabin on the ocean floor, a slice of the wing that, serving as a life-raft, had floated her daughter serenely out to sea. Or perhaps Louise had already staggered to shore somewhere, with no memory and no ID.

Louise, I had discovered, was a graduate student in astrophysics, heading to Cornwall to observe an eclipse. I castigated myself for my earlier, possibly racist, assumptions, based on Louise's photograph, her service-industry smile. But pictures are so misleading, so many square inches of disinformation. If you saw Eleanor's passport

photo, with her beauty-salon hairdo and her string of
pearls, you might take her for a kindly matron, someone
whose large, soft body would be comforting to hug. The
truth was that Eleanor hated to be touched, that she
stiffened into a simulacrum of Harlow's wire monkey
when an embrace was required. She'd hug you with her
palms against your upper arms, as if to push you away.

She always hated her body, I thought, she dragged it
around as if it were a dead, bloated thing that didn't
belong to her. And now it is a dead, bloated thing, a
biohazard. My mother's body is a biohazard, I thought.

Dog handlers were being brought in, the medical examiner had said, to patrol the beaches. To sniff out any, uh,
remains that might have washed up. I pictured a dog with
a spoiled, meaty bone, then let my mind go blank.

After a while I realized I'd been gnawing, hard, on my
hand, on the webbed, fleshy part between forefinger and
thumb. I stopped, dried my hand on my pants, looked
around. There was a growing restiveness in the room,
an ugly, muttering mood. You've got a thousand people
here in shock, I thought, a thousand people who haven't
slept, a thousand people whose lives, in a split second,
were blown apart. Not exactly a split second, but close
enough: the explosion had occurred, according to Harold,
in the interstices between radar sweeps, between 8:31 and
45 seconds, which showed one "hit" for Flight 770, and
8:31 and 57 seconds, which showed two. Then, as the
plane broke up, a shower of tiny plus signs. Adding up,
I wondered, to what?

A woman from the Red Cross, looking fresh and officious
as if she'd just arrived, was introducing someone from the

FBI, I didn't catch his name, who was in charge of the investigation, Deputy-something of the New York office. I didn't care about titles, offices, job descriptions; I wanted information. I wanted explanations. I wanted them now, and so, I could feel from the agitation, the escalating tension in the room, did everyone else. Ullman, that was his name, stepped forward, eschewing the podium and opting instead for a single microphone on a skinny metal pole. He looked vulnerable, exposed, a stocky man in khakis and navy-blue blazer, his hair wet, as if from the shower, raked with comb marks. He had heavy pouches under his eyes, demarcated, this morning, with dark streaks that gave him the look of a lugubrious raccoon.

"I'm afraid," he said, "I don't have much that's new to tell you, I wish to God I did. One thing you can be sure of, though. We will keep working day and night, travel to the ends of the earth if necessary, to find the cowards who did this." He sounded as if he meant it. He reiterated the number of bodies recovered, 103, adding that a massive search effort was under way to "recover" the rest, to "recover" the wreckage, the black boxes. "We have not yet found the pingers with the pinger locator," he said. I had no idea what he was talking about. He went on about the debris field, about grids and quadrants, about the C130 Hercules, the HH-60J Jayhawk, the HH-65A Dolphin, the Naval MR2 self-propelled search vehicle. Also the cutter, *Vigorous*, whose very name made me feel better, more vigorous.

Two high-tech Navy salvage vessels, with divers, were on their way, he said, the *Grasp* and the *Grapple*. Who named these things, I wondered. Guys, with comic books? The *Pow*, I thought, the *Wham*, the *Gotcha*.

"Cut the crap, Ullman!" somebody began yelling from near the front of the room, a red-faced man I thought I recognized. "We don't want to hear your bureaucratic shit, your stonewalling, we've had enough of that from the fucking airline. What are you guys doing RIGHT NOW to rescue them? Why aren't there divers down there right now? Not tomorrow, now! What if you've got people still alive in the cabin, still breathing that, that air, that oxygen, down there?"

A babble of voices broke out at once, people shouting hoarsely, some climbing on to their chairs.

". . . you guys get off your asses and bring in submarines. They could be trapped down there . . ."

". . . a crane or something to lift out the cabin. Where's the cabin? Why haven't you found it? That's where the survivors are, and time's running out." A wave of unrest was rising, a transmission of disquiet through the crowd, an instant, tacit end to decorum. I felt it in my own blood: I wanted to shriek, I wanted to be heard, I wanted to make something happen. Ullman, raising his right palm pacifically, was trying to respond, opening and shutting his mouth but failing to make himself intelligible above the din.

". . . translators for the Greek families, the Swedish families! They can't understand what's—"

"And what about the missile?" someone shouted directly behind me, startling me. "When are you going to talk about that?" I turned and looked him full in the face, a tall bony man, cantilevered above me, spitting in fervor, cheeks flushed, eyes bright with tears. He had a big beaky nose, a ponytail. He spoke with some kind of accent, French perhaps, and was stumbling over his words. "What about the missile on the radio, I mean, radar? The bleep?"

His voice, too, was drowned in the general uproar, but he continued, addressing himself directly to me. "It's on the radar tape, many people have also sin it with their own eyes, many many people, a strick of light."

"Really?" I said. I was trying to determine whether this man was deranged, or whether, somehow, he'd come into possession of privileged information. "So they think it was a missile, then?"

"Everyone knows, everyone has sin it, it's on the tape. But the FBI, the American government, they are covering it up."

"Well," I said, wearily, "I don't see how they can be covering it up if everyone already knows about it—"

"Did he talk about it, did he tell us, this, this FBI?"

"No, but—"

"Ah, voilà."

"No, but we hardly gave him a chance. Before we all started yelling. I mean, listen to this." We were silent for a second. A tumult of angry voices, a furor of release. "And they're just beginning their investigation, you know, they're probably just covering their asses."

"Their asses?" He looked shocked.

"Uh, being careful, making sure they don't put their foot in it."

He still looked blank. He appeared to be picturing feet and asses, in various configurations.

"I mean, waiting till they're sure, so they don't get into all kinds of trouble, saying the wrong thing."

He made a snorting expostulation with his lips, such as a horse might make. "They are covering up because of the Olympics, in two wicks, to make a smiley-face for the world."

Okay, I thought, no point in arguing. He might be right, for all I knew. And if he wasn't, so what? I felt numb, weary, profoundly apathetic. Missile, bomb, malfunctioning coffee pot—what did I care? It made no difference. Eleanor was dead, and I, Kim, had killed her. Had blasted her with the explosive force of my rage, expelled her into the chill air of a lonely death. If it hadn't been for me, she would never have been on that plane, would never have been hurtling in a flimsy metal tube three miles above the earth, and I didn't even say goodbye. Didn't even say I was sorry. Just let her get out of the car, carrying her own bag, and let her go.

I began, covering my face, to weep.

"Ah no," the man said, his features crinkling in distress, "ah no, I beg of you. Please excuse me, my words . . ." He looked helplessly around him, fumbling in the pocket of his jeans.

"It's not you," I said, accepting the linty tissue he offered, "not the missile or anything."

"I know," he said. "It's . . . ?"

"My mother."

"My brother. Michel."

He told me, haltingly, that his name was Paul, he was an architect, he was from Paris, he'd rushed to Roissy upon hearing the news, his parents being too old and devastated to make the trip. I reciprocated with parallel information about myself. I was tired of explaining, and the clamor in the room was making it difficult for us to speak. With shrugs of apology, postponement, we soon abandoned the attempt. He grasped my shoulder briefly, firmly, for a second, then I turned my back on him, facing the front of the room, where Ullman, grim and flushed, was trying to regain control of the situation.

"How could you let this happen?" a man was screaming. "How could the FBI not know these people were going to do this? What right do . . . I don't go to their countries and kill their families, do I?"

"I want my daughter's body back," a woman wailed. "That's all. I want my daughter's body back and I want to go home."

"Okay, folks," Ullman finally managed to say, seizing upon a lull, one of those odd, synchronic silences that descends upon any group of people all talking at once. "Okay folks, okay, okay, okay. I understand that you're very upset, I understand that you want answers, and I don't blame you. I don't blame you at all. But you have to believe me, we're doing everything that's possible right now to recover the, uh, victims, that's our number-one priority. Number two, to recover the wreckage, so we can begin a careful, systematic analysis of what brought that plane down. No jumping to conclusions, that's not our job. There's no point in having an answer unless it's the right one." He paused after this line; I felt he had used it many times before.

"If it was a bomb, we'll know that very soon. You get a distinct signature in metal from a high-velocity explosion.

You get torturing, feathering, you get pitting and tearing. And if some kind of, some kind of projectile was involved, you'd get petaling. Around the point of entry. And so on. Okay, you don't need all these technicalities right now, God knows. My point is that we will know, we're committed to knowing, we'll be able to determine what happened with a high degree of accuracy. But it's going to take time. Once the Navy gets here and starts hauling pieces out of the water, then we can really get to work, kicking tin. But right now, and I repeat, our number-one priority is recovering the bodies."

Torturing, feathering, petaling—the language of metallurgy. Beautiful, almost, in an austere, otherworldly way. Beautiful to imagine metal marked with the filigree of a quill, metal unfurling like a flower. Not so beautiful, though, to imagine it torn and tortured like a human being, opening a wound with jagged teeth.

I decided to leave. There was too much craziness in the room, too much rage and blame, and I craved, suddenly, to be alone, to be in my sealed, featureless hotel room, watching television, which seemed much more real to me at that moment than the mob of strangers that surrounded me, the absurd discourse about feathering and flowering. I craved, suddenly, to call Anna. Ullman seemed to be wrapping things up, anyway, informing the families that agents would be dispatched to interview us—"with your consent, of course"—over the next week or so, and that rooms had been set aside at the Ramada and the Sheraton nearby for interviews with the pathologist's office. "Regarding, uh, identification. Distinguishing marks, medical records, and so on."

I whispered my goodbyes to Harold and Bernice, who'd been silent and ashen throughout, Bernice with her face in her hands, Harold blankly intent, and, as I was squeezing past Bernice's walker in the narrow space between rows of chairs, I turned and gave Paul the ghost of a wave, a flex of the wrist. He responded with a grave nod.

Room 310, this time, felt comforting, a pod of silence and cool air after the near frenzy, the pheromonal broth of the ballroom. I splashed my face with cold water, noting, as I did so, how it had hollowed out, become pointy and strange, wolfish. I put a call through to Anna, but Angus answered and said that Anna wasn't doing so well just then, that she was having "a bit of a crying jag." I had expected Angus to be at work, importing and exporting or whatever it was that he did, but then, on second thoughts, why would he be bringing in job lots of mattresses at a time like this? He'd be with his wife, of course, providing solace. I always pictured other people dealing with life alone, I realized, always pictured them solitary and stoic, like myself.

I told Angus what little news I had, asked him to start rounding up the medical records, asked him to have Anna call when she felt up to it. He would, he assured me, in his gentle, attenuated burr, not to worry, love. I wondered what Angus would be feeling now, at the news of Eleanor's death, what cocktail of emotions. Eleanor had made life difficult for him, dismissing him, out of hand, as a drinker and a ne'er-do-well; she'd even expressed to Anna, on the eve of Angus's heart surgery, the hope that he would die. Anna had forgiven Eleanor this, as she forgave all Eleanor's cruelties, something I could never understand. "That's just how she is," Anna had said later, tearful but resigned, "she says some terrible things."

Somehow Anna never reached a limit with Eleanor, Anna never said no. I could picture Anna helping Eleanor pack for her trip, this final trip, picture Anna running around the house in the inevitable last-minute frenzy of Eleanor's departure, following impossible, contradictory orders, taking the blame for things that had gone missing or wrong, bearing the brunt, as always, of Eleanor's distress.

The medical examiner had explained how, for each victim of the crash, investigators had established a cardboard box. Into this box, he said, went every item— wallet, passport, wedding ring, piece of clothing, and so on—that could be linked to that individual. Of course, he added, thoughtlessly, there were "mountains" of personal belongings that had no obvious owners—"orphaned" bits, he called them. But as each item was identified, it went into the box.

I tried to picture what might end up in the cardboard box labeled Eleanor Lilian Roth, which items Anna would have assembled and packed, with care, for her. Eleanor, I knew, never traveled anywhere without the makings of tea—an infuser, mug, and tea bags—or without a sizeable first-aid kit (remedies for travel sickness, aching muscles, colds, flu, constipation, diarrhea, high blood pressure, and snakebite; a stash of vitamins and Band-Aids; antiseptic swabs for toilet seats and the mouthpieces of public telephones). An inflatable neck pillow, for the plane.

Tweezers, for plucking her brows every morning into
that strange, thin line, her Oil of Olay, the coral-colored
lipstick she'd been wearing all her life, and her Coty
powder. Her comfy slippers, flowery nighties, girdles and
hose. Heated hair-rollers, with an arsenal of electrical
adapters. A big fat paperback to read on the plane.
Chewy fruit candies, Sugus, they were called. Little wads
of banknotes and travelers checks secreted in various
pockets, to thwart thieves. And Joy eau de toilette, her
one extravagance in life.

I wished she'd had more, more extravagance, more
joy. I wished she'd owned more beautiful things, jewelry
and scarves and Italian shoes. I wished I'd given them
to her. I pictured Eleanor's ancient hair-curlers bobbing
to the oil-slick surface of the Atlantic, some man in a
moon suit and surgical mask tossing them into a box.
I felt something inside me, some retaining wall, begin
to give.

Both Ullman and the medical examiner had warned their
audience—the Families, as we were now known, with the
implied, pious upper case—to stay away from the TV. The
coverage might be "distressing," the examiner had said; it
was "irresponsible," Ullman had added "sensationalistic."
But, compared to the stage-managed insanity of the Rococo
Room, it seemed like my only access to the real. Reality,
at that moment, was everything outside the Ramada.
Everything outside my own head.

CNN was interviewing local people, fishermen and
weekenders, who, responding to news of the crash,
had leapt into their whalers, their whatevers, bringing
blankets and wives, and headed out to help, to pull

survivors from the drink. Only, as it turned out, there were none. Now, a day later, with drawn faces and a distant gaze, they described the scene: the eye-stinging haze, the blast-furnace heat, the sulphurous smell. The throng of marine traffic, a cat's cradle of flares and searchlights against the night, and radio calls crackling from every direction.

The station played tape, picked up on a marine frequency. "There are so many bodies, so many bodies," a man's voice was repeating, "so many bodies, you just wouldn't believe."

"It was real ugly," one rescuer said. "It was not a nice scene. I've never seen anything like that in my life, and I hope I never do again." He'd seen no "live humans." He'd seen wallets, tray tables, diapers, a child's T-shirt, a page from a Spanish textbook, chunks of insulation, body parts.

"I'm not looking forward to looking in my net," a fisherman had said, setting out at dawn. "You get a bad feeling."

A construction contractor, a pot-bellied man in too-tight jeans, had been one of the first to arrive. "When my neighbor and I headed out in his Sunfish, we thought we were going to find survivors," he said. "We came upon dead bodies, but we kept looking for people who were still alive. Then we realized nobody was alive. I saw legs, a head. I said 'Please, God, don't let me see a kid.' Then I saw a kid." He rubbed his eyes, hard.

"There were legs and internal parts floating around. It smelled like rot," the neighbor said, tersely. He'd reached

into an oil slick to pull out a woman's body. Her head
fell off.

Woman's body. Whose?

"I tried not to get a good look at them, at their faces,"
another man said. He was shaking his head, like a wet cat.
"I didn't have time to think about what I was seeing—we
were out there looking for survivors. And by about 3 a.m.
it became apparent there were none."

"I told my crew, don't look at the faces," said a fisherman who was also a war veteran. "You'll be reminded of
someone you know."

"Try not to think of them as people," a Suffolk County
cop had advised the less experienced members of his
team, "that's the only way you can handle them, bring
them in."

A young Coast Guard commander had stared at the
ground. "There was this fishing boat," he said, "wanted
to use a gaff. But I said no. I said, Be gentle with them.
Be careful with them. They're human."

I watched this all quite calmly, propped against four
huge pillows on the gargantuan bed. It seemed to have
nothing whatsoever to do with me. Nothing to do with
Eleanor. I felt a numb, appalled fascination, a vacant,
mechanical registration of information. Body parts, tray
tables, gaffs, uh-huh. Insulation. Something about the
precision of these nouns appealed to me. The words
multiple anatomical separations scrolled through my
brain again, the words *torturing* and *tearing*. I thought
about Ella, hoped she was okay, that Lauren had been
in to feed her. I felt an odd gaping sensation in my gut
that I couldn't name. I went to the bathroom and drank

a glass of cloudy water from the tap, then retched it right up, gasping and panting over the shiny Ramada sink, where the miniature soaps were arrayed, the mouthwash, the shower cap. The little card that asked, "Forget Something?"

THE AVIATION RADIO ALPHABET

A = Alpha
B = Bravo
C = Charlie
D = Delta
E = Echo
F = Foxtrot
G = Golf
H = Hotel
I = India
J = Juliet
K = Kilo
L = Lima
M = Mike
N = November
O = Oscar
P = Papa
Q = Quebec
R = Romeo
S = Sierra
T = Tango
U = Uniform
V = Victor
W = Whiskey
X = X-ray
Y = Yankee
Z = Zulu

Alpha, Bravo, Charlie

My mother taught me to read, at three and a half, or so she says, and I believe her. I remember nothing of this except a single image from my alphabet book (the colors in my memory elegantly attenuated, mimicking, perhaps, the action of time): the letter N, a needle with its wavy, wayward thread forming the downstroke and the second upstroke. By contrast, I recall only too well my reading sessions with my father, when I would routinely be reduced to tears by the exploits of three squirrels named Nig, Nog, and Nug, unable, to my utter frustration, to distinguish Nog from Nug, or vice versa. (Nog and Nug sound like characters from Beckett. But who, I now wonder, in the South African context, was Nig?)

Delta, Echo, Foxtrot

My mother once, with uncharacteristic compassion, stayed up most of the night to finish knitting a royal-blue tea cosy, my Handcrafts project in the third grade, which I, with my left-handed lack of dexterity, had abandoned tearfully in a tangled mess. Not only did she complete the cosy, crowned with a pompom, but, in a gratuitous gesture, went on to crochet two sky-blue daisies which she affixed to each side (thereby definitively exploding the fiction that this was my handiwork, but never mind: it was a sight to behold).

Golf, Hotel, India

On Sunday, if she was in a good mood, my mother would

make crumpets for tea, standing at the stove producing batch after fresh, steaming batch, which Anna, my father, and I, seated like royalty at the dining-room table, would slather with butter and apricot jam, stopping only when we felt—exaggerated groaning and clutching—fit to burst. Then Eleanor would emerge from the kitchen, untying her apron, and sit down to what was left, the crumpets cooling now, turning leathery and tough. It never occurred to any of us (except Anna, much later) to learn the simple art of crumpet-making so that our mother could sometimes sit at the table, too, and be fed.

Juliet, Kilo, Lima

As a child, I read non-stop. That was how, other than fantasizing that I was the star of a Clairol commercial, I managed, most of the time, to screen out the fact that I was living in Johannesburg, South Africa (rather than, say, London or Paris), with parents who bickered constantly, and with a mother who, most of the time, seemed to resent my very existence. One day, in one of her energetic phases, Eleanor set up a sunny corner of the glassed-in verandah with bookshelves containing my entire library of *Secret Seven* and *Famous Five* books and an ancient little sofa, which she recovered in colorful chintz, making, as a finishing touch, curtains to match. Though I never actually spent much time reading there (preferring to lie on my bed with my cat Bonkers), I knew that she had wanted to give me something, create something—a private space—for me.

Mike, November, Oscar

My mother sewed most of my clothes, and there was little

in my childhood equal to the delight of going to the pattern shop and flipping through the rows of Butterick patterns—arranged in bins the ways CDs are now—to choose the one for my next dress. It took me years to grasp the conceptual distinction between the dress pictured on the cover of the package—sketched on some grinning little miss with upturned nose and upturned hair—and the essential, Platonic pattern of that dress: I always based my choice on the colors, the fabric, the lace, the very buttons that the illustrator had drawn in. Then there would be the corollary delight of making a trip to the Indian stores downtown (Eleanor anxiously clutching her handbag) and poring, with great deliberation, over bolt after bolt of fabric—fresh, peachy smell of new cotton—to pick out the perfect two yards.

Papa, Quebec, Romeo

Shopping was, for my mother, a symptom, a discharge of otherwise free-floating desire. Shopping was an end in itself, a pastime, a way of killing off a long Saturday or an endless weekday, a way of defying the tedium of her life, of imposing her will on the world. It was the main way that Anna, Eleanor and I spent time together, and it was almost the only way during my adolescence that my mother and I could endure each other's company. When Anna and I were children, shopping was an unambiguous delight, an adventure involving our "good" clothes (in case we ran into anyone we knew), tea at John Orrs (pastry for Eleanor and Anna, a toasted cheese and Coke float for me), and then the rapt somnambulation through the stores, intoxicated but at the same time intimidated by the objects that hovered in the perfumed air, too perfect, too luxurious, too glamorous, surely, for us.

Sierra, Tango, Uniform

When I began graduate school in California, my mother sent me, as a gift, a set of linen dish towels that were identical in design—some kind of stylized tulip, I believe—to one that I, in a fit of extravagance, had recently bought myself. At a distance of 10,000 miles, with all the dish towels in the world to choose from, she had chosen for me the very ones that I had chosen for myself, a coincidence that both moved and frightened me. Did she, in fact, know me? After all? And if she did, what might that mean?

Victor, Whiskey, X-ray

When I graduated from Berkeley and got my first real job and first real apartment, in Chicago, my mother made me a quilt. She'd heard that the winters were bad there. The design was called "Around the World." In one corner, on a dark red square, she'd embroidered *For Kim*, then the date, then her signature, *Eleanor Roth*.

Yankee, Zulu

A few years ago, for no apparent reason, my mother sent me in the mail something I'd had as a child: two white china figurines, a tiny girl (barely an inch and a half high) with her even tinier cat. The girl had two blue dots for eyes and a demure red dot for a mouth; her hands were clasped, clutching a painted bloom. The cat stared out from the two brown dots on its wedge-shaped head with an air of blank astonishment; a sprig of wildflowers was painted on its back. I'd forgotten that this girl, this cat, ever existed, but the sight of them rolling out of the bubble wrap pierced me with sadness, a surprise attack.

7

Thursday, July 20

———

"What about footprints," the woman asked, pen poised in the air, a left-hander, I noted, like myself.

"Footprints?" I said. "Why in the name of God would I have my mother's footprints? I mean, how . . . ?"

"I don't know, some people do. You know, if you're goofing around with paint, sometimes. Or if she sent you the outline of her foot so you could buy shoes for her. People often do that with their kids' feet, actually."

"No," I said. "No footprints." My mother and I had never goofed around with paint, not even when I was a child. The image was absurd, Eleanor on hands and knees with her skirt hiked up, her bare soles daubed fire-engine red, bobby's-helmet blue. Eleanor did not "goof around," period—she had little capacity for play. Part of her brain always seemed occupied with the silent, ongoing calculus of anxiety; even when she smiled, her brow neglected to unknot itself. Except, I thought with a pang, on those rare occasions, usually after an unaccustomed glass of wine at Christmas or New Year, when she would become giggly and silly, quite undone, wiping tears of laughter from an unfamiliar, unclenched face, and, for a second, I glimpsed what my mother might have looked like if she'd ever been happy.

"Tattoos?" the woman asked, and we both laughed, the woman kindly, myself with a bark of release. The interviewer from the pathologist's office, Cherry Levine, was small and wiry, in her thirties, I guessed, athletic-looking, but at the same time, if you didn't notice the ropy forearms and wrists, the muscly calves, almost frail, vulnerable-seeming, with a gentle voice and a level, contemplative gaze. She took off her glasses to look at me when she asked a question, then put them back on to write the answer on her clipboard. She wore some kind of lab coat with a name tag, her wavy brown hair was tucked neatly behind her ears, and she looked tired, pale-lipped, but used to it, as if fatigue were her habitual state.

"Toenail polish?" she asked. "I'm serious. In that Ethiopian Airways crash, the one that was hijacked, you know, like, ten years ago, this woman was able to identify her friend among all the injured people by her toenail polish. Blue, I think."

I had to stop and think. Toenail polish? I scanned the small conference room, the putty-colored walls, the bad botanical prints. I stared down at the fake walnut table where I sat angled from Cherry, close enough to read the forms. We'd already done age (64), sex (F), race (Caucasian), hair color (greyish brown), eye color (brown), wedding ring (yes) and pierced ears (no). Smoker? No. Implants, pacemaker? None. Now toenails. I stared at my own small, neat toes in their black Italian sandals, then back up at the table—the listing stack of folders, which I longed to straighten and align, the water pitcher, the fax machine from whose mouth, like a lizard's tongue, a long document curled.

Toenail polish? Yes, definitely, when Eleanor was younger: I could still picture the white sandals she liked to wear, the squished, sausagey toes, the chipped coral paint. But now? I strained to remember Eleanor's feet—in the car to Sag Harbor, for instance, applying imaginary brakes as I drove, or that night, after the theater, when she'd kicked off her pumps in her hotel room. I could see the flowered sofa where she'd sat, could see her feet, puffy and red-indented in their nylon sheaths, the bunions that she'd rubbed with visible relief, but not the toes.

"Don't know," I said. "Maybe. Another thing to ask my sister." I made a note. It made me feel more competent, in control. Cherry had already asked about medical records, dental X-rays, recent photographs; Anna would send them, Anna would provide. Medications: Anna would know. Recent illnesses: all I could remember was the broken thumb and the flu. Did craziness count, I wondered, bouts of depression, paranoia? Never diagnosed of course, never named, because in Eleanor's culture, Eleanor's day, you didn't admit you were ill, you didn't ask for help, you covered up instead. Everyone covered for you—Mom's having a lie-down, Mom's a bit tired today, Mom's upset, don't upset your mom—until it was too late, Mom was afraid to leave the house, Mom was lashing out with a leather belt, Mom was screaming from the car window at pedestrians, but no one could do anything then, no one could put a name to this, because that would mean admitting you'd all been lying all along. Simpler, in the long run, to decide that you were the defective one, that you'd been born rotten, unlovable, the way some people are born with a wall eye or a club foot. Simpler never to put it to the test.

Birthmarks? No birthmarks that I could think of, but scars we'd discussed. The long barbed gash across Eleanor's belly, a double purple welt that had terrified me when I was a child and had seen, on the folds of my mother's flesh, what it might cost to give birth. The word "Caesarean" had sounded punitive, severe. "What are bosoms for?" I'd asked, afraid, seeing Eleanor naked, unimaginably fat. Afraid that one day this fate, this disfigurement, would befall my own flesh.

It felt obscene to remember my mother's body this way, in so much detail, the way a lover would. Obscene to dismember it like a pathologist: toes, ears, organs, scars. A tremor of nausea passed through me. "I don't think I can handle much more of this," I said, propping my forehead on my fingertips and kneading my temples, hard. "Are we almost done?"

Cherry took off her glasses, looked at me with mild, greenish eyes. "Almost done," she said. "Hang in there just a few more minutes if you can, Kim. Just some contact numbers, some release forms, and I can let you go."

Someone would be sent to my apartment to dust for fingerprints, the traces of Eleanor's touch. What had Eleanor handled there, I wondered: a teacup, a doorknob, the telephone? The Thai water pot some lover had brought me from some trip: "What is this funny thing?" she'd asked, picking it from the shelf and squinting at it. The cushion that she'd plumped up on the couch, the medicine cabinet door.

But not, I thought, my skin. If they dusted my body down, they'd find no prints. Just ancient bruises, ancient scars.

"Something else you need to know," Cherry said, taking her pen in both hands and see-sawing it slightly, a grave but clumsy gesture. "If we ah, if we don't have success, don't make a positive identification, we'll have to go to DNA. Eventually. Then we'd need samples from her, samples from you. Blood from you, and from your mom, you know, hairbrush, toothbrush, something like that. Underwear. Even a pen she'd chewed." As Cherry paused, I was picturing Eleanor's gnarly, matted hairbrush sealed and labeled in a Ziploc bag on a lab bench somewhere. The image came close to undoing me, unknotting the hard weave of grief inside me. Not now, I told myself, stay focused, this woman is trying to help. The earpieces of her sunglasses, that's what Eleanor would have chewed.

"Not a pen," I said, "probably not a pen."

Cherry looked taken aback, blinked, then continued. "Well, that's not something we have to deal with right now, okay? It's just a possibility that I want to prepare you for. We're not there yet," she said, placing a hand, for a second, on my arm. "It's still early, let's hope for the best." The best, in this case, being a dismembered corpse with enough pieces left to go on, a ringed finger, a painted toe. Otherwise, I thought, the long slow demotion from *body* to *remains*, from *remains* to *biohazard*. From *biohazard* to *tissue sample*, from *tissue sample* to *DNA*, a smear in a vial. My mother in a vial, essence of Eleanor: all the necessary information about her, all the code she passed on to me. Nice girls don't hang about the cinema on a Saturday afternoon, here's how you make a roux, here's how you make a crêpe-paper flower, always wear a slip, always have enough money with you for a telephone call and a taxi home, you can't trust Jewish doctors, you can't trust men, you can't trust anyone, marriage is two rats trapped in a sack, gnawing at each other because neither can escape.

"She would just die if anyone saw her underwear," I said, a non sequitur even to myself.

"This is hard, I know," the woman said, after a beat. "I know it's hard."

They hadn't even used her name when they had notified me. They'd come to my door at the Ramada, Christina Barnes and a man in a suit. Barnes had placed her hand on my shoulder, the man had said, "Ms. Roth, we now have the final list and I have to inform you that your loved one is on the list." I wondered what I should be feeling. They asked me if I needed anything. It took, perhaps, forty seconds.

As Cherry stood to shake my hand, signaling the end of our interview, she bumped the table with her knee, dislodging a folder from the stack. A slew of brightly colored tags slid out, like a hand of cards.

"What are these?" I asked, picking one up by its coarse raffia string. I thought I could guess, though: it showed a crude line drawing of a human body, back and front views, neutered, open-palmed. You were supposed to tie the tag on an injured person, then show, by drawing on that cheerful nude, where the damage was. Below the body was a chart, for vital signs, then, horrible, four vivid perforated strips— green, yellow, red, black.

Green was outermost, a bright leafy green, marked with the Roman numeral three and a little white ambulance,

crossed out: *not serious, no need to transport*. Above
that, sunny yellow, traversed by a tortoise and a Roman
two: *second priority, take your time*. Number one was
red, with a leaping hare. And innermost, the one that
would be left when you'd torn off all the rest, a black
strip, a white zero, and a shovel combined with a cross.
Daggerlike, signifying death.

"Triage tags," Cherry said, tersely, taking it back. "For
disaster scenes, you know, when a lot of people are injured.
But we didn't need those. In this incident. After all." For
the first time she looked flustered, said a kind but hasty
goodbye.

Sphygmomanometer, I thought, numbly, as I walked
out, as I awaited the elevator next to a brass plaque that
hailed Verna from housekeeping as Employee of the Month.
That's what those things are called, those blood-pressure
things. There'd been a pictogram of one on the triage tag.
Sphygmomanometer. I filled my mind with the word.

I'm going home, I decided, as I slid the key card into
the door, waiting for the little eye to wink from red to
green, I'm going home, that's it, there's no reason for me
to stay here.

The world outside the cab window was like a halluci-
nation, an assault on the senses, a harsh brilliant space
swept by a disquieting breeze and a roar of sound. As
I sat stupefied in the back seat, having struggled for a
few seconds to recall my address, I experienced reality
as a dangerous and alien place, swarming with beings,
shimmering with the violent colors of their clothing, their
hot shining machines. On the expressway, in cars, buses,
vans, limousines, staring straight ahead of them, or in

the huge red-brick complexes of Queens, stacked one on top of another like eggs in a carton, or, just ahead, in that red-and-white moving truck, Moishe's, trundling to a job, the choreography of other people's lives continued, everyone going somewhere, everyone busy, hurrying, intent on some private purpose, as if, I thought, nothing had happened, no one had died. I felt insulted, appalled; I felt outrage foaming up in me. How could they be conducting themselves like this, in this mundane fashion? I wondered, as the cab slowed on the streets of Manhattan, allowing for close-ups, snapshots of people I'd never seen before and would never see again, that Chinese deliveryman on his bicycle, that doorman in his bizarre brocaded cap, that fat sweating father struggling to fold a stroller. I felt as if I were returning, from a long journey, to a world emptied of significance, a spectacle that had nothing to do with me. It hurt my eyes to look at it. I felt raw, frangible with fatigue. I didn't know how I was going to get out of the cab.

"Here we are, miss," the driver said, "222 West 79th. Need a receipt?"

The super, Haxhi, waved at me as I walked into the vestibule, checked, reflexively, my mail. Then he went on mopping the floor. I'd half expected him to ask how I was, where I'd been. But how, I thought, would he know I've been anywhere at all: I don't have any luggage. I haven't missed a day's newspaper, a day's mail. I haven't even been gone for twenty-four hours. It was—I checked my watch—just after six.

As I unlocked the apartment door, I listened, automatically, for the plop of Ella jumping off the bed, the high-pitched little cry as she padded out to greet me.

But there was silence, or what passed for silence in the city, the subliminal background roar. "Ella?" I called. "Where's my Ell?" The apartment felt stuffy, stale, and, with the curtains still drawn, seedy somehow, evocative of hangovers and regret. I yanked the curtains open, pulled the windows all the way up. Lauren had been there, I could tell: the newspaper, retrieved from the doorstep, lay on the kitchen table, next to a jugful of orange zinnias.

"Ella?" I called again, entering the kitchen, which looked oddly denuded. I soon understood why: Ella's litter box was missing, the blank square of its absence sketched by a scatter of stray grains, which meant that Lauren had taken Ella to her place, rather than merely stopping in to feed her. It made sense—Lauren hadn't known how long I would be gone, and it was quite a trek from Alphabet City to West 79th every day—but a howl of reproach rose up in me, a surge of self-pity, as if there'd been a terrible misunderstanding. I'd meant Ella to stay here! Here! I needed her here.

I walked back into the living room and looked around. I literally couldn't think what to do next. Without Ella, the apartment suddenly felt empty, depopulated. There was, I realized for the first time, a faint echo in the large, airy room, the kind you hear in a vacant house, or in a bathroom when you've taken all the towels for laundering. I needed more rugs, more furniture, why hadn't I realized that before? The spare, austere decor on which I prided myself—white walls, sheer linen drapes, black-and-white photographs, a few elegant, oversized pieces of furniture— suddenly looked meagre, miserly, as if there wasn't enough

of anything, enough things, enough comfort, enough dis-
order, enough love. I sank into the enormous sage-green
armchair where I usually liked to curl up with Ella and
a book, but felt lost in it, dwarfed, as if my feet might no
longer reach the floor.

I tried to think what to do next. I could call Anna, but
it was past midnight in Johannesburg. I could call Miles,
but he would have left the office already, heading home
to Boerum Hill, his roommate, and his dog. I could call
Lauren, but she'd be at her tango class, three nights a week,
six-thirty to eight. I could call Bernice and Harold at the
Ramada, but I knew they would have called me if they'd had
any news. We'd exchanged numbers before I left, of course,
promising to stay in touch, but I missed them already,
missed Bernice's stubborn patience, her slow, deliberate
gait. Missed Harold's theories, his enfolding hug.

A sense of unbearable loneliness flooded over me, a
feeling, which I'd never experienced before, of being alone
on the earth, sole. The pleasure I usually took in my
solitude and self-containment, the relief I felt on shutting
the apartment door, shutting out the clamor and demands
of other people, had evaporated, vanished, as if it had never
been anything but a shabby delusion. Sorrow engulfed
me, desolation, like a physical pain. I can't do this any
more, I thought, I can't go through life alone. I was
staggered to find myself thinking this, staggered by the
sudden revelation of my loneliness, as if it were an illness
that had inhabited me for years but never been diagnosed,
never been named.

If I sit here any longer, I thought, I'll bay like a wolf,
I'll rend my hair. I'll writhe and flop like a landed fish. I

could actually picture myself doing this. If I start weeping, I thought, I might never stop.

I sprang up and headed for the telephone, in the dining alcove off the kitchen that I'd turned into a work space. A million years ago, I thought, I sat here, at this big old oak desk, in my T-shirt and boxer shorts, and heard the woman from FIN say I'm so sorry miss, but, yes, we do have an E. Roth on the list from the gate. Five messages, the red digital display informed me: why hadn't I thought to check?

The first was from Gabriel, at Organica Hair Care, confirming my appointment for color at 5:30 "tomorrow," whenever tomorrow was, or would be. Then the voice of my mother's friend Maude, which I couldn't bear to listen to, dreading not only Maude's grief but (irrationally, I knew) some terrible accusation. I skipped and saved the message, with a pang. The next three were from people at work, people I didn't know very well: Deborah, a fellow senior VP, platinum blonde and fur-coated like a villainess in a soap opera; Tony, the computer guy, sweet, chubby, and gay; and Courtney, a recent Brown graduate who coordinated the Attitude and Usage Studies but was secretly plotting a career in the futures market. They were all so very sorry to hear the news; they were all thinking of me; I should please let them know if there was anything they could do. I felt touched, weepy, to hear their voices, but at the same time unreasonably annoyed: what did they know about Eleanor, about death? What, for that matter, did I?

I needed to talk to someone. I wished I still had a shrink, though I'd never had much luck in that department. I thought briefly of Christina Barnes, who'd given me a card and a beeper number, but balked at the thought of her relentless compassion, her to-do list for the bereaved. In a frenzy, in a fervor, with the urgent sense that if I wasn't occupied I would fall apart, I began making calls, working through my address book, leaving messages for my friends—Matt, Irina, and Joyce in New York; Rosario and Tom in Boston; Pin, Walter, Pat in Los Angeles; a distant cousin in Cincinnati—using the same formulation each time—"Hi. Just calling to let you know some very bad news . . ."—which still sounded like a lie, a grotesque bid for attention. Odd that no one was home, that no one ever picked up the phone. Then again, neither did I.

Now what? I left a message for Lauren saying I was back, that she should let me know when I could pick Ella up. I went into the kitchen, got a dustpan and brush, and briskly swept up the spilled kitty litter. I tried the 800 number FIN had given the Families but it was busy. I thought of Cherry, from the pathologist's office, her soft voice, her long monkeyish hands. I thought about fingerprints and looked around the room, trying to remember what Eleanor had touched. I tried to picture Eleanor in my apartment, Eleanor walking around and looking at things, but was suddenly unable to visualize my mother's face. There'd been too much talk about smashed skulls, about the damage fish and crabs could do, about burned flesh sliding off the bone. I could no longer see my mother's face whole. In a panic, I dashed to the hall closet where I kept the photograph albums.

Sinking, cross-legged, to the floor and hoisting one of the heavy volumes to my lap, I had a quick flash of

rainy afternoons when Anna and I used to entertain ourselves with the family albums, accompanying the images
with a narrative that, familiar, reiterated, became the
truth, whether it was or not. Those albums were the
old-fashioned, leather-bound kind with pages made of thick
black card, on which you had to glue little corners to
affix the photos to the page. Eleanor, for years, had
faithfully dated and annotated the pictures with a special
white ink, rich and dense as icing. It wasn't until I was
well into my teens that I noticed that the date on my
parents' wedding picture had been altered, that beneath
the date inscribed there lurked another one, smeary, spec-
tral, indecipherable. I couldn't understand why I'd never
noticed it before, but, at that moment, a whole sequence
of things made sense: why Eleanor and Roger, despite
their flamboyant incompatibilities, had married in the first
place; why Roger's mother, a proud and arrogant woman,
had refused to attend the wedding; why family mythol-
ogy had ascribed a premature birth to me, so premature
that, by rights, I should have emerged blind, languageless,
and gilled.

My own albums were the ugly, modern kind, with gold-
stamped fake-leather binding and plastic pockets, but I
seemed to have inherited my mother's archivist tenden-
cies, printing neat little labels to identify time and place.
Flipping through them, I was astounded to see how few
pictures I had of Eleanor. None, that I could find of the
two of us, just the two of us, together. Maybe others
had existed and I'd thrown them away. Or maybe they
hadn't.

The album, carefully edited, was a shrine to my self-image,

with, where possible, only glamorous pictures allowed, pictures of me looking slender and tanned, my wavy hair streaked with gold (either from the sun or from Gabriel's ministrations) and, over the years, inching upwards from shoulder-length, to show off my long neck. Pictures of my travels, the trips to Belize, to St. Petersburg, to Kenya, the Galápagos. Pictures that made me look pretty rather than odd and angly, as I often did, a face out of Picasso or Almodóvar, with my high cheekbones, my aquiline nose, my slanted, peeled-looking eyes. Pictures of parties and celebrations, of Ella in various poses, of friends and lovers—Chris, the beautiful younger man; Len, the charming psychopath; Malcolm, who'd lasted two years. But none, or almost none, of Eleanor.

The most recent one I could find dated, shockingly, from the day of Roger's funeral: it showed me, Eleanor, Anna, Angus, and their two girls, Bridget and Sally, on the steps of Anna's suburban house. Bridget and Sally, seven and five, were standing in front of Eleanor, one step below her, shielding her body from the camera. They looked very smart in their school uniforms, the two little girls, scrubbed and shiny but strained, as if their hair had been so tightly braided it was pulling their features out of whack. Eleanor, heavily sedated, wore a navy-blue two-piece. Her eyes were puffy and pouched, her skin the color of clay. Next to her, their shoulders touching, stood Anna, plump, anxious, and exhausted-looking, in a floral dress with our grandmother's pearls, her hair set in a stiff and unfamiliar style. And, on the far edge of the group, next to Angus, I stood, looking washed-out, with my New York pallor, in the South African sun, ridiculously overdressed in a black suit. I was frowning, severe, and thin. I looked as if I had no idea where I was. I looked as if I came from another species, another gene pool altogether, as if Eleanor's DNA and mine would never make a match.

DNA: WHAT IS IT?

DNA (deoxyribonucleic acid) is a chemical structure that forms *chromosomes*. A piece of a chromosome that dictates a particular *trait* is called a *gene*.

Structurally, DNA is a double helix: two strands of genetic material spiraled around each other. Each strand contains a sequence of bases (also called nucleotides). A base is one of four chemicals (adenine, guanine, cytosine, and thymine).

The two strands of DNA are connected at each base. Each base will only bond with one other base, as follows: adenine (A) will only bond with thymine (T), and guanine (G) will only bond with cytosine (C).

What is DNA Fingerprinting?

The chemical structure of everyone's DNA is the same. The only difference between people (or any animal) is the order of the base pairs. There are so many millions of base pairs in each person's DNA that every person has a different sequence.

Using these sequences, every person could be identified solely by the sequence of their base pairs. However, because there are so many millions of base pairs, the task would be very time-consuming. Instead, scientists are able to use a shorter method, because of repeating patterns in DNA.

These patterns are able to determine whether two DNA samples are from the same person, related people, or non-related people. Scientists use a small number of sequences of DNA that are known to vary among individuals a great deal, and analyze those to get a certain probability of a match.

How is DNA Fingerprinting Done?

The 'Southern blot' is one way to analyze the genetic patterns which appear in a person's DNA. Performing a Southern blot involves:

1. Isolating the DNA in question from the rest of the cellular material in the nucleus.
2. Cutting the DNA into several pieces of different sizes.
3. Sorting the DNA pieces by size. The process by which the size separation, or "size fractionation," is done is called gel electrophoresis.
4. Denaturing the DNA, so that all of the DNA is rendered single-stranded.
5. Blotting the DNA. The gel with the size-fractionationed DNA is applied to a sheet of nitrocellulose paper and then baked to permanently attach the DNA to the sheet.

The Southern blot is now ready to be analyzed.

In order to analyze a Southern blot, a radioactive genetic *probe* is used in a *hybridization reaction* with the DNA in question. If an X-ray is taken of the Southern blot after a radioactive probe has been allowed to bond with the denatured DNA on the paper, only the areas where the radioactive probe binds will show up on the film. This allows researchers to identify, in a particular person's DNA, the occurrence and frequency of the particular genetic pattern contained in the probe.

The fit of the probe to the DNA does not have to be exact.

Sequences of varying homology can stick to the DNA even if the fit is poor; the poorer the fit, the fewer the hydrogen bonds between the probe and the denatured DNA.

VNTRs

Every strand of DNA has pieces that contain genetic information which informs an organism's development (exons) and pieces that, apparently, supply no relevant genetic information at all (introns). Although the introns may seem useless, it has been found that they contain repeated sequences of base pairs. These sequences, called variable number tandem repeats (VNTRs), can contain anywhere from twenty to one hundred base pairs.

Every human being has some VNTRs. To determine if a person has a particular VNTR, a Southern blot is performed. The pattern which results from this process is what is often referred to as a "DNA fingerprint."

A given person's VNTRs come from the genetic information donated by his or her parents; he or she could have VNTRs inherited from his or her mother or father, or a combination, but never a VNTR that either of his or her parents do not have.

8

Friday July 21

———

Eleanor, her hair aflame, her skirt filled with air like a flamenco dancer's, was falling from the sky: a shower of people was falling from the sky, all fully dressed, all perfectly vertical, as in a Magritte painting, falling like rain, and I was running, arms extended, to catch my mother, stumbling through the stony dark, gasping with panic and exhaustion. "Hold on," I yelled, "I'm coming, I'll catch you," I cried, though I knew already that I wouldn't get there in time, that I was too far away, lost, lame, bruising my bare feet on the rocky ground. My whole body convulsed and I awoke with a yelp which, in the dream, I felt, had been a long, reverberating scream.

I lay there for a few seconds, emptied of identity, of anything but a raw prickling terror, until, gradually, like blood rising in a syringe, self returned: time, place, memory. And, with it, pain, resuming residence like a familiar: remember me? I was here yesterday, I haven't gone anywhere, I'll be here today, tomorrow, next week. Nothing has changed, Eleanor is still dead, you're still alive.

The room was dark, with the absolute, authoritative dark

of the middle of the night, and I put my hand out blindly, feeling for Ella's warmth on the pillow next to me. I tested the weight of the bedding at my feet, Ella's other designated spot. Then I remembered that Ella, too, was gone.

The bedside clock, when I turned towards it, read 2:14. Damn, I thought, realizing that I'd been asleep for less than four hours, when I'd hoped, succumbing at last to sleep as if I'd been trepanned, decorticated, for a long stretch of oblivion. But I was awake now, wide awake, with a ragged, scratchy consciousness in a body that felt somehow incomplete, disassembled, as though the moths had been eating it, as though a thin, cold wind were blowing through.

Eleanor is dead, I thought, my mother is dead. This is the first time I've had to wake up and know that.

There wasn't much I could think of to do at two in the morning. Pulling my robe around me, I went to the front door and opened it, checking, absurdly, to see if the paper had been delivered yet. It hadn't, so I plopped down on the sofa, missing, at the edges of consciousness, Ella's arrival at my feet, the little annunciatory cry, and then the long, inscrutable feline calculations, the eyeballing of distance and obstacles, before the oddly clumsy, go-for-broke leap up into my lap. I miss her, I thought; who'd have thought I'd miss her so much?

As I clicked through the channels, I saw that most of them had sneakily reverted to normal programming in the middle of the night, old movies and real-life veterinary emergencies, weight-loss schemes and devices for trimming the hair out of your nose. CNN was rerunning footage I'd seen before, a calm-looking man in military fatigues being

escorted from the Coast Guard station at East Griffiths.
Shortly after the crash, he'd shown up in US Army Reserve
uniform, name tag and all, and, using his own illuminated
batons, began directing helicopter traffic. "I'm running
the takeoffs and landings in this operation, and if someone
doesn't follow my instructions, I'll wave him right off
the site," he'd declared grandly. He'd done a fine job
for several hours, before anyone thought to question his
credentials.

I felt like an impostor myself, a confabulator, someone
impersonating a woman who'd lost her mother in a plane
crash. I didn't know what to do, what to feel: Anna
is the one, I thought, the real one, the daughter, the
motherless child. I felt an odd surge of envy, an emotion
that surprised me, an archaic emotion—the emotion (rage,
dismay, disbelief) of the one-year-old confronted by the new
sister, the warm new bundle, in the mother's arms.

Perhaps because I'd been thinking about the family photo
albums the night before, a picture that I hadn't seen in
years came back to me, with sudden eidetic clarity. The
picture, taken when Anna and I were about three and four,
showed us, hand in hand, approaching an amazing thing,
a big scary thing, something neither of us had ever seen
before: a horse, its long face leering, wide-nostriled, over
the stable door. I even imagined I could remember its damp
harumphing, its warm dusty creaturely smell. Although
Anna and I looked almost identical, with our wide faces
and pudding-bowl haircuts—people mistook us for twins
all through our toddlerdom—our demeanor couldn't have
been more different. Anna shrank back, eyes and mouth
round with apprehension, her entire body contracted into

a flinch of avoidance. I, on the other hand, stepped boldly forward, one hand behind me, holding Anna's, the other reaching toward the huge, lippy face of the horse. My brows were scrunched with misgiving, but my nose and chin pointed defiantly up.

And that, I thought, became my face, pointy, defiant, poking into things, while Anna's stayed round and soft, with cushiony cheeks and a button nose. No one mistook us for twins any longer: people were surprised, these days, to learn we were sisters and usually mistook Anna—less well preserved, more sun-damaged—for the elder one. Nonetheless, I thought, I'm the one who's alone at two in the morning. I suddenly felt chilled, so, grateful for a task, I went into the kitchen and put some water on to boil, standing numbly next to the kettle until it screeched. Then, while my ginger-ginseng tea bag steeped, I read the fine print on the box. This ancient brew, it said, was guaranteed to stimulate the *qi*. If ever I needed my *qi* stimulated, I thought, it's now. Taking a tentative sip, I speed-dialed Anna's number.

Anna's voice sounded weak, as if she had laryngitis, as if her vocal cords were worn out from weeping.

"Hi, Kimmie," she said, performing an imperfect subtraction to establish New York time. "Isn't it, what, four in the morning there? Can't you sleep? Is there . . . ?"

"Slept already," I said, "for a few hours. I'm fine."

"Any . . . ?"

"No, no news."

"God," said Anna, "when will there *be* some?"

"Don't know," I replied, thinking: what kind of news do you want? The news that a skull, crushed like an egg, or a stray limb, swollen and strange from the sea, has been positively identified as that of Mrs. E. Roth, please come and pick up your property? Then what? I wondered, feeling a wave of dread and helplessness wash over me at the thought of everything I'd have to do, to endure, to negotiate and organize, in the days and weeks ahead. While Anna sat safely in Johannesburg, not having to deal—as usual, I thought, bitterly, and, I realized, unfairly.

"Angus is going into town this morning," Anna said, after a pause, "to pick up the stuff, the X-rays and all that. Then he's going to DHL it to you, I think it takes a day or two."

"Okay, great. Whatever's quickest. I'll pay for it if you—"

"No, no. It's fine."

There was a silence during which a whole menu of unmentionable items scrolled through my mind and, I supposed, Anna's as well: Angus's failing business, which had operated for years in the interstices of economic sanctions but was shriveling up now, in the light of open trade; Bridget and Sally's school fees, a constant source of stress; the fact that, with six rands to the dollar, I seemed rich by South African standards whereas, by Manhattan standards, with my mortgage and my loan payments, I was barely scraping by. Usually Anna and I didn't discuss money, but soon, I realized, we'd have to.

"Anyway . . ." I said.

"Anyway . . ." said Anna, at precisely the same moment. We both stopped, then Anna, after a pause, continued. "I had to tell the girls last night." Her voice cracked, became thick and teary. "It was terrible. Horrible. You know how close they were to their nana, especially Sal. She just got

really quiet, sort of shrunk into herself, wouldn't talk. I
don't think it's really registered yet, you know, what this
means. What really happened. I'm keeping them home
today, but I'm not letting them near the TV. The coverage,
my God, it can make you ill . . ."

"Yes," I said, trying and, for some reason, failing to
visualize my nieces, to remember what they looked like.
I kept seeing the taut, scrubbed faces in the photograph
from five years back, at the funeral, the cowed look of
children negotiating some adult catastrophe. They'd be
ten and twelve now, I realized, embarking on adolescence:
Bridget was probably wearing strawberry-flavored lip gloss
or sparkly nail polish by now, probably had posters of
Leonardo DiCaprio on her bedroom wall. Sally was the
more meditative, meticulous one; she'd recently developed
a precocious passion for bonsai, tending her five little pines
with finicky care.

"It said on CNN," Anna continued, "that twelve bod . . .
twelve victims had been identified so far. Oh, Kim," and
she started to weep, "how long do you think this will take?
I just want her back. Back here."

"Don't know," I replied, feeling, from nowhere, a spurt
of anger, bad chemicals in my blood. "I have no idea. I
don't know any more than you do." And also, I wanted to
add, but didn't, have you thought of the logistics, what it
will take to get her—or what's left of her—back to you? I
felt exhausted, utterly overwhelmed, I wanted to lie down
on the floor and sob.

"No, no, I know," Anna said, in her habitual placatory
manner—years, I thought, of dealing with Eleanor. "I know
you don't. It's just, you know, so hard."

Try doing it alone, honey, I thought. At least you have a husband, children. Someone to hold. The thought shocked me: I'd never consciously wanted, or allowed myself to admit that I wanted, a husband. A lover, yes; a companion, a mate; but not a husband, the very word smacking to me of tedium, of entrapment, of constant petty bickering, of dirty socks on the floor and a sexless bed. Of a Dagwood-like figure recumbent on the couch. Of middle age, the end of passion and the end of hope. As opposed to what? I wondered, bitterly. My life, which is so full of passion and so full of hope?

During one of our set-tos a few years before—I could no longer keep them apart in my mind—Eleanor had called me, among other things, an "old maid." She'd been in full screeching frenzy, spewing out the usual sequence of insults (selfish, ungrateful, think you're so much better than everyone else, well, just you wait, my girl, and so on). Then, visibly ransacking her word-hoard, she'd sputtered and stammered for a few seconds before triumphantly ejecting the most damaging epithet she could find. "And," she yelled, as if that clinched everything, "you're an *old maid*." If anyone else (who? I can't even imagine) had referred to me as an *old maid*, I would have laughed out loud, recognizing one of those terms—like, say, *hubby*—that can no longer be deployed without irony. But when Eleanor hurled it at me, it hurt. It hurt because it was intended to hurt. It hurt because I knew it was her way of telling me that—advanced degrees and fancy jobs and assorted lovers notwithstanding—I was, in her mind, defective. Defective merchandise, left on the shelf. Unlovable is what she meant, what *old maid* meant to her.

"Yes," I said, belatedly, to Anna. "It is. It's hard, and it's only going to get harder. Have you thought about that?"

"What d'you . . . ?"

"Have you thought about what happens when they *do* find her? What we'll have to do then, everything that will need to be done? Have you thought about that? What *I'll* have to do?"

"Oh God, Kim, I don't even want to . . ."

"No, I know you don't. That's reality. That's adult life. That's my department, isn't it?" My sudden viciousness shocked me, shamed me into silence. Space roared between us like the sound inside a seashell, or inside your own ear, whichever it is.

Why am I doing this? I wondered. Why now? If ever we needed the *entente cordiale*, we need it now.

"I'm not sure . . ." she said, weakly, then stopped.

"I mean . . ." I said, then stopped too. That sound, I decided, that roaring sound, definitely originates inside your own ear. "I mean—oh, forget it."

I searched my mind for something to say. Something grown-up and helpful, something polite. Something that didn't originate from some indefinable rage. Then Anna, the conciliator, spoke up.

"It says, um," she ventured, "it says on CNN that they're going to send the divers down, soon as they can, soon as the weather calms down."

"Calms down?" I asked. "What do you mean, calms down?"

"Isn't there some kind of storm going on there? Something to do with that hurricane, the tail-end of it?"

"Don't know," I said, picking up the phone and walking

toward the window. "Didn't hear anything. I'm looking out now."

Seventy-Ninth Street looked slick, varnished, with a litter of freshly fallen leaves. Across the way, a couple of stunted trees nodded and tossed, but I had to focus on the building opposite, on a blank square of concrete, to see the actual stripes of rain. Otherwise, the night was ambiguous, unreadable, a damp, shiny haze traversed by the intermittent whirr of tires, a succulent, peeling sound, like Velcro.

The ocean must be like that too, I thought, restless, soupy, treacherous—how could they dive? And what would they find? I imagined, for some reason, a diver in a diving bell, drifting blindly, dreamily, into the deep, like a fetus in the amniotic sac.

"Yes," I said, "it's rainy, kind of windy out."

I walked away from the window, seized by a sudden panic, wondering what I was going to do with the next few hours, the next few days, now vacant but non-fungible, like a voided check. Sit around and wait for the phone to ring? Watch CNN, the same three-minute segment over and over again? Pursue every rumor and crackpot theory on the Internet? Call people in different time zones? Drink?

"Anna," I said, "it's just going to be difficult, okay? A lot of waiting."

"I know." Then, pleadingly, "But really, it won't be too long, will it, once they start diving?"

"Don't know. Let's hope. I mean, let's hope they find what they're looking for, right away . . ."

The image of the diver came back to me, descending, in his antique contraption, toward the wreck of the plane. His helmet like an oversized head, with its single enormous eye, an O of apprehension.

"Anyway," I continued, "we should probably get off the phone, free up the line." I glanced at the TV, as if Anna were keeping me from it, preventing me from getting what I wanted. "See what's on the news."

"Yes," said Anna, sighing, "And I should go see what those girls are up to."

I hit the remote before I put down the phone, forestalling even a second's worth of reflection, a nanosecond of vacant consciousness.

A Navy commander was speaking, a leathery man in brilliant whites. "—and so you have to be aware of where your body is and where your umbilical cord is," he said, gesturing vaguely towards the Atlantic, "and make sure you don't get tangled." He was, I began to understand, describing the perils of "hard-hat" diving. Hard-hat diving was when divers were tethered to huge oxygen tanks on board ship, rather than being restricted to the oxygen they could carry on their backs, like scuba divers, who had to resurface every fifteen minutes. The hard-hat operation was scheduled to begin once the weather cleared up and the *Grapple* arrived, he said, squinting pugnaciously at yesterday's smudgy horizon, as if to issue it an order. Then he looked down at the heaving grey water.

"There's a lot of debris down there," he said, "with a lot of sharp edges, and you have to make sure you don't get snagged on it."

I sipped at my tea, now cold. I pictured Eleanor trapped down there in the dense silent gloom of the seabed, her broken body enmeshed, like a fly's, in a web of wires and cables: there were 150 miles of wiring in a 747, I'd read. Then I pictured the diver approaching her, moving like a moonwalker with his weighted vest and boots, stirring up clouds of silt with every slow step, the light on his helmet sending out a thin, lonely beam into which, every few feet, nightmares reared.

I didn't even say goodbye, I thought, just let her get out of the car and walk away. And the time before that? The time before that had been three years earlier, when I'd made a dutiful trip at Christmas time, laden with Nike sneakers and Beanie babies for the girls, Clinique cosmetics for Anna, good-quality nightgowns for Eleanor ("The stuff we get here these days is such junk, you know, made for the Afs,"— "Afs" meaning "Africans," Eleanor's current substitute, when she thought about it, for the now-tabooed "kaffir" of yore). The Yuletide cheer had lasted about thirty-six hours, until—in the course of an argument about who should go in which car to the Carols by Candlelight—Eleanor had hurled an ashtray at me, missing me and breaking a china angel on the mantelpiece instead. I had packed my bags, still bulging with beribboned packages, moved on to Anna's sofa, and sworn, quite calmly, never to spend another night under my mother's roof.

And now, I thought, I never will. The thought filled me with a terrible, choking sadness; I never will, because I never really tried, never tried, as Anna did, to accept her. Never let go of my pride and self-righteousness, always sitting in judgment, primly biting my tongue, waiting for her, out of fear and resentment, to come to a boil, waiting for her to lose control so that I could too, and it would always be her fault.

I leapt up, clicked off the TV, and, electric with anxiety, began making calls. Lauren wasn't home, Bernice wasn't in her hotel room, the 800 number was busy. I redialed a few times, needing to hear a human voice, then thought of Paul, imagining him as even worse off than me, in crazier, lonelier free fall. After a short triage session with the hotel operator (I had misremembered his last name), I reached him in his room. He said he'd call me back, that he was expecting a call from Washington, some federal lab. The radar tape, he explained, "there is big news." Okay, I said, talk to you soon.

I put the phone down and stared at it. I knew I had to call Maude, couldn't put it off much longer. Maude DuPlessis was my mother's oldest friend, pretty much her only one these days, as Eleanor had had a lifelong pattern of staging a huge blow-out with anyone within a certain radius of intimacy—friends, relatives, the house servants, even the family doctor—and instantly severing all connection with them. She hadn't been on speaking terms with any of her brothers for years and had maintained a silent, vicious warfare with her own mother for over a decade, until Belle had died. Eleanor and Maude, too, had had a falling-out that lasted almost ten years—I couldn't remember the details, something about a tablecloth—but lately, thanks to Maude's persistent efforts, they'd repaired it.

Maude didn't pick up, to my relief. I left a brief message: no news at the moment, would be in touch. I suspected she'd already spoken to Anna. But I knew that at some point I was going to have to talk to her. I couldn't imagine what I would say, what she might think of me—the bad daughter, who'd just dumped her mother out of the car, who hadn't even said goodbye. This thought made my head swim, as if it were filled, to bursting, with black air.

Stop this, I told myself, and reached for the remote.

". . . 120 feet," another uniformed official was saying, "right at the limit of diving capacity." He was pointing to a chart, a three-dimensional schematic that showed the ocean like a slice of pie, with the seabed as the crust, the surface like whipped cream. Two tiny black divers were heading down, like ants upon the pie. "So you have a choice. If you focus on the grief of the families, then you bring up bodies. If you focus on the investigation, then you're primarily concerned with the black box. The wreckage itself."

The so-called black box, the flight data recorder, I had learned, was bright orange, with two white stripes, made of steel and titanium, about the size of a large shoebox. It kept track continuously of the plane's internal operations, spying on itself, even after failure, catastrophe, explosion, an avionic Richard Nixon, taping compulsively, compiling a comprehensive self-indictment. Air speed. Air pressure. Oil pressure. Heading. Roll. Pitch. Fuel flow. Deviation from ideal approach path. Vibration and fire.

Once ejected from the body of the plane, it transmitted a ping: even under a hundred feet of water, it transmitted a ping, a piteous sound, I imagined, like a kitten's cry. Listen to me, I imagined it pinging, I could tell you a thing or two.

Eleanor had hurled the ashtray at me—a heavy, squarish one, made of some grey-green South African stone—and I had simply moved my head to one side, my mind calm though my heart was pounding, so that it shattered the white china angel on the mantelpiece behind me. Eleanor

had wept, literally gnashing her teeth with rage and frustration—"That was my favorite," she kept saying, "my favorite
one"—and I had looked on, like an anthropologist, taking
notes: So this is how they do it, how they comport themselves
still, on the planet of the mad. Had looked on the way, I
knew, that men had sometimes looked at me, lovers, when,
in the late, burned-out butt of the night, in a kitchen or
on a street corner, flooded by a terrifying rage, I'd turned
on them, shrieking, with the man—if it were toward the
end and he'd seen this all before—regarding me, amid
the passion and the pounding hearts, the anger and the
bafflement, with that same quizzical distance, wondering
who I was.

This is my true inheritance from you, Eleanor, I thought,
the code you transmitted from your body to mine. That's
how my blood knows it's yours, when it's possessed by the
same fury that drove me from you. In those moments, the
moments that I've lost myself, I know I'm yours.

If I sit here any longer, I thought, if I think like this, I
will go insane. I pictured the pressure of my thoughts as
an aneurysm, an overfilled vessel that threatened at any
minute to burst and flood my mind with blackness, like
blood. I found that I couldn't breathe, that my breath
stuck pinched and shallow in my throat. The words "scare
air" came into my mind and at first I couldn't remember
where I'd heard them, what they meant. Then I did: the
Navy official, a diving term. Scare air was when something
went wrong with your air supply, when you could no longer
breathe underwater. A scuba diver, in a crisis—hose sliced
or blocked—would have a spare, plus a partner nearby
with a surplus mouthpiece. But a hard-hat diver was all

alone down there, tethered to his distant air supply. If his hose snagged on debris, he had to signal the ship to switch oxygen to an auxiliary hose. If that didn't happen fast enough, he would die.

9

Saturday July 22

———

Lauren showed up at nine the next morning, looking harried and overburdened, holding Ella's carrier in one hand, two shopping bags in the other, and, squished under one arm, a bunch of yellow tulips, which looked, with their pale, parted lips, as if they were gasping for air. A bulky object shrouded in a shiny black garbage bag was sliding out from under her other arm, but I caught it, in a deft swoop, before it crashed to the floor. Then Lauren dropped everything, tulips and all, and hugged me hard, long, wordlessly. I was conscious mainly of the hard edges of the garbage-bagged thing, Ella's litter tray, pressing into my chest. I tried to remember when I had last eaten; I felt bony and empty, my ribcage frail as a bird's.

Extricating myself from Lauren's embrace, I knelt, still without a word, on the hallway rug, where the blue plastic cat carrier had been dumped. Tufts of tabby fur extruded through the mesh of the door as Ella butted her head anxiously against it.

"My sweetie," I crooned, unlatching the door. "You're home now. Everything's all right." Ignoring me, the cat shot out of the case, paused for a moment at a safe distance to lick fussily at one flank, and then began to prowl the perimeter of the room, sniffing with particular interest at my sandals, abandoned, in third position, next to the couch.

"I fed her this morning," Lauren said, "like, not even an hour ago, so she should be fine."

"Thanks," I said, "but I think I'll give her a little snack, just so she knows she's home." In the kitchen, I dished up a few spoons of canned food from the fridge, a stinky, unidentifiable mush that turned my stomach. Remains, I thought: fish remains. Ella wolfed it down, then repaired to the living-room rug to lick her paws.

"That stuff is gross," I said, rinsing my hands in the kitchen sink, still sensing, in my throat, the ghost of a gag reflex. Lauren unwrapped the tulips, took down a vase. She nodded agreement, crinkling her nose.

"I picked up a few groceries," she said, hoisting the bags on to the counter, pulling out a triplet of bananas, a pumpernickel loaf. "I figured you wouldn't have time." She stashed a carton of milk and a wedge of Jarlsberg in the refrigerator, bumped the door shut with her hip. "Just the essentials," she added, producing, with a flourish, a slab of Belgian chocolate.

"Thanks," I said, absently drying my hands. "You're so sweet. Thanks so much. But I do have time, I have plenty of time. That's the terrible part. That's what's driving me up the fucking wall right now, the waiting." Lauren's demeanor changed, became serious, solicitous. She filled the kettle for tea.

"Where's the . . . ? Ah, got it." Her voice switched to

a deeper, more tender tone. "I know, honey. It must be so hard, I can't even imagine. Any news? Since last night, I mean?"

"No, nothing, just what's on the TV. They've only done about thirty autopsies so far, something like that. And the bodies are pretty smashed up, from what I hear. There was something on the Internet about one face that was in twenty-five pieces. Don't know where they get this shit, but it's out there. Anyway, they won't even have her medical records yet. So I'm not holding my breath."

"No . . ."

"They photograph them and number them when they get into the county medical office, and you know what the weird thing is?"

"What?"

"They number the first body 5,000, don't ask me why, that's part of their disaster plan."

"Hmm. Seems odd."

"And you know what else? It said on NPR this morning that the Department of Environmental something-or-other has been busy mapping out all the nesting areas for endangered species. In the search area. So no birds get hurt."

"You're kidding."

"No, and, okay, listen to this, for dinner on the plane, in coach, they would have had a choice of beef Mediterranean, whatever that is, with carrots and, I don't know, some kind of pasta. Or roast turkey, with sage-and-onion stuffing, mashed turnips, and mixed veg. Eleanor would have chosen, um, the beef. No, the turkey. Because of mad cow."

"Kim . . ."

"And do you know what movie they were going to show? *The Birdcage*. Almost worth crashing and burning to avoid that."

"Come on, Kim," Lauren said, after a pause. "This isn't going to help. It's better if you talk about it. For real, I mean, not like this." We had moved, by now, into the living room, where I crouched, trying to coax a purr out of Ella. I had, I recognized, been jabbering in an odd, compulsive manner, so I stopped. Lauren sat on the sofa, worriedly gathering and folding the strewn sections of *The Times*. It was Friday's so, in addition to all the crash coverage, there was a fat arts section—reviews of the latest alien-invasion blockbuster, of an installation at the Dia that consisted, apparently, of a roomful of hair. Also, where to find the best caipirinhas.

"So," Lauren ventured, after a while, "when does Anna get here?"

"Anna?"

"Your sister?"

"My sister? She's not . . . I mean, what gave you the idea that she was coming?"

"Well, I don't know . . . I'm sorry, I just kind of assumed." Lauren, flustered, placed *The Times* in a neat pile on the coffee table, then knocked it out of whack with her foot as she recrossed her legs. She was wearing a long Indian-print skirt that caught on things, big jangly earrings, an ankle chain. "I just thought . . . I mean, if, God forbid, something like this happened to us, then Ben would fly right out here. So we could be together, go through the whole thing together."

"No," I said shortly, "she's staying put." I realized that

Anna and I had never even discussed the possibility: I'd known, without asking, that she would want to stay with Angus and the girls, that she would be afraid to fly, afraid of New York. Anna had never left South Africa, except for the occasional long weekend at a Holiday Inn in Swaziland, where Angus liked to gamble. I tried to imagine her here, in my apartment, the two of us sitting around waiting for the phone to ring, Anna tanned and tearful in some kind of summer frock, not knowing what to do with herself, getting up to make tea, to wash dishes, to sew on a button or feed the cat, utterly out of place, out of scale, in the small bare space of my life. And myself with my knees tucked under me on the big green chair, staring out the window at the brick façade of the building opposite, undergoing the slow, involuntary petrification of my emotions that always occurred in the presence of my family, everything shrinking and shriveling inside me, until my heart felt as small and dead as a dried pea.

When had it begun, I wondered, this distance between Anna and myself, this cordial but effortful connection, as if we were two people in separate rooms trying to communicate by means of tin cans and string? Long before I'd left South Africa and translated my distance from my family into geographical terms—long, even, before I'd left for university, raging, rebellious, and self-righteous, heading for Cape Town because it was as far as you could travel from Johannesburg without dropping off the continent, off the very tip of Africa where the two oceans meet, the warm and the cold, in a blue-and-green swirl. I'd wanted to be an actress, then a radical lawyer, then a photojournalist. I graduated instead with a degree in economics—more fungible, I'd found, especially if you were planning to leave. Meanwhile, Anna had stayed home, gone to the local teacher-training college, created a life for herself within a five-mile radius of her childhood home.

As girls, though, we'd been as intertwined as twins, whispering to each other in our shared bedroom every night after lights out, retelling the plots of movies we'd seen, lingering on the costumes and the kisses. And, in the afternoons, after Eleanor had picked us up from school and we'd shrugged off our sweaty uniforms, unbraided our hair, we'd played together for hours, intricate private sagas like long-running soap operas.

Our favorite, for years, had been Tea Party, in the little garden shed through whose imperfectly joined boards the sun pierced in dazzling stripes. There was an ever-changing cast of characters—Maureen the stuffed rabbit, assorted golliwogs and teddy bears, Barbies, Skippers, and Kens, invisible Mrs So-and-Sos from Next Door—though the menu was always the same: muddy water in the dolls' cups and torn-up yellow tissue representing scrambled eggs. (Dried leaves were served too, as toast, and violence often broke out among the guests.) And, before Eleanor had stopped taking us there, we'd played Shop in our grandmother's bedroom, all her costume jewelry dragged out and displayed on the gilded dressing table, with Anna as the eager saleslady, Kim the imperious, never-satisfied customer.

In the winter, inspired by Roger's equestrian interests, we used to play Showjumping on the lawn, with broom-sticks for horses and upturned buckets as hurdles, taking long dramatic spills on to the ground, so that, when we ran inside for supper, our lungs burning from exertion and the cold thin Highveld air, the dry grass would be clinging to our sweaters like patchy fur. And in the summers we rarely changed out of our bathing suits—blue for Anna, red for me—baking beside the pool all day long with a tinny transistor radio. We'd invented our own version of water polo, which consisted mainly of trying to hold the other under water until she struggled, sputtering, to the surface, thrilled by the brief intimation of what it might feel like to drown. Then Eleanor would come out of the house, frowning, dish towel in hand, telling us to be careful, to come inside for tea.

Water Polo, Showjumping, Tea Party, I thought—there's a colonial childhood for you. I'm surprised we didn't also play Firing the Maid or Showing the Garden Boy Where to Dig.

My heart gave a little ping of distress, muted, like a signal from the bottom of the sea, as I thought of how distant it seemed now, my childhood with Anna, simultaneously unreal and hyperreal, like a diorama in a museum. With Anna as the little figure in the diorama, an anthropologist's reconstruction, poised in mid-gesture with an eager, frozen smile. Perhaps this is what happens when you leave your native land, I thought: your own past becomes imaginary, an installation under an arc light. Or perhaps it's just what happens when you grow up.

We grew up on different calendars, Anna and I, the year's age gap between us opening like a fault line in the earth. There I was suddenly, at eleven and a half, on the far side of it, with new, puffy breasts and a bulky Kotex held in place by a truss-like contraption. (It had metal suspenders, I recalled, like suspenders for stockings, which I also began to wear, in the frosted pastel colors that were fashionable then, ice-creamy colors straight from the British teen magazines that Roger brought home every Thursday night.) Meanwhile, Anna, at ten, remained a little girl, still content to spend hours combing her doll's hair. In the grip of a sudden, nameless irritability, a nervous, scornful agitation, I was no longer interested in adorning dolls or riding a broomstick around the back lawn; it was much more thrilling to wrestle with the neighborhood boys from the apartment complex nearby, the "rough" boys of whom Eleanor disapproved, to spend all day with them at the over-chlorinated public pool, shoving and being shoved, instead of by the tranquil lake-shaped one on our own property, from whose surface Daniel, the gardener, would fish floating leaves every morning, in graceful, dreamlike strokes, with a long-poled net.

The phone rang, shrill; both Lauren and I froze but neither of us made any move to pick it up, Lauren regarding me questioningly as I sat with head cocked, listening for the machine to click on.

"I'm not dealing with the phone," I said, "unless I have to." Lauren nodded. "The FBI is supposed to call this morning, set up a time to come over here."

"Hi, Kim . . ." a hesitant voice began. "I don't know if this is a good time, but I just wanted to say how . . . how horrified I was to hear your news, how sorry I am. It's Pin, in LA, got your message last night. I, I don't really know what to say, other than how sorry I am, but please call if there's anything I can do. Or if you just feel like talking, okay? I'll call again later, hope you're doing okay, okay, bye." A hasty, relieved clatter, then a beep.

"It's that," I said, gesturing toward the phone, "that I can't deal with right now."

"Well, you don't have to," Lauren said. "People will understand." Then, after a pause, "For what?"

"For what?"

"The FBI."

"Oh, some kind of interview. To find out if Eleanor had a secret life as a terrorist or something." I giggled, despite myself, at the image of Eleanor, in her nice navy-blue suit, with a stocking mask over her head, toting an Uzi. Threatening a planeload of people with brusque commands.

"They doing that for all the families? Interviewing them all?"

I nodded.

"Wow, that's going to take a while. Two hundred people, all over the world—"

"You know, though," I said, pursuing a private line of thought, "in a way she was."

"Was what?"

"She terrorized us, when we were kids. Me, anyway."

"What do you mean?"

"I mean, you never knew when she was going to blow up. Or why."

Lauren was silent, having heard some of these stories before. Eleanor's temper, the way she would lash out. The things she said.

"And God help you if you were within an arm's length of her when she did." Lauren had heard these stories too:

the hairbrush across the back of the leg, the table napkin across the face at dinner. The chair pushed over with me in it, the letter shredded that I'd given her to mail. The sneaker that had left a purple tread on my thigh. We'd debated, once, whether this constituted child abuse: Lauren had said yes, definitely, nodding her curly head for emphasis; I, shrugging, had argued that child-rearing practices were different then. And there, in the colonies. It wasn't so unusual to smack your children, I said. Okay, but did any of your friends go to school with bruises, like you? Lauren had asked. I had shrugged again, poured another glass of wine.

"But in the meanwhile . . . ?" Lauren asked, after a pause.

"In the meanwhile?"

"What are you going to do? After I leave? You can't just sit around here alone all day."

"I really don't know," I said. "I just feel so . . . wiped out." I thought about taking a shower, which I needed— my armpits felt stale and sour, my feet gluey between the toes—but I couldn't imagine standing upright for so long, the sheer physical effort of it. I was wearing the grey T-shirt I had slept in and a pair of sweatpants with bleach stains where I'd once spilt Ajax, in a bathroom-cleaning spree. My hair was clumpy and uncombed. I had gunk in the corners of my eyes. "I don't know," I repeated. "Call Harold and Bernice, see what they've heard? Watch CNN? Get on the Internet? Wait for the FBI to call."

"Who're Harold and Bernice? And, honey, I really don't think you should be watching TV right now. You never know what you might see. It could be, well, you know, really upsetting."

"That's what the grief counselor told me, but screw it. My imagination has got to be worse than anything I'd see on TV. And the worst thing is just not knowing, feeling so cut off. So helpless . . ." Tears smarted in my eyes again. "Oh, fuck this."

"You could get some meds," Lauren said gently. "To help you sleep. Just to help you through the next few days."

"No," I said. "No meds." I mistrusted, in life, anything that made me feel better, that tampered with my brain's own stingy, stoic capacity to endure.

After Lauren had left, having begged me repeatedly to let her cancel her workshop and stay for the day, and I had repeatedly refused, I stood in the entryway, motionless, as if boxed into a cube of space defined by the closing door. When, at last, something caught my attention—Ella's tail slinking around the doorjamb into the bedroom—I didn't know how long I had been standing there. I felt like a survivor of that sleeping-sickness epidemic of the nineteen-teens, brought to life, after decades of immobility, by a shot of L-dopa.

It was almost noon. The sun, I noticed, was beating in through the tall windows, parching the African violets on the windowsill. I thought about giving them some water, but didn't. I drew the sheer drapes and, in their soft, filtered light, clicked on the TV. I discovered that I had a vicious headache, that same black puff pressing behind my eyes.

The diving had begun, I saw, feeling vaguely annoyed

that I'd missed the beginning of it, like someone arriving late to a movie. An enormous grey ship towered out of the water—the *Grasp* or the *Grapple*, I supposed, though there was another one, I'd read in *The Times*, called the *Rude*. Pronounced "Ru-dé," but still, too fucking bizarre, these Navy names. I giggled aloud, realized I was becoming silly, giddy, and turned my attention soberly back to the screen. From a smaller boat alongside the looming vessel, men in black wetsuits pulled on their masks and, like a grim chorus line, fell one by one into the sea.

Eleanor is down there somewhere, I thought—what's left of her. Somewhere down there among the razor-edged hunks of metal, the web of cables and wires, the shreds of human beings. Under 120 feet of water, in the dark silty place where life began, where creatures live who have never seen the light. It made no sense to me. It was never going to make any sense to me.

Almost nothing about my mother's life was clear to me: she'd spoken so little about it, holding her life story in her mouth like a cat with an evil-tasting pill, waiting to spit it out in secret. Perhaps she'd told more to Anna, I wasn't sure. I understood only that she'd seen herself as trapped, without options, at least since her marriage and perhaps before—the marriage which I, by my inconvenient conception, had occasioned and for which, obscurely, she seemed to blame me. "You were a colicky baby," she'd say, as if it had been my fault. "You cried all the time, you made my life hell."

But Roger had been trapped too, I thought, and I grieved again for the young man he'd been, emigrating to Africa at twenty-two, on a whim, following a woman and the whiff of a job. The woman and the job had evaporated, but he'd stayed, finding himself swallowed, somewhere in middle management, by a huge multinational. And then finding himself married, too soon, inhabiting his marriage like a jail—resisting it at first through faithlessness, fecklessness, and deceit, but later, as Eleanor grew crazier, more needy, devolving without protest into her keeper.

After apartheid ended, she'd become almost housebound, turning their small townhouse into an elaborate cage of window bars and burglar alarms, afraid to go out for a library book or a loaf of bread. "They" were everywhere now, "they" had the run of the streets, the right to shop in the same shops, to try on the same dresses or sit at the same cafés. "They" no longer had to yield to her on the sidewalk, they even dared to meet her eye. It was the world she'd dreaded all her life, a nightmare world now flaunting itself in daylight. So Roger had, increasingly, become her emissary and errand boy, taking it upon himself to protect her from the world, and, as far as possible, to protect the world from her. They'd talked, often, about leaving South Africa and starting a new life elsewhere—in England, perhaps—but they were afraid of being poor; anyway, she said, it was too late. She was afraid to stay, but equally afraid to go.

I thought of them both, enmeshed in the wreckage of their lives. A bleak sadness came over me, a sense of waste. But if I'd been the one who'd died in a crash— as, I now understood, anyone could, at any time—what would I have had to show for mine? An apartment, a cat, a career convincing people to buy hairspray?

For the rest of the afternoon, I stared at the television, clicking restlessly when the images started to repeat themselves, dozing thinly at times, waking with a start. Reporters were trying to explain about side-scan radar, multi-beam sonar, how they worked, how they were used to identify "targets" that divers were then sent down to investigate. How sonar bounces well off metal but not so well off "soft targets" like flesh. How a laser device, towed methodically up and down its designated quadrant, like a lawnmower on a suburban lawn, was being used to peer to the bottom of the sea, to spy on that silent, devastated world. How this very device had previously been used to scan underwater sewage pipes for leaks, to photograph rare worms in the Gulf of Mexico. Sewage pipes, rare worms, and Eleanor, I thought; strange bedfellows, seabedfellows.

An over-made-up young woman, her hair unmoved by the marine breeze, reported breathily from the deck of some boat. One of the earliest "finds," she said, had appeared as a "grisly" video image, which divers were sent down to investigate. The video showed two objects, shaped like, well, like a torso and a pair of legs. But when the divers got down there, she said, brightly, as if delivering the punchline to a joke, what they found was— a shirt and a pair of trousers! Each still on its hanger, escaped from a garment bag, on the bottom of the sea!

The coffee-maker from the first-class galley had been found, I learned, still in the "on" position. A heap of car tires, illicitly dumped. Some human remains. The divers were supposed to attach evidence tags to the scraps and float them up to the surface.

That idea, somehow, was the one that did me in, made me mute the TV and get up to call Bernice, extricating the number, on a sheet of Ramada paper, from the pocket of the khakis I'd been wearing that day. Only, what, two days ago? I had a fleeting thought of Paul, picturing him lonely and ranting in his hotel room. I wondered briefly whether I should call, see how he was holding up, then decided it would take too much energy, more than I could muster.

"Sweetheart!" Bernice exclaimed when I got through to her room—room 800—bringing the sting of tears to my eyes again. "We miss you here, honey, so much. Have you . . . ?"

"No," I said. "I miss you too, it's just me and the TV here. Waiting for the FBI."

"Us too," Bernice said. "They haven't got to the eighth floor yet."

"Any . . . ?"

"No, nothing. Harold's out there, downstairs, talking to the press, talking to the families, badgering the airline. He needs to know every little thing, keep hassling them, it's his way of dealing. He just can't sit still. In this room."

"And yours? Your way of dealing?"

"I'm praying," Bernice said. "I know she ain't gone."

I could think of no response.

"Oh, hon?" Bernice said. "Here he is, he just came in. With a whole pile of . . . You want a word?"

"Sure."

Harold sounded breathless, agitated, as if he'd just climbed several flights of stairs; I was suddenly worried about his health, what would happen to Bernice if he keeled over. He was on the heavy side, I remembered,

with a full, firm-looking belly; he needed to be careful—
heart attack, stroke; I wanted to warn him, make him
sit down.

He, too, called me "sweetheart," asked if I'd heard
anything, reeled off a slew of information: the next scheduled news conference, the addresses of two websites, one
maintained by the FBI, the other by the Families ("to get
the truth out there, not this crap the airline is feeding
us"), the number of bodies recovered so far (112).

"How much you want to know?" he asked.

"Everything," I said. I wondered, as I said this, whether
it was true.

"Okay," he said, "listen to this." Then, louder, "Bernice,
honey, you block your ears or something, go into the
bathroom. You don't want to hear this, trust me." A
pause, a low grumbling in the background, and then he
continued. "Okay, well, I got this off a reporter in the bar
downstairs, who got it off a Coast Guard guy, who said one
of the Navy divers had seen it with his own eyes. They're
not going to print it, obviously—too embarrassing, makes
them look like jackasses."

I listened, numb, as he explained how pairs of divers
were escorting the bodies, one by one, from the bottom of
the sea. I pictured it so clearly, the macabre underwater
ballet, the dark-suited divers with their pale, unresisting
partners, ascending toward the surface in a languid pas
de trois.

"So," he continued, strangely excited, as if none of this
had anything to do with him, "one of the very first ones,
okay, they're down there, they spot him, still strapped into
his seat, you know? Unstrap him, bring him carefully up,

the two of them, each holding an arm, like they do. So they get to the surface and there's a boat, police boat, I think, waiting to load him on. This one diver gets the body bag off his belt, that's where they keep them, okay, so they're struggling with the bag, treading water, struggling to get him into the bag. So *finally* they do and just as they're handing him up to the boat, in the bag, the zipper comes undone, and the guy slides right out, right down to the bottom of the sea again."

I was silent for a second and then asked, "Are you sure it was a guy?"

"Who?"

"The one who fell out."

"No, I don't know, I'm just saying 'guy' like 'some guy,' you know? Some one. Some person."

I wished I hadn't asked. Because now I could imagine, imagine terribly, that it had been Eleanor. Eleanor's body buckled into its seat on the ocean floor, like a crash-test dummy. And Eleanor's body at the surface, refusing capture. Spurning the shroud as if it were a straitjacket.

"And," he said, "but you really have to keep this to yourself, okay, you know what else is really weird?"

"What?" I anticipated that he was going to say something about a missile. More and more people, on TV, were talking about a missile.

"When they were examining the bodies, at the coroner's, it was just too weird, they didn't know how to explain it. They'd open the eye, you know, push up the eyelid, and there'd be all this glitter."

"What do you mean, glitter?"

"I mean, glitter, like you sprinkle on things, like kids glue on stuff. Like you'd put on your face. One of the bodies, apparently, shows up covered in glitter from head to foot."

"Glitter?" I couldn't attach any meaning to the word.

"Like, I don't know, for carnival. For costumes. Comes in a tube, or at least it used to, when L, Louise was a kid." His voice faltered at the mention of her name, and I felt oddly relieved. The way he'd been gabbling, rushing from one gruesome bit of information to the next, I'd almost begun to fear that he'd forgotten his daughter. Forgotten that he'd ever had a daughter, that she'd been on that plane, that she was dead. Perhaps, I'd thought, the mind could just decide to wipe out such information, like a wet sponge on a chalkboard, leaving a slick, merciful blank.

Harold continued, in the same overexcited tone. "And when the divers go down there, you know what they find?"

I shrugged, invisibly.

"The wreckage is just covered with glitter, they can't believe their eyes, it's like fairyland down there."

"But how . . . ?" I felt sick, as if I were, or were about to be, the victim of a practical joke.

"It turns out," he said, triumphantly, "that, in the cargo, there was 800 pounds of glitter. Eight hundred frigging pounds, all in different colors! Some circus in Italy had ordered it."

He continued, enumerating some of the other cargo that had been in the hold—cash registers, live turtles, bowling pins—but I wasn't listening. I was picturing, again, the sunken wreckage on the ocean floor, but now, in my mind,

the water was alive with glitter, like brilliant plankton—
red and green and silver and purple and gold—sifting
down, like a blessing, upon the tortured metal and the
tortured flesh, upon the dead.

10

Monday, July 24

———

Though the headline was sober—SEARCH FOR EVIDENCE
CONTINUES IN FIN CRASH; 230 CONFIRMED DEAD—the photo-
graph shocked me, robbed me of air. I couldn't believe *The
New York Times* would publish it.

The front page showed, in color, a boat of some kind—
whaler, cutter, what did I know?—official-looking, crowned
with lights like a police car. In the foreground gleamed a
strip of dark sea water, flecked with fire; on the boat stood
three men, one, in a hard hat and lab coat, staring out of the
frame, and the other two, in Coast Guard vests, crouched
over a corpse. They held it—slung it, like a side of beef—by
the arms and legs, face down, splayed and sharply bowed,
its head hidden behind part of the stern. The body—
the carcass—was naked except for a small undergarment,
strategically placed. The more I examined the photo, the
more convinced I became that the neat triangle of briefs
had been drawn in afterwards, just so the picture could
be published. It made me sick to think of it: of the airbrush
artist or computer-graphics guy, hunched over the image,
shading it in.

This corpse is somebody's, I thought, this body belongs to somebody. And that somebody belongs to somebody else.

I was still upset, still shaken, when Lauren stopped by on her way to work. She'd brought me a pie: people seem to think that, when you're bereaved, you need a pie.

"Look at this," I said, showing her the paper in a trembling hand, "it's obscene, fucking obscene."

"I saw it," she said, quietly. "I thought of you. It's not right, I'm going to send them a mail." She took it from me, examined it more closely. "You can't even tell if it's a man or a woman, can you, it's just, I don't know—" I had the feeling that she was going to say "a piece of meat" but stopped herself in time.

"Anyway," I said, "it's not her."

Lauren raised her eyebrows, gave a nod.

"Too young," I said. "Too slim."

"That's good," she said. She paused, ran her hand through her already unruly hair. "Oh shit, that sounds terrible. That's not what I meant—"

"It's okay," I said. I could feel tears, weak, sullen tears, gathering somewhere.

"Oh shit," she said again, dropping the paper on the table and giving me a big, dramatic hug. I shrank away; it was too hard, too much. I felt as if my body were held together by old rubber bands, that it might easily come apart.

She seemed a little offended, backed off.

"Sorry," I said, "I just—" I sat down at the table, propped my head on one hand. The tears felt imminent.

"I know, sweetie," Lauren said, consolingly, rubbing the curved place where my neck met my shoulder. Her touch irritated my skin, made it feel raw.

"I'm just so tired, you know? And I just wish," I added, to my own surprise, "I just wish my dad was still around."

"You must miss him," she said, sagely, shaking her head. "Especially now, poor punkin."

"No," I said, crankily, "I don't *miss* him, you know, most of the time. I could just use some—help." I wanted her to leave, before I wept.

She said nothing, continued kneading my neck. "It's funny," she said, after a while, "how you call him your dad, but you always call her Eleanor."

"I do not," I said.

She shrugged, stopped rubbing.

"And anyway," I continued, "if I do, it's just, I don't know, a cultural thing. What am I supposed to call her? Mummy? Mother? Like something out of, I don't know, bloody *Winnie-the-Pooh*?"

She looked at me mistrustfully. I could see her thinking that bereavement didn't necessarily bring out the best in people. I could see her deciding whether to stay or go.

"I'll have to be heading up to City soon," she said, after a few moments, looking at her watch. "Office hours. But I hate to leave you alone like this—"

"I won't be alone," I said. I stood up, to hasten her progress towards the door. "I'm having a visitor today, from the FBI. An Agent—" and here I consulted a scrap of paper from the pocket of my jeans—"A. Garcia."

From the movies, I'd formed a persistent, if un-examined, notion of what FBI agents looked like—im-passive men in suits—so I was surprised when Agent Garcia turned out to be a young woman with a ponytail and short, curly bangs. She was wearing pressed khaki pants that fit snugly over her full hips, a yellow oxford cloth shirt, and loafers without socks, a look I had never much cared for. But Garcia looked crisp and uncrumpled, despite the noonday heat, and, with her flawless café-au-lait complexion, her pretty upturned nose, and her small pearl earrings, she looked as if she should be setting out for a shopping trip at J. Crew rather than interviewing people whose family members had been blown to bits.

Or had suffered, I'd learned through a rogue site on the Internet, something called "internal decapitation": assaulted by 400-mile-an-hour winds, the human spine snaps, severing the head from the body within the skin. You might look, I imagined, as if you were whole, except that your brainstem had been unplugged. And the plane, too, had been decapitated, its front section breaking off and plunging with the first-class passengers into the sea, while the headless, pilotless stump rose blindly for a few seconds more.

A plane, I thought, has a head, a nose, a belly, a spine, ribs, an aluminum skin. The plane is a body, containing other bodies.

I became absorbed by this idea, lapsing into the kind of distracted immobility that had been afflicting me lately, when I noticed that Garcia seemed to be looking around for somewhere to sit, somewhere to rest her clipboard. The living-room, I realized, was a mess, stale-smelling, littered with newspapers and tissues, scraps of paper, empty cups. A gnawed bagel lay on the sofa and the big armchair was matted with Ella's fur, so I gestured toward the dining table, gathering up a few days' worth of tabloids to clear a space.

"My place is usually really neat," I said, with a shrug.

I felt weak and numb, as if I'd never have the energy to bring order back into my life. Never have the strength even to pick a sock off the floor.

"That's okay," Garcia said, sitting down. "I completely understand. I'm not even paying attention to that—I'm from the FBI, you know, not, what's her name, Martha Stewart. Well, actually, the FBI-NYPD Joint Terrorism Task Force."

"Terrorism?" The word sounded definitive, peremptory. "So they've decided that's what it was?"

"No, no," the woman said, flipping her ponytail over her shoulder with one hand, "the investigation's just beginning, nothing has been determined yet. I'm just here to ask you a few questions about the passenger." She glanced at her clipboard. "Roth, Eleanor Lilian? Your mother?"

"Yes."

"First, let me say how sorry I am for your loss."

"Thank you." I shifted in the hard wooden chair, wished fervently for this to be over, this conversation, this situation, this phase of my life. Wished to be back in a narrative of my own invention, which was how I'd seen my life for the past fifteen years.

As I leaned back, conscious of the chair rung cutting into my spine—I was getting too bony, I needed to eat—Garcia leaned forward, elbows on the table, hands clasped compassionately together. "I know this must be very hard for you," she said.

Just get on with it, I thought.

The routine questions came first—Eleanor's date and place of birth, sex, marital status, and so on. I answered like a pro. Height I knew (a whisker over five feet) but

weight defeated me: Eleanor's weight, a constant source
of stress and distress, had never been named, and I found
myself unable to gauge, afraid that I would grossly over-
estimate. I'd always seen Eleanor's body as alarming,
immoderate, risen and swollen like dough. Too much of
it, I thought, always too much, claiming too much space.
And now it's gone.

"Don't know," I said. "A lot. Overweight. The medical
records are on their way."

Maiden name: Blomet. Distinguishing marks: abominable
scars. Abdominal, I mean. Occupation.

"Housewife," I said, after some hesitation. "I mean,
homemaker, whatever you're supposed to say these days."
Whichever word you used, it had been, in suburban white
South Africa, a role without a function, a recipe for bore-
dom and bridge parties, for compulsive shopping, for long
siestas with Sugus and sticky-jacketed library books, for
slowly and almost imperceptibly losing your mind.

"Employment history?" Garcia asked, pen poised, not
looking up.

"No, I just told you . . . Well, I guess she did work as a
bookkeeper once, for a newspaper. Before she got married.
Got pregnant. Whatever. With me."

"Which newspaper?"

"Which newspaper? This is almost forty years ago, do
you really need to . . . The *Sunday Express*."

"In Johannesburg, South Africa?" She pronounced it
with a soft "J": Yohannesburg.

"Uh-huh."

"And thereafter employed as a homemaker, is that correct?"

"Yes. If 'employed' is the right word." How to explain to this young woman, this ponytailed employee of the FBI, that white South African women of Eleanor's generation didn't have jobs, except under financial duress, that a wage-earning wife was a shameful sign? How to explain that, with a live-in maid and gardener and a laundrywoman three times a week, Eleanor had, basically, nothing to do, no essential function to fulfill, except—once she'd overcome her fear of driving—that of chauffeuring her daughters around? No wonder she'd wanted a different life for us, insisted on it, and yet resented every scrap of freedom and accomplishment that came our way; no wonder she had, with one hand, pushed us out into the world as her proxies and, with the other, yanked us back, kneecapped us. She'd indulged us, then envied us; given, then begrudged. Her attention was fickle, short-lived; it spoiled quickly, soon turned sour, as milk does in a hot climate. Had Eleanor been born a generation later, or in a different place, I thought, she would have been able to put all that anger and combativeness to work, that nagging, niggling intelligence, rather than have it, over time, turn upon itself, turn upon her. Like an autoimmune disease, I thought, an autoimmune disease of the soul, and an immense sadness filled me, hollowed out my throat.

"So she had not recently lost a job or been fired from a place of employment?"

"No," I said, shrugging. "Obviously not . . . This is all kind of silly." I stared at the floor, like a sullen child. "I'm really tired," I added after a while. "My mother didn't blow up that plane, you know."

"I understand," Garcia said, meeting my eyes. "I'm

really sorry. For everything that's happened to you, for all of this. There are just certain questions I have to ask everyone."

"I haven't been sleeping well," I continued, feeling, to my embarrassment, tears beginning to burn at the back of my eyes. "Hardly getting any sleep. Well, what happens is I go to sleep, because I'm exhausted, then I'm wide awake a couple of hours later and my mind is racing and that's it for the night."

"I understand," Garcia said. "That's completely normal, you know, a normal reaction." She made a neat little doodle, an ameba-like shape, on the margins of her pad, a gesture of patient solidarity: take your time, I'll just draw amebas here for a while.

"Okay," I said, after a moment, swallowing hard, "let's get on with it."

Tax returns and credit records. Another chore for Anna. Insurance policies. Eleanor was insured up to the eyeballs, I said, indicating with the ghost of a gesture, hands at eye level, parallel to the floor.

"And who would be the beneficiary, do you know?" Garcia asked. "Beneficiaries?"

"Not me, that's for sure." I thought about it. "My sister, her kids? We've never discussed it, but who else would it be?" I hadn't accepted a penny from my parents in twenty years—a matter of some pride—while Anna, I knew, still received regular infusions. When the import-export business was lagging, when Bridget needed riding lessons, Sally new shoes. When they all needed a restful weekend in the Drakensberg or at the beach. "My sister and her kids," I repeated. All of them still umbilically connected, one generation to the next, I thought, while I've managed to cut loose, subsist on my own air supply—on what I can carry with me—thin and spare as it at times has been.

I wanted to put my head down on the table and weep. This is crazy, I thought: I'm regressing. I wanted to put my head down on the table and wail, beat my fists. I wanted to wail, like a child, for more.

"You'll verify that, will you?" Garcia asked, making something that looked, at that distance, like an extra-curly question mark.

"I'll verify that," I said. "Soon as I can."

"Good. Okay. Now, to your knowledge, was, um, the passenger, your mother, involved in any problems with the law?"

"You mean," I asked, "did she have a criminal record?" I pictured Eleanor, defiant and disheveled, in a mugshot, front and side views, a sprung lock of hair surmounting the height marker behind her, the sixty-inch line. I wanted to laugh but I wasn't sure what sound would come out if I did. I remembered Eleanor's shame when I'd been arrested during an anti-apartheid demonstration at the University of Cape Town, her mortification when my name had appeared in the Johannesburg newspapers. "This is very bad for Daddy's job," she'd told me, angrily, by phone. "You'll do anything for attention, won't you?" As if, somehow, the anti-apartheid movement were all about her. Well, now it's you, Eleanor, I thought, now it's you getting the attention. Here's the FBI, filling out this form, this big thick 302, all about you. This is probably the most attention you ever got in your life without throwing a tantrum.

"Divorce proceedings, for instance?"

"I told you, she's a widow."

"Got that. I mean, divorce proceedings involving other parties."

Eleanor? In a lover's triangle? The idea was laughable. Somehow, because of the deep loathing I sensed in her of her own body, I'd always thought of my mother as sexless; not unsensual, but sexless, deeply afraid of sex. Someone who'd long ago ceded the sexual arena. I knew, of course, that this wasn't entirely true: I'd heard my parents having sex a couple of times in my early adolescence, an experience that had made me go cold all over, with a kind of primal horror, an experience I preferred not to revisit, even in memory. But otherwise, Eleanor's self-presentation, by her early thirties, had been that of a matron, a woman whose body had been ruined by childbearing, a woman, in other words, out of the sexual running. Whereas I, in my thirties, presented myself as a woman very much in the sexual running—good body, good clothes, good line in sophisticated banter—but, in fact, rarely had sex.

Too much wear and tear, I'd begun to feel, to let someone in, only to know that somewhere down the line you were going to have to let them out again. And then wait, patiently, for your solitude to reconstitute itself, for a new epidermis to grow over the abraded surfaces, the exposed nerve endings, the myriad unmanageable longings of a body that's been touched.

Garcia was looking inquiringly at me, pen poised. I was thinking about bodies, my mother's body, my own. The ways in which desire is circuited and short-circuited, the ways in which the wiring goes bad. Eleanor *had* been part of a sexual triangle, I realized: the idea wasn't so absurd,

after all. That had been, in fact, the configuration that had
defined her marriage. From the time Anna and I were very
young—for, in fact, as long as I could remember—Eleanor
had felt compelled, every now and then, to sit us down, in
our nightgowns or school uniforms, wriggling and giggling
in discomfort, since we knew what was coming, wriggling
like worms on a hook, and tell us that, at that very moment,
our father was with another woman. Sometimes she'd tell
us who it was, sometimes not. Sometimes she'd tell us
where: which hotel, whose house, whose car. I could never
decide whether she really knew these details or was just
imagining them, making them up, tormenting herself with
possibilities. Could this really have happened, I wondered
later, the mother giving the daughters information they had
nowhere to put, that would poison them if they took it in,
information against which they clenched their minds like
teeth against the spoon? Out of what mixture of spite and
loneliness, out of what need for love and revenge, had she
told us this?

Anna's way of dealing with it had been to comfort her
mother, cleave to her. Mine had been to dismiss Eleanor
angrily, to reject everything she said as crazy, paranoid,
delusional, to throw in my lot with Roger, even if that meant
loving a liar.

It wasn't difficult: he was charming, after all—a rac-
onteur, a playmate, an attentive and devoted dad. If he
cheated on my mother—and I would admit that idea only
as a hypothesis, a big "if"—well, who wouldn't: she'd
become, hadn't she, the fat, nagging wife right out of
the comic strips. Why wouldn't he flee her grumbling,
her accusations, her long, hectoring diatribes? And, more

to the point, he remained faithful to me. He took me to the theater or to see Shakespeare on film; he bought me silver bracelets and books of poetry; he taught me about chess and heraldry; he bought front-row tickets for Margot Fonteyn; he lavished praise upon my grades, all As. Why shouldn't he cheat on Eleanor, especially with me?

This Freudian romance got me through my childhood and my teens. But by the time I reached my twenties, I'd gained enough distance and enough experience—with, predictably, men who lied—to understand that my mother's version had been, if not wholly accurate, true enough. Roger had been a common or garden philanderer, no more, no less. That was how, I understood, my father had stayed married. Why then, I'd wanted to ask both of them, why then stay married, stay married to gnaw and rip at each other, to disembowel each other on the installment plan, to drag the other drowning person down with you, rather than both swimming free?

Why did you stay married? I'd always wanted to ask Eleanor, more as an accusation than a question. I still wanted to ask her that, wanted to dredge her bloated and crab-nibbled corpse from the seabed right then, prop it up right there, at the dining table, where Garcia was sitting, and force Eleanor to answer, force her to sit there, salt-puckered and waterlogged, with seaweed sticking to what was left of her blue-white skin, and answer. Force her to open her mouth and, in a stream of sea water and small sea creatures, give me a response. I wanted to ask her the question I'd never dared pose directly because I thought I knew the answer and the answer would be more than I could bear: we stayed together for your sake, for your and Anna's sakes. So you could be part of a family.

A family, I thought, that would convince you that no other kind is possible.

"No," I said. "No divorce proceedings, nothing like that, that I know of."

"Okay," said Garcia, making a check mark in a box. "And, as far as you are aware, had she been threatened in any way? By anyone? Even as a joke?"

"No," I said. "As far as I know. Look, I told you, I wasn't very close to my mother. I hadn't seen her in three years. We had a . . . difficult relationship, you know? You should talk to my sister."

"You're the one who's here," she said mildly. "This is fine, we're doing fine." She tapped her pen down the page, as if skipping a series of questions (which? I wondered. Was she allowed to do this?). "Only one other thing I need to ask you about, and this might be difficult, so take your time. Had the passenger, your mother, ever been treated for a mental illness?"

"Treated? No." That was easy.

"Had she ever, to your knowledge, suffered from depression—a serious depression, you know, clinical depression."

No, Agent Garcia, in our house it was called "feeling a bit blue" or "having a bad day." It was called "having a lie-down," "going to bed early," feeling "not quite up to par." It was only when I, at twenty-five, found myself suddenly unable to leave the house, lying for days in a leaden bleakness like a suit of armor, that I began to understand what my mother's life had been like.

"Oh well," I said, "probably no more than most people.

They didn't have Prozac in those days, you know, so people didn't tend to talk about it much. Didn't go running off to shrinks."

"Is that a yes or a no?" she asked, pen poised.

"A . . . sort of," I said. "A yes, sort of."

"And had the passenger ever, to your knowledge, forgive me for asking, made a suicide attempt?"

"No," I said. "No way." No matter how joyless her existence, Eleanor, I felt instinctively, would have wanted to stick around, if only for the meager satisfaction of being right, of confirming that things had turned out as dismally as she'd expected.

"So, to your knowledge, again forgive me for asking, she was not in a suicidal state of mind at the time of the incident?"

"The incident?" I asked, with a quick guilty stab. How, I wondered, did Garcia know about that, the lacerating, unforgivable things I'd said, the long silent ride back to the city, Eleanor hoisting her suitcase out of the car, her effortful, hunched gait as the hotel doorman had hastened out to help, that being, if only I'd known it then, my last glimpse of her on this earth?

"The in-flight incident," she said, looking puzzled. "The crash?"

"No," I said, sick at heart. "I don't think so." I only ever thought about how my encounters with Eleanor affected me, I realized, how they left me eviscerated, gutted and filleted like a discarded fish. I always imagined her as rageful and unyielding, never allowing myself to think that she might feel gutted, too, sorrowful, ashamed. "Again, not as far as I know. How would I know?"

Garcia nodded, made a few additional annotations and then, leaning back in her chair, began gathering her papers, tapping them into alignment, paper-clipping them, scribbling something across the top. "Thank you, Ms. Roth," she said, sliding them efficiently into a blue plastic dossier, "you've been very helpful. I know this hasn't been easy for you and I want to thank you for your cooperation."

"Haven't given you much to go on, though, have I? Nice older lady from Johannesburg, visiting her grown daughter. Not much to work with there, in terms of international terror."

"True," she said, standing up, "but you'd be surprised. Almost everyone on that plane, almost everyone you'd ever meet, has got something that can get your imagination going."

"Really?" I asked. I tried to think what, in Eleanor's profile, might excite the imagination of the FBI. The South African connection? The estranged daughter? The suspiciously blameless life—no criminal record, no divorce, no bad credit? "Like what, for instance? In my mother's case?"

"Well, no, I'm only speaking hypothetically here."

"Okay, then, hypothetically."

"No, no, no," she said, with a tight little smile, waving the suggestion away as if it were a wasp. "Let me thank you again for your help, and I'll be on my way."

As I stood up, partly because I didn't want her to leave yet and partly because this might be my one shot at inside information, I asked her about the missile. More and more people, on TV and the Internet, were speculating about a missile, about a trail of light seen arcing up toward the plane just before it exploded. Scores of witnesses, including pilots of nearby planes, had reported seeing an ascending streak of light, like fireworks or a flare.

"What we saw was a vapor trail, like fireworks going off," one man had said, sweeping his hand lavishly across the sky. "A stream of white smoke, you know? They ask me, Was it like a missile? I don't know, I've never seen a missile."

"What d'you think," I asked Garcia. "Any opinion on that?"

"It's all speculation," she said, shortly, "nothing but speculation. Not enough evidence yet for anything. We're just beginning our investigation and you'd better believe it will be thorough. We're the Federal Bureau of Total Investigation, not the Federal Bureau of the Obvious. Or the Wacko. But you know," she added and shrugged, "there'll always be some theory that fits the lack of evidence."

This seemed profound to me, though I couldn't say why.

"And anyway," she added, unwarily perhaps, "from what we've seen so far, the, uh, the catastrophe seems to have unfolded from the inside out." That seemed profound too.

As soon as Garcia had left, I went straight to the computer, gratified by its friendly ping of greeting, and logged on to altexplanation.com, a website that had begun to obsess me. People with odd preoccupations and too much time on their hands: it gave me something to think about, filled the frightening black spaces in my brain.

The Navy, I read, had been scheduled to conduct extensive exercises, including missile tests, on the evening of

the crash, in military zone W-105E, off the coast of Long
Island, right where the plane had blown up. Coincidence?
Clearly, it was a massive cover-up, a case of friendly fire.
The missile's radar, blinded by heavy electronic jamming
in the area, must have "acquired" the doomed plane by
mistake.

No, someone else insisted, a huge bubble of natural
gas had risen from the sea and swallowed the plane in a
fiery gulp. The President had ordered the plane destroyed
because disgruntled Secret Service agents were on their way
to Rome to tell the Pope everything they knew. The true
target had been Henry Kissinger, who (very few people
knew this) was scheduled to have been on board. A UFO had
been spotted in the area, just before the crash, hovering,
with intent, in an iridium haze. A meteorite had struck
the plane.

Someone claiming to be an expert on meteorites—more
likely a twelve-year-old boy with a search engine—explained that we don't know how many meteorites strike the
earth, because most of the earth's surface is uninhabited.
However, he said, based on what we do know, we could
expect a meteorite to hit a plane in flight once every 59,000
to 77,000 years. "So you can't rule it out," he concluded,
"just like you can't rule out the possibility that a chicken
will lay a green egg."

Indeed, I thought. You can't rule anything out, a chicken
laying a green egg, Eleanor giving birth to me, a plane
ejecting the body of my mother from its belly. Bodies
hurtle into and away from each other all the time. They
collide, they separate, they survive or they don't. I wanted
my mother's body back, that was all, the missing body of

my mother. It might be, at that very moment, drifting away on an ocean current, blowing away as vapor or ash. I wanted it back. As for the rest—meteorite, missile, falling star—what did I care? Certain types of missile were called "fire-and-forget," I'd read, because they were so simple to deploy. Maybe someone had fired one and forgotten. Maybe there was another one still out there, fired and forgotten, roaming the desolate sky, seeking heat.

DALLAS-FORT WORTH, TEXAS, 1988

CAPTAIN: Did you see that bird?

FLIGHT ATTENDANT: Yeah.

COPILOT: He just got jet blast.

FLIGHT ATTENDANT: Yeah, he did. He got it.

COPILOT: Ah, what a crash.

FLIGHT ATTENDANT: [Bird must have said] what in the world was that?

COPILOT: Ever go out to Midway [Island] and see the gooney birds? They're something to watch.

FLIGHT ENGINEER: [They] crash and look around to see if anybody saw 'em, you know . . .

COPILOT: Yeah. They would . . . If you would do a [engine] runup, and the gooney birds would be back there in the prop wash just hanging in the air, you know. And then they pull the power back and then [the gooney birds] would just . . .

Cabin: Laughter.

COPILOT: . . . Hit the ground, you know. They were hilarious. They'd send a truck out. You'd get ready to take off. They'd send a pickup truck out and they'd go move the birds off the runway so you could take off.

FLIGHT ATTENDANT: Oh, really? Oh, how funny. Where are they? Where was that?

COPILOT: Midway. Midway Island. They come back and they nest in exactly the same spot they were born.

FLIGHT ATTENDANT: On the runway?

COPILOT: Yeah, whether it was a runway or what[ever] it was. They come back to the exact same spot and, ah, so there's some kinda law or something that you can't build anything on the island any more because . . .

FLIGHT ATTENDANT: Uh-huh . . .

COPILOT: It's a sanctuary for the birds or something.

FLIGHT ENGINEER: (*on public-address system to the main cabin*): Good morning, ladies and gentlemen. We're number four for departure. Flight attendants, prepare the cabin, please.

FLIGHT ATTENDANT: We're ready.

FLIGHT ENGINEER: Thank you.

Cabin: Cockpit door is closed.

CAPTAIN: Might as well start.

COPILOT: Number three.

FLIGHT ENGINEER: Start valve open.

Cabin: Sound of engine starting.

Thirty seconds go by.

TOWER: Eleven forty-one, taxi position runway eighteen left and hold . . .

FLIGHT ENGINEER: Shoulder harness.

COPILOT: They're on.

FLIGHT ENGINEER: Flaps.

COPILOT: Fifteen. Fifteen. Green light.

FLIGHT ENGINEER: Flight controls.

Crew goes through pre-takeoff checklist.

TOWER: Eleven forty-one, fly heading one eight five, runway eighteen left, cleared for takeoff.

COPILOT: Eleven forty-one, one one eight five, cleared for takeoff.

Brakes are released, power is applied, and the aircraft begins its takeoff roll down the runway, picking up speed rapidly.

Cabin: Sound of engines spooling up.

COPILOT: Power is set. Engine instruments look good. Airspeed is coming up both sides. Eighty knots. Vee R, Vee two.

Cabin: Sound of snap, sound of the stick shaker.

Without warning, the aircraft rolls violently to the right.

CAPTAIN: Something's wrong! Oh . . .

Cabin: Sound of engine stall.

COPILOT: Engine failure.

CAPTAIN: We've got an engine failure. We're not going to make it. Full power.

Cabin: Sound of first impact; sound of second impact; sound of third impact.

Cabin: Screams.

Cabin: Sound of fourth impact.

End of tape.

11

Tuesday, July 25

The next morning, with a start, I saw Paul on TV. He had
ventured out of the Ramada, past the police barriers, to
the sodden horde of journalists who were encamped there
in the rain, like guppies in an overcrowded tank, swarming
snappishly at any tidbit that came by. He wore dark glasses,
despite the drizzle, and his long damp hair was combed
straight back, giving him, with his pale, beaky face, the
air of a minor European movie star. Accompanying him
was a grey-haired businessman from Texas, husband of one
of the flight attendants on the plane, a cordial, articulate
fellow I'd seen interviewed before. Somehow, these two had
become the spokesmen for the Families, the thousand or so
people still held captive in the Ramada, in a limbo of daily
briefings and politicians' visits, waiting for something—a
chip of bone, a smear of DNA—to set them free.

"We are coming directly to you," Paul told the mass of
microphones, "because we, the families of the victims, are
extrem, uh,"

"Extremely dissatisfied," the Texan interjected, "with the,
uh, pace of the recovery efforts, with the response, if you

could call it that, that we're getting from the airline and the FBI."

"But isn't the mayor doing something about that, sir? Aren't the families getting daily updates now, twice a day, sir, over here, sir?" a reporter called, agitating her mike like a panhandler's paper cup.

"*Tree* times a day," Paul replied, with an exasperated shrug. "They tell us this and that, you know—how many dives, which pieces of wreckage came up today. We get lots of informations. But we don't want the information they give us. We want the bodies and we want to go home."

"We have prepared a list of . . ." the other man began.

"The problem is now the body," Paul interrupted, his voice beginning to falter. "Anything we take will be all right."

The Texan, Joe Midler, explained that the Families were concerned that the FBI and the NTSB were focusing more on investigating the cause of the crash than on returning and identifying the, uh, loved ones in a timely manner. Moreover, he said, organization and communications were poor. We families, he said, have had just about as much as we can take. So here, he continued, speaking slowly and clearly into the cameras, blinking erratically, is a list of our immediate requirements:

"Number one, we want more assets on site." I had no idea what he meant. "Number two, we want a live communication link between the crash site and the family center at the Ramada. It's unbelievable, in this day and age . . . Three, daily flyovers of the crash site for the families. Four, a list of names and room numbers for all family members, can you believe they haven't even . . . And five, name tags. For all of us."

Name tags, I thought. These people want name tags.

"We must have the body," Paul burst out again. "We cannot, you know, make a memorial without the body. Without the body is not a memorial. Just people sharing sadness. And the empty place."

Neither of them mentioned the special briefing that afternoon, at three, a briefing that Harold had urged me, very strongly, to attend. "I hear they've found something," he'd said. "The black boxes, is my guess. This won't be the usual bullshit, the usual blah, blah, blah, I think they may actually have something to tell us." I'd agreed to go out to the Ramada, in fact I wanted to be there, in the thick of things, but I wasn't sure how I was going to leave the house. Except for the occasional late-night trip to the corner store, I hadn't been out of my apartment in almost a week. Just couldn't quite imagine how it could be done, how to summon the energy or the will. My body felt unreal, phantasmagorical, my skin oddly tender, too tender to clothe. I wore an old silk bathrobe and roamed the Internet instead, hunched for hours over my Mac, obsessively hitting link after link in case I missed something.

People had brought food—Lauren, a roster of colleagues from work, even, touchingly, my geriatric neighbors—more food than I could eat. The fridge was full of untouched casseroles, moldy pies. I hadn't even removed the foil from most of them. Every time I looked into the refrigerator, I thought about something I'd read, about a nurse at a hospital in rural Georgia where scores of burn victims had been treated after a DC-9 had crash-landed on the highway.

For two weeks after that, he said, he couldn't eat: couldn't get the smell of burning flesh out of his nose. "The only way I could bring myself to touch anything," he said, "was to sit in the dark." I'd tried that and it didn't work.

I'd also tried leaving the house a couple of times, had even, foolishly, called Miles on Monday and told him I'd be coming into the office later that afternoon. Then I'd had to call back within the hour to say I wasn't, as it turned out, feeling quite up to it. He understood, he said, of course, he understood how distraught I must be, it was silly even to think about work at a time like this. Please, please to stay home and rest, take care of myself. How to tell him that I didn't feel distraught, just vacant and spacy, not quite real? It was the idea of getting dressed that had defeated me, the idea of washing my hair, putting on shoes, a gargantuan, superhuman effort.

It occurred to me, finally, that I might need some help.

"We'll have a car for you there at two," Christina Barnes said, clacking the keyboard as she spoke. I pictured her holding the receiver in place with a cocked head, exacerbating some chronic neck problem. "Two sharp, okay, someone from the Family Escort Program."

"What's that?" I asked, weakly. A corps of employees and volunteers trained to attend to the needs of survivors, she said.

"I'm a survivor?" I asked, confused.

"You are, Kim, and, believe me, you will be. Need any groceries or medications?" she asked. "Catfood?"

I was touched that she remembered, though I supposed it was part of her job. As I put down the phone I glanced at Ella's bowl and noticed that it was indeed empty, save for a few dried, adhesive shreds of fish. I poured in a small avalanche of pellets. I'd given up, a while back, opening the cans—that rank metallic smell, like something that's been rotting on the bottom of the sea.

Energized by the phone call, by the idea that someone was coming to get me in a car, I moved purposefully to the bathroom, rehearsing in my mind the steps necessary to take a shower. I wanted, suddenly, to go outside, breathe new air; I felt a fresh yearning to be back at the Ramada, in the tacky splendor of the ballroom, among those bereaved strangers, accidental kin to me. I felt I knew them all well by now, knew their missing ones, had committed them all to heart. I'd spent hours poring over the photo spreads in the papers and news magazines, the memorial websites, scanning the pictures, searching for clues as to which, in this throng of smiling dead, might have been the last face my mother saw, before deafness and blindness burst upon her, before her brain was pulped like an exploded fig.

In their published photographs, all the passengers looked happy, as if they'd been happy all their lives. The thirteen-year-old girl at the piano, ponytailed and serene. The Italian newlyweds, his chin resting intimately on her shoulder as he ducked behind her to bring their faces level, radiant, cheek to cheek. The bottle-blonde, born-again homicide detective from St. Louis, striking out on her own after a divorce. The beaming flight attendant, on her first overseas flight, who'd left a trip's worth of frozen dinners, marked by day of the week, for her husband and son. The crewcut missionary from Salt Lake, the attractively tousled interior designer from Milan. The Harvard hockey star with his enormous padded shoulders and crooked teeth. The Asian woman with her little dog, who'd chosen FIN so the dog could travel under her seat rather than in the cargo hold. The little girl, shuttling between divorced parents, who'd been found with a few dollars still tucked into her sock. The family of four headed for a bat mitzvah in Tel Aviv, the TV producer who'd called his girlfriend from the airport, just before the flight, to propose. "His greatest fear was deep water," she'd wept. "I just want to know he's no longer in the water."

I had a sudden impulse to call Anna, to give her some kind of reassurance, but I didn't have much to offer. One hundred and eight bodies had been recovered as of that morning, according to the medical examiner, seventy had been positively identified, forty-five released to families. Clearly, we were not among the latter. I tried to think of something that might make her feel better.

"The Families are really organizing," I said. "Starting to kick butt around there, shake up those bureaucracies."

"Good," she said flatly, without affect. I tried to think of something else to say, something like, I'm having terrible nightmares Anna, airplane seats falling, empty, from the sky, are you having them too? "Oh and," she continued, in that same flat tone, "I've got almost all those documents together for the FBI. You know how Eleanor was always convinced she was going to die."

"Wake up dead in her bed," we chimed together, a family joke.

"So everything was pretty much organized, all in one place, in the safe. Will, insurance stuff, house stuff, everything. Even the warranties on her appliances and so on. Things she didn't even own any more, you know, vacuum cleaner from thirty years ago. Only thing I can't find is the birth certificate."

"Well, that's probably not so important," I said. "I mean, it's pretty clear that she was in fact born. Otherwise, how did we get here?" My own grim cheeriness grated on me, made me sick. I wanted to cry out instead. I wanted to turn on the shower, deafen myself, take a pounding.

"It's on the list, Kim," she insisted, in a dogged, humorless way, "for the FBI. Your FB bloody I." Anna didn't often use language like that, or did she? I knew so little about her these days, so rarely saw her rattled.

"It's not really *my* FBI," I said, after a pause. "If it was *my* FBI, this whole thing would be solved by now."

"You're the American," she said, sullenly. "It's your FBI that's making everyone run around in circles like this."

"Excuse me," I said. "I'm not an American."

"You may as well be," she said. "You've lived there half your life, almost half your life. You hate coming back here, like it's not good enough for you."

"I'm not an American," I repeated. "I still have my South African passport. I don't get to vote. I don't eat popcorn in the movies, I don't wear sneakers in the street, I know what irony is . . . I'm not an American, okay?" Her hostility had unnerved me, made me jabber like a fool. I didn't know how to talk to this Anna. The other Anna, the Anna I needed, was docile, cheerful, accommodating.

"Well, anyway," she repeated, "it's on the list. And I'm trying to follow the list." I'd never heard her like this, stubborn and obstructionist. That was, or had she forgotten, my role in the family, my rightful tone.

"Okay," I said, "well then, keep looking, I guess."

"Listen to you," she said, "'*I guess.*' You *are* a bloody Yank."

"Well, I'd rather be a bloody Yank than a bloody South African," I retorted, without thinking. At that moment, my own voice began echoing back to me, as it still sometimes did, courtesy of my cut-rate long-distance server. "Bloody South African," I heard myself say, unnervingly flat and foreign.

"What do you mean by that?" she asked, speaking over the echo, audible only to me. "Apartheid's over, in case you hadn't noticed."

"I've noticed," I said. "Look, I'm getting that weird echo thing again, so maybe we should talk later, okay? It's too hard to hear you like this." I felt oddly disoriented as I hung up, even more at sea.

My naked body looked strange to me, bony and white, barely human, barely flesh. It looked, I thought, like a chicken carcass in the freezer case, sectioned and re-assembled. As the water from the shower crashed down on me, I feared my body might come apart. I thought, again, of multiple anatomical separations, of spines blown out of bodies, of femurs stripped clean of meat. Then I thought about the Styrofoam box of human corneas that had been placed in the cockpit just before takeoff, a medical delivery, last minute. Which had later bobbed to the surface, in the soup of carnage, intact.

The volunteer from the Family Escort Program turned out to be a retired FIN pilot, a tall rangy man with close-cropped silver hair, an awkward stooped posture, and not much to say for himself. I was downstairs, by the front door, just before two: my hair was still damp, my pants were drooping off my hipbones because I couldn't find a belt, I had forgotten my sunglasses and my cellphone, but I was there. Though the day was overcast, the light pierced my eyes, paralyzing my brain, making my whole body feel hollow and squeamish. The traffic noise seemed menacingly loud. "Thank you," I said, when he pulled up in his Saab. "Yes, I am," I said. "People have been very kind," I said.

Once he'd ascertained that I didn't want to talk about the Loved One, he lapsed into silence for a while, maneuvering alertly in the crosstown traffic. Then, as we slowed to a near standstill on the bridge, he began talking about planes. There were six million parts in a jumbo jet, he told me. One hundred fifty miles of wiring, which I already knew: I'd had nightmares about cables squirming in the deep, as if they were tentacles, as if they were alive. Flight 770 had had a flight range of 5,290 miles. The capacity of its fuel tank was 48,445 gallons. The plane had weighed half a million pounds on takeoff. I wondered how he could remember all those figures, what they meant.

"She seems to have been very well maintained," he said. "No one's seen any signs of aging issues here."

He was a kind man. He wanted to help. He wanted to offer me something, so he offered information. He gave me his card, too, Pat C. Klein. "Call anytime," he said.

The inside of the Ramada, the gauntlet that the Families had to walk to the ballroom for briefings every day, had been transformed into a bazaar, a souk of social services, with tables for all the various agencies—city, state, airline, FBI, NYPD—staffed by tired but friendly-looking people, offering help and brochures. There was also a Mary Kaye

Cosmetics sales rally going on somewhere, right next to the
kickboxing tournament. The scene had the misplaced buzz
of a workplace health fair, minus the cookies and balloons,
the free blood-pressure tests, and I feared, as I stumbled
by, that eager volunteers might call out to me like carnival
barkers.

Somehow, by the time I had gained entry into the Rococo
Room—establishing, by means of my driver's license, that
I was legitimately bereaved—the briefing had begun. Stepping into the ballroom, I had a brief moment of shock—
I was in the wrong place, surely, a shabby, shrunken
hall jammed with chairs and people and electrical cords,
instead of the vast glittery space my imagination had been
inhabiting since the night of the crash. Hesitating, seeing
nowhere to sit, I leaned against the wall near the door,
scanning the crowd for a familiar face. These, I thought,
were the Families, my Family, my new, imaginary kin, this
mob of exhausted-looking, irritable, unshaven people, these
people subsisting on rumors and room service, people whose
days and nights unspooled alike in the thin grey light of
nightmare.

"—placed immediately into coolers filled with fresh
water," a short, rumpled man in an NTSB windbreaker
was saying, staring intently at the floor, like someone more
accustomed to listening to the last fractured sounds of
human and mechanical life than to hearing himself talk.
Two large photographs of surprisingly intact, surprisingly
banal metal objects were propped on easels to either side
of him. So Harold had been right: the black boxes, found,
improbably, within minutes of each other, one by a hard-hat
Navy diver in Debris Field #1 who'd accidentally stepped

on it, releasing it from its shroud of silt, and the other by a small robot, a ROV, which had pointed its camera right at it. Since I had no idea what it was, I pictured the ROV absurdly, anthropomorphically, as a silvery homunculus zipping around the seabed, filming whatever caught his fancy. The NTSB man was talking about the chain of custody that had been established for the tapes on their flight to D.C., about the process of washing and drying tape in the NTSB lab, but he was losing his audience, his timing was off. All we cared about was the punchline: what the tape would say, what secrets it might, like a ditched lover, reveal.

Slowly, pedantically, peering almost grumpily at us through his black-framed, Buddy Holly-style glasses, he came to the point. The flight data recorder, he said, showed that no instruments malfunctioned before the explosion. But all electrical systems seem to have stopped at almost the same instant. He repeated this, "almost the same instant," as if it were significant, but didn't explain why. And as for the cockpit voice recorder, he said, pausing, then shrugging, "well, there isn't much to tell you, I'm afraid. There's just a little noise at the end, sort of a click. A final loud sound before the power died."

This information was repeated in French and Italian by smiling, overdressed interpreters, both female, and then, for good measure, in American sign language. During the brief agitated silence of the latter, I felt in my own body what I felt in the room, an ebbing and emptying, a queasy suspended feeling. That was it? Electrical failure, a little click? I had, we all had, expected the black boxes to tell us what we needed to know, to give us an answer

of some kind, to make catastrophe intelligible. It was
only in the gradual, bleak realization that this was not
going to occur that I understood how much I had been
counting on it.

The official refused to take questions, emphasizing, as
they always did, that these findings were preliminary—
"we wanted to get the info right out to you, as soon as
we pulled that puppy up out of the water"—and that
was the end of that, leaving, in the room, a babel of
unanswered questions and, somewhere in the centre of
my body, a hollow sense of yearning, a vague, unlocatable
rage. It was sharp, like hunger or like lust; it agitated
me into action. I looked around the room for something
to do, someone to latch on to, something to smack up
against. Harold and Bernice were nowhere to be seen.
Nor was Christina Barnes. Somewhere near the front of
the room was a small knot of people, talking or arguing,
and somewhere in that knot was Paul, with an overstuffed
red-and-white FIN folder under one arm, gesticulating. I
wasn't sure if he would recognize me—I wasn't sure what
I looked like any more—but as I made my way toward
him, ducking and weaving through the traffic patterns
of distracted people, he acknowledged me, first with his
eyebrows and then with a vague, inclusive motion of his
free hand.

They were talking about a spike. Something on the tape,
some acoustical spike. Just like Lockerbie, someone was
insisting, the exact same spike.

"Paul," I said, edging in beside him. The top of my head
reached only to his sternum, which made me feel small and
insubstantial, breakable, like a doll. "You been—?"

He shrugged.

"I saw you on TV," I said, stupidly. "It's good that you're—"

He nodded. He seemed to be listening with half an ear to the discussion about the spike, what kind of explosion it might suggest, high intensity versus low intensity. High, I gathered, would mean a bomb.

"What do you—" I began. I realized I'd forgotten how to speak to people, other than to receive their condolences, how to hold a conversation. "What do you think about this all, the boxes?"

"They are not telling us everything, of course," he said, his attention still elsewhere, like a dog straining to hear something you can't. I noticed how haggard he looked, how pained, as if consciousness were an ongoing ordeal. "That sound, the spike. They aren't . . ."

"Yes, but—"

I realized, in abandoning my sentence, that I didn't care about the black boxes any more. I didn't care about the spike, the missile, the bodies, the bomb, the crash. I didn't want to talk about any of it any more. I didn't want to talk. I wanted, suddenly, to be very drunk.

"Paul," I repeated, grasping his upper arm to secure his attention, "when you're done with this, with them," indicating the now dispersing group, "you want to get a glass of wine? I could really—"

The bar at the Ramada was dark, dark at 3:30 in the afternoon, wood-paneled, with some kind of nautical motif conveyed by the anchor-shaped cutouts on the chairbacks, the limp swags of netting on the walls. Candles burned glumly in globes of amber glass. A crew of journalists had already commandeered the narrow bar and its wide-screen TV—sports, full volume, violent Fauvist color—so, moving through the thick air as if drugged, I steered Paul toward a small table at the back. We didn't speak, other than to order a glass of red wine apiece. He grimaced as he took the first sip.

"California," he said, shaking his head, as if California were the name of a disease.

I stared at him. He was an odd-looking man, no doubt about it, all angles and agitation. I drank most of my wine in two gulps. I felt that I should make conversation but had forgotten how. Or why. He stared somewhere beyond the candle, his eyes unfocused but intent, as if trying to conjure one of those stereoptic images off the page. Then he looked straight at me and, continuing some urgent internal discourse, said, "The missile, you see, if it exploded *outside* the plane, could cause a, how do you call it, a wave of high pressure. And this pressure, this is what causes the explosion. The spike."

"Maybe," I said. I drank down the rest of my wine.

"But yes," he said, emphatically. "But they will never tell this, will they? Not in one million years, this American army."

"Navy," I said, "whatever." I looked around for the waitress, torpidly examining her fingernails at the service bar, signaled another round. "Paul," I said, "why don't you tell me something about Michel? I mean . . ." He withdrew his gaze, stared down at the tabletop, which was stained like a Venn diagram with intersecting rings. "If you feel like it," I added.

"Well, he," he began, then stopped. "My brother, you know? Twenty-six years." The relentless, manic quality that drove his talk of missiles and conspiracies and spikes had deserted him; he used instead the halting, stumbling speech of a person trying, in a language not his own, to say what could barely be said in any. He shredded his cocktail napkin as he spoke.

Michel, it turned out, was a blues guitarist, trying, after some success in Europe, to make it on the American scene. And he was close, Paul told me, so close; he'd played gigs at this club and that club, names that unfortunately meant nothing to me. So talented, Paul said, it could break your heart. He'd been living in the East Village with a slew of roommates, tending bar at some bistro, occasionally playing for change at the Union Square station, the uptown N platform, Paul specified, "perhaps you might even have heard him once, no?"

"Perhaps," I said. "It's quite possible. There are some wonderful musicians who . . ."

Paul's eyes filled with tears. He scrubbed them away angrily with the remains of his napkin, scrunched it in his fist, dropped it on the floor. We were on our third glass of wine by then and I was contemplating a fourth.

"Was he on his way back to Paris?" I asked. "I mean, how did he end up . . ."

"Old girlfriend," Paul said, bitterly. "He was going to make a visit with an old girlfriend in London, you know, then on to Paris. For the vacation of August, with my parents, in Normandy."

I imagined an empty guitar case, resting open, as if to receive coins, on the bed of the sea. I pictured its once velvety lining, dark blue. I saw the occasional sea creature flitting in and out of its open mouth. And then, like a commuter when the train arrives, a departing current tossing, in valediction, a handful of silver glitter.

"Let's get another glass of wine," I said. "It seems to help."

His room was on the eleventh floor, overlooking a parking lot, and it smelled of cigarette smoke and unwashed socks. Also something stale and oniony, food or sweat, I couldn't tell. There were ziggurats of Xeroxes, newspapers, faxes, and pink message slips on every surface—further evidence, if I needed any, of his craziness, his overweening need to build a case. I envied him, vaguely, his energy, then lay down on the bed.

His body was hard, bony, and so, on a much smaller scale, was mine, so we clashed, bone on bone, my hipbone whacking his, his kneecap digging into my thigh, my elbow cracking against his collarbone as I reached up to grasp his face. He twisted his hand into my hair, yanking my head back as he covered my mouth with his mouth, devouring my lips, my tongue, devouring me in a way that had nothing to do with me and everything to do with grief. I could feel the sudden frenzy of sensation in his body as sharply as, suddenly, I felt it in mine, the pull in my hair, the abrasion of his stubble against my skin, the pressure of his knee against my thigh, my nails scraping the smooth flesh of his back. He sucked my nipple until it burned, until I cried out and pulled his head away. I was wet and gasping, fists and jaw clenched, heel hooked around his lower back. "Just fuck me," I said, so he did, hard and quickly, came without a sound, collapsed on my shoulder and wept.

It lasted, perhaps, four minutes. No condom, what did I care. No conversation. I was covered with sweat and I wept too.

12

Thursday, July 27

———

There were 318 new messages on my office e-mail. Three hundred and eighteen unread, it said, redundantly.

"Miles," I said, "I don't think I can do this."

I swiveled my chair away from the computer screen and looked across the desk at him, my blank shiny desk with its in-tray and its out-tray, its lone white rose, placed there by Miles, in a bud vase of gentian blue.

"Seriously," I said, "I don't think this is an option right now." I couldn't imagine where to start. I also couldn't imagine what a single one of those 318 messages might say that I could give a hoot about, a damn, a flying fuck.

He leaned forward in his chair, recrossed his legs, and made a gesture that involved a slight shrug, a slight pursing of his lips, a slight downward tilt of the chin. "Okay," he said, amiably, "I can see that that would be a bit overwhelming." He paused, selecting a file from the neatly labeled rainbow of them on his lap. "Would you rather just go through the phone stuff, then? Of course there've been media calling every day, still are, but we don't even take anything down. Just tell them you're unavailable, home number is unlisted, please respect your privacy, so long, goodbye."

I stared out of the large showy window that didn't open, stared at the Manhattan skyline, as glamorous and eye-catching as an expensive piece of art, stared at the signed Louis Stettner print on the wall. Stared at the telephone dial pad, so function-laden that I could imagine myself piloting a 747 with it.

"I'm surprised they haven't tracked you down anyway, the creeps," he continued. He looked up, gave his trendy wire-rimmed glasses a tweak, right where the earpiece met the frame.

"No," I said, after a moment. "I don't think you understand. I don't think any of this is an option right now."

I'd thought, until then, that I'd managed it, the make-up and the pantyhose and the blouse and the skirt, the taxi ride across town, the briefcase filled with urgent, obsolete reminders, the crammed elevator to the seventeenth floor (familiar morning smell of toothpaste, shaving cream and hair gel), the gauntlet of well-wishers between reception and my door with its discreet, burnished plaque: Kim J. Roth, Senior Vice-President of Business Development. I thought that, with Miles's efficient help—everything was annotated, flagged, and prioritized for me—I'd sit right down and barrel through it, eight days' worth of mail and messages, worldly concerns, money and products, a welcome distraction, surely, from the waiting. From the daily body count and the nightmares (she was alive, she had something she wanted to tell me but I couldn't hear it, couldn't reach her in time, the phone was out of order, the train was pulling out of the station, she was floating off, terrified, in a hot-air balloon).

But now it was clear to me, utterly clear, that I couldn't do this. Couldn't do it now, or probably ever again. Christina Barnes had warned me, in our most recent chat—she'd been calling every day to check in—that people in my, uh, situation often felt impelled to make "impulsive" and "inappropriate" life changes and that I should feel free to run anything major by her, any major decisions, okay? But this didn't feel impulsive. This felt sure, like something falling into place, like the soft but decisive plop of a ripened fruit.

I was never coming back to this job, I could see that now. I'd never wanted it in the first place, never dreamed of a career in market research, never aspired to be VP of anything. Market Metronics had made me the best offer after grad school, and I needed a job and a green card, so I took it. I'd been good at it (endless attention to detail, knack for reducing complex data to catchphrases, nice interface with clients), had made a lateral move to Hite Consulting after five years, and was on a conveyor belt to the top. But now, suddenly, I felt free to leap off the conveyor belt while it was still moving, even, perhaps, at the cost of a twisted ankle or broken leg. Eleanor was dead. And my only real aspiration, I now understood, had been a negative one: not to become her. To avoid her fate. Not, in any way, to replicate my mother's life.

I'd never learned to cook, for fear that, the moment I stepped into a kitchen, I'd metamorphose into her, fat and sweaty and put-upon. I'd never learned to sew, garden, bake, arrange flowers, make curtains, ice a cake. I abhorred shopping. I abhorred housekeeping. I loathed the idea of marriage and, especially, of children—each one, in my imagination, a ball and chain.

I'd worked on myself, made myself, I thought, spare and strong, self-sufficient, light on my feet. I'd learned to do without, to breathe thin air. I could provide what I needed, manage my own air supply—no need for a diving partner there in the deep, an oxygen tank on the mother ship. I could survive, I had survived—depending, I now saw, on how you defined "survive." I was thirty-nine years old, sitting at my big shiny desk on the seventeenth floor, and I had no idea, I realized, what I wanted or how to live.

Perhaps, I thought, it was time to find out. The idea was giddying, vertiginous, as if champagne were circulating in my veins. As if my blood were composed of tiny bubbles, instead of the stubborn coils of the double helix. I felt like laughing out loud, whinnying like a horse.

"Dirk in?" I asked Miles, who was regarding me with some concern. Dirk Hite Jr. was my immediate boss, a genial, tennis-playing Yalie, lover of good cigars and Irish setters, unburdened, like the latter, by excessive IQ. Dirk was in, as it turned out, eager to see me and to welcome me back; within twenty minutes, to his bemused dismay, I'd negotiated a three-month leave of absence. Bearing Barnes's words in mind, I hadn't burned my bridges, but I knew I'd never be back. I made Miles a gift of my Palm Pilot on my way out.

My apartment felt stuffy, heady with the scent of lilies and roses, the large, white, waxy arrangements people had been sending me, as if I were dead. I threw open the windows, letting in the roar of Amsterdam Avenue and alarming Ella, who'd been snoozing on the windowsill in a parallelogram of sun. I pulled off my pantyhose, ripping them, a brand new pair, bloody Donna Karan. I stepped out of my skirt, tossed my pricey little blouse across the room, unhooked the scratchy lace bra. My bathrobe felt delicious next to my skin, cool and soft, and, though it was barely noon, I poured myself a tall vodka and turned on the TV.

For a while, in a celebratory spirit, I watched the cartoon channel. Everything seemed hilarious, every character, no matter how badly drawn or how crudely colored. So what if their squeaky little voices weren't synchronized with their lips, so what if their antics were designed to divert five-year-olds? Here was a world in which everything was vivid, frenetic, and reversible, where broken objects reconstituted themselves and the creature flattened by the steamroller stood up and walked, in two dimensions, away. Where the worst that could happen was a *boing* on the head. But after about half an hour of this—of boings and biffs, of diminishing returns—my merriment began to pall, my attention began to stray, and, in a chastened mood, I switched back to the news.

There, on CNN, was a hunk of wreckage, a big flat Lego-like piece, being hoisted, dripping and tilted, out of the sea. What surprised me, as I sat back and sipped my drink, was how colorful it was: an edible celery green on the ends, a deep lipstick rose for the rest. I'd expected everything to be grey—the engine, the fuselage, the functional parts. Seeing that they weren't, that they were lush and vivid inside, was a thrill of sorts, like discovering that a dull-looking person has a riotous inner life. I didn't really think about what that particular piece might be.

The phone rang and I ignored it. A man's voice came on the machine and I ignored it. Raising my glass festively in Ella's direction, I clicked to another channel, a local Long Island station that had pretty much given itself over to coverage of the crash. An academic from MIT was explaining why, according to his information, the streak on the radar tape was not, in fact, evidence of a missile—was, in fact, evidence of nothing at all. "These are just little twinkles that pop up and go away," he said, dismissively. "We call it 'anomalous propagation.'"

Anomalous propagation, I thought. A lot of that going around. The vodka was announcing its presence in my brain. I felt, at the same time, oddly free and oddly compelled, as if everything might be significant, if I only knew how. As if everyone on TV might be talking in code. Anomalous propagation. Proximity sensors. Uncommanded rolls. Thrust reversers. Controlled flight into terrain. I topped up my drink and took a long sip.

After a commercial for frozen crabcakes, an official from the NTSB came on to explain the organization of the investigation, the various working groups, from Metallurgy to Human Factors. Metallurgy looked mainly at fractures. Human Factors examined how people behaved—how, without knowing it, they brought disaster upon themselves, in an "event cascade."

The Cabin Interior group would study the "disposition of interior artifacts." That is, where everything flew and fell, how the snug world of the cabin burst apart in a hail of popping rivets. The Trajectory Study group would produce a "wreckage diagram." "Of course," the official said, "we add more wreckage items as they come in."

Then, he said, there was the Wire Group, whose task was to untangle the miles of snarled and broken wiring, determine where it belonged in the reconstructed plane. Unlike most components of the 747, the wiring was never replaced. So the wiring on Flight 770 was over twenty-five years old; it might be damaged or corroded, might reveal what he called a "latent failure."

"A latent failure," he explained, "is, ah, a failure that goes undetected for years, decades maybe, until something happens. Unusual circumstances, you know, an unusual combination of circumstances. Then you get an incident."

I stood up. My feet were pins-and-needly from sitting cross-legged, my calf muscle in a cramp. I needed a good long walk but that seemed unthinkable, like space travel. I needed a yoga class but could barely imagine touching my toes, let alone adopting the warrior stance, supposed to conquer inner turmoil, summon dignity and strength. What I really needed, I decided, was another drink. As I cracked the ice free from the tray, sliced up a lime, it occurred to me that I might never leave the apartment again, that I might sit here in my bathrobe, tippling, until my savings ran out. The idea was exhilarating, like a draught of laughing gas. Let Anna deal with Eleanor's corpse. Let Anna deal with the FBI, the NYPD, the Suffolk County Medical Examiner's Office, with FIN, CNN, and Christina Barnes. Let Anna surrender her DNA. I would just sit in my bathrobe and drink.

There had been a memorial service the day before, at Roberts Point State Park, the sliver of shoreline nearest the crash site. As soon as I'd heard what was planned—the scrupulously ecumenical service, the guitar and harp, the 230 white doves—I'd decided not to go. Bernice was going, but then Bernice believed in God. Harold was going, just, he said, "to tell my girl goodbye." Paul, I surmised, would not be there. Barnes had counseled me, gently, to attend, suggesting that the ceremony might bring some kind of "closure." "I'm not a suitcase," I had said, picturing the click of an old-fashioned hasp. In the moment of silence that followed, I wondered what professional empathy providers did when they just wanted to smack someone.

Now, as I watched footage from the event, I raised my frosty glass to the screen and toasted my decision to stay home. The beach itself was shabby, stony, swept by an irritable wind, the kind that would fling grit into your eyes. People huddled on rickety white chairs, facing the ocean and a makeshift stage. First came the politicians, in a flurry of platitudes. We should "remember not only the tragedy of their deaths," the governor said, "but more importantly what they gave to our lives." The mayor said, "All of us have learned many lessons from you who have lost your loved ones, and the chief lesson is love." The CEO of FIN claimed that the passengers had been striving, through international air travel, to "live up to their God-given potential." There was also a lawyer, retained by some thirty of the Families, who spoke to reporters before the ceremony. He said, "We have felt from the start that this was a good strong product liability case."

A priest and rabbi recited Psalm 23 together, another priest said a prayer in French, a boys' choir sang some awful John Denver song. Then, in the only moment that moved me, the mourners headed to the water's edge, rolling up their trousers, hoisting up their skirts. They waded knee-deep into the surf and, with clumsy flinging motions, scattered long-stemmed white roses into the sea. They held each other, rested their heads on each other's shoulders, dropped letters and photos into the foam. They stared into the wavelets, and they wept.

They were there, I realized, because they wanted to remember. I was here, in my bathrobe with a vodka tonic, because I didn't. Didn't dare. I'd become afraid to think about my mother save as a problem of retrieval and identification, afraid some terrible howling sadness would beset me if I did. I could feel the sadness out there somewhere, like several tons of ocean water, and I was just hoping that my hatches would hold.

But the vodka was working on me, the sight of those mourners in the surf. I let myself think about it, in a maudlin way. If I had been there at the service, let's say, if I'd flung a rose for Eleanor, if I'd written her a letter and sent it eddying toward where I imagined her bones might be—now coral, now pearl—what would it have said? Dear Eleanor, I began in my mind, I'm sorry. I don't know why we couldn't love each other. I think we both tried.

I stopped to think about whether this was true. Perhaps I'd never really tried hard enough. Or perhaps I'd tried, but failed, failed over and over again, failed every time. The flaw must be in me, I thought, it must be my wiring that's faulty, frayed, susceptible to sparks.

I thought it was our differences, Eleanor, that pushed us apart. Now I know it was our likeness, the way the blood rises and pounds in each of our brains, the desolating rage that engulfs us both. Bad chemistry, dangerous fumes.

In order for an explosion to occur, I'd read, you need

the following elements: heat, the right proportion of fuel to air, a container to pressurize, and an ignition source.

Oh, Eleanor, I finished my letter, that was us.

If only, I thought, taking a long cold sip, it were that simple. Even I could see that my letter was no good, that it explained nothing. Goddamnit, Eleanor, I thought, the blood surging to my face, you made it so hard.

I stared out of the window at the fire escape of the building opposite, so rusty I couldn't see it saving anybody. I thought about my childhood, how little I could recall—a few images, with nothing in between, like postcards from the void. I thought about Anna, how she seemed, for better or for worse, continuous with herself, the same little girl who'd played Tea Party in the shed. Whereas I, right from the start, had felt something splitting off inside me, some part of me retreating, like a creature with a shell, to a private, armored place.

But I'd needed that place, I thought, that shelter, like a person living under constant threat of aerial bombardment: the blast could come without warning and it could blow you to bits. Growing up, I'd identified fiercely with the domestic servants—the "girl" and "boy," live-in housemaid and gardener—when Eleanor, in a fit of fury, would turn upon them, screaming abuse for some real or imagined infraction, calling them stupid, calling them kaffirs, calling them baboons, and giving them—poor Cynthia, poor Regina, poor Paulina, poor Daniel, sole supporters of large families in distant homelands—one hour to leave the house.

By the time I was twelve, the rage between my mother and myself, which was form—which existed and would have existed anyway—had found its content. We fought about politics, apartheid and race, fought violently and bitterly about that, as we did about everything else (clothes, boys, curfews, make-up, food, motorcycles, "foul language"). Arguing about politics was one way, I suppose, of arguing about power, about recognition, about who had what kinds of rights over other people's bodies. I knew I'd never change her mind—she was raised as a racist and would die one— but I could never prevent myself, in full adolescent throttle, from wrangling and remonstrating, battering and bullying. I was raging and self-righteous; she was like a cornered rat. Roger would cower in his study as we came to blows, then emerge to console, conciliate; sometimes he just got in his car and drove away. I stabbed her once, with a pair of scissors, a feeble, glancing blow on the forearm, pure theater. Once, to Eleanor's utter mortification, the neighbors called the police. That was when she dragged me to a psychiatrist and demanded tranquilizers; I spat them out, like Ella, on the sly.

There were times I feared that one of us might actually kill the other, out there in the suburbs, with nobody around to witness or to intervene—Anna at swimming practice, Roger at work, the servants on lunch break, the neighbors not home. Sometimes I would run out of the house, barefoot, and hitchhike the ten miles into town, just to get away. It would never end, I understood, until I left: her rage was ancient, indestructible, as was her fear.

That's what, I thought, still staring at the rusty fire escape, it's taken me a lifetime to understand: that my mother was afraid. That she'd always been afraid. Afraid, when she was younger, of not having enough. And later, with the husband and the house and the servants and the swimming pool, afraid of having too much, which might then be wrested away. Afraid that the world was a dangerous, fickle place (which it proved, at 15,000 feet, to be). And afraid, her whole life, of being found out, unmasked—even by her own children—as an impostor, a class pretender. The same fear, perhaps, that had afflicted me at graduate school, when I found myself rising among the entitled, raking in the rewards, without, I felt, any real intellectual capital to call my own.

I drained the last of my vodka; my eyes and throat burned. I felt grief opening up inside me like a wound. I'd known it would be a mistake to dredge all this up, to sit here, sloshed, and recall, in one moment, how much we'd been alike, Eleanor and I, similarly charged, and then, in the next, how different, fissionable. Bodies that had repelled each other, right from the start. There's no solution, I thought, no blame either—nothing, in the end but the double-crossing double helix.

Any more of this, I thought, thumping my glass down, and I might really go mad.

The phone rang again and I made no move until I heard Anna's voice, tentative, on the machine. "Kim? Kimmie? You there?" Then, in an awkward scramble, tripping over the sash of my bathrobe, realizing I was pretty far gone, I ran for it.

"Yeah, I'm here."

"Oh. Thought you might be at work, weren't you going to . . ."

"No, I'm home. Let me call you right back." We'd

arrived, tacitly, at a convention whereby I always bore the cost of a call.

"So what's up?" I asked her when she picked up again, before I'd even heard a ring. "Kids doing okay?"

"I think so," she said. "I'm watching Sally carefully, you know, because she's the one who keeps it all inside. Bridget'll just throw a tantrum, so you know where you stand. They're talking to the counselor at school, though Sal apparently doesn't say too much."

"And Angus?"

"He's all right. Sort of. Not sleeping well, with all the worry. Sits up half the night watching TV."

"Yes, I . . ."

"Drinking a bit."

"Oh," I said. Imagine that.

"But I'm back at work now," she said, after a pause. "Which helps, some of the time. Keeps your mind off it. Though some of the other teachers, you know, they just want to talk about it all the time, oh, have you heard anything new, is it a missile, is it a bomb."

I thought about Paul, about how I was probably never going to see him again, except on TV. I thought about how that was perfectly fine. We'd done what we needed to do, that was all. I felt as if I never wanted to see anyone again, as if the attentions of other human beings were a wearisome imposition. Lauren could just keep her casseroles, Christina Barnes could just empathize off, and the UPS man could just leave my parcels with the super downstairs.

"Oh, and we saw the service," Anna said, after a few moments, trying to keep things going. "Part of it, on the

news. It looked lovely. I didn't let the girls watch 'cause I
thought it would be too sad. Though maybe I should have,
you know, because we don't know if we'll ever . . ."

"The service?"

"The memorial. That they had at that beach."

"Oh yes."

"I hope you threw a rose for us. Roses." She sounded as
if she was starting to choke up.

"Um," I said. "Well, actually. I wasn't there."

The silence roared, intercontinentally. "You . . . ?" she
said.

"I wasn't there. I didn't go."

"Kim . . ." she said. Her voice was definitely teary,
becoming tearier.

"You know I hate that shit," I said. I could feel myself
snapping into defensive mode, insistent, overemphatic.
"You know I have no time for that crap, organized religion,
politicians, the whole Department of bloody Platitudes."
Anna, I knew, was raising her children as Anglicans; Angus
was a deacon at the local church, doing, every Sunday
morning at nine, whatever deacons do. I didn't know
what, if anything, Anna believed in, other than living a
respectable life. It occurred to me that we'd never talked
about it—strange, under the circumstances (death having
moved in with plenty of luggage, death parked in our living
rooms like a doddering relative, death pacing the house at
night, death listening in on the phone).

"Yes, but . . ." Anna began.

"Wild horses couldn't have dragged me there. There
aren't enough wild horses in the state of New York to drag
me to that kind of, of . . ."

"You just don't care, do you," she said, quietly. "You never did care about her."

I felt the air leave my lungs, felt something like a jolt of electricity surge through my body. I thought, somehow, of the electric chair.

"Oh," I said, "is that so?" My voice suddenly sounded whiny, like a petulant teen. I could feel myself regressing by the second. Any minute now, I thought, I'll be resorting to adolescent sarcasm: *As if*, I could hear myself saying. *Oh yeah? I don't think so.* Soon I'd be sticking out my tongue at Anna, calling her Little Miss Perfect, Mama's Girl. Soon I'd be three, two, the child who wails inconsolably when her mother leaves the room, believing she'll never see her again. "Is that so?" I continued. "Well, a fat lot you know. And anyway, what the hell difference would it have made? Did she ever care about me? Tell me that."

"You know she did, Kim," Anna said, her voice quavering. "You know the whole thing with you broke her heart."

"No I don't know that," I started to yell. "How would I know that? How would I ever have known that?" I wanted, badly, to weep.

"You know it did, Kim. She tried, she kept trying. She came to New York, didn't she, she tried. You just didn't give her a chance. You never did. And now look what's happened . . ." Anna then did, in fact, begin to weep.

"I didn't give *her* a chance? Oh, for God's sake." Another giant surge of rage jolted through me. "She was impossible, you know that. She was crazy, insane, mentally ill, whatever you want to call it. Sick. I know we're not supposed to say that but it's true. You know it, Dad knew it, but God forbid anyone should ever actually say it."

"That's not fair, Kim," she wept. "You didn't even know her."

"I knew enough," I said. "Enough to know a crazy person when I saw one."

"That's not fair," Anna repeated. "She was just a little . . . tense all the time. Tense, unhappy. She just didn't have good coping skills, never learned to cope, the poor old thing."

"I'll say. I'll say she was unhappy. But did she have to go out of her way to make everyone else unhappy too?"

"No, no, Kim, you never really understood. You just couldn't see . . . You didn't really know her."

"I knew enough," I repeated. "Enough to get away."

Another silence, loud and staticky, the sound of space.

"Yes," she said. "You got away. You got away, okay. Leaving me here, to deal with her, to deal with everything."

"Oh, really," I continued, unable to stop, "is that so? Is that so? Then who's dealing with everything here, doing all the work? The shit work? The paperwork, the FBI, the this request and that request? Who's running around here doing the depressing stuff? Dealing with reality? Which, God knows, isn't your forte. If you're such a good daughter, if you were so happy living in Eleanor's pocket, like a, like a baby kangaroo, then why the hell aren't *you* here? Why aren't *you* taking care of things?"

"Oh, Kim," she wept, "you know that's not fair. You know we don't have the . . ."

"Well, you know what, Anna? Fuck you. Just *fuck you*,

Anna." With that, I slammed down the phone, knocking
over, in the process, a jar I'd filled with pennies. Ella
awoke, startled, and sprang off the windowsill. I had, I
realized, been yelling, screeching like a fiend. My throat
hurt. I was trembling and tingling all over. I felt a burst of
exhilaration, *schadenfreude*. There was a tinge of dread in
the mix, too, but I'd deal with that later. In the meanwhile,
I decided, I'd head for the fridge and fix myself a drink.

PERMITTED AND
RECOMMENDED COMMUNICATIONS

As you communicate over the airwaves in an emergency situation, remember to:

- Speak calmly and slowly enough to be completely understood. Identify yourself.
- Use complete sentences and language that you know and understand, but be brief.
- Use correct terminology when it is appropriate. Speak as a professional: no joking, singing, profanity, etc.
- Do not use individuals' names. Use unit, dispatch, and hospital identifications.
- Always monitor the channel before speaking so that you do not interfere with another unit's transmission.
- Speak distinctly, but do not shout.
- Always acknowledge a transmission promptly. If you cannot take a long incoming message, simply acknowledge the call with "Stand by."
- *Never* pretend to understand a communication if you do not. Ask for a repeat in other terms.
- Be certain of the message received; if you are unsure, ask for repetition of the message.
- Do not cut off the sender until you have received the complete message.
- Be brief and concise, and know what you are going to say beforehand.

- Do not try to transmit if other personnel are using the channel, or if the dispatcher is sending to you.
- Sign off at the end of the transmission.

13

Monday, July 31

Total decompression will disrupt the anatomy of the body,
the pathologist said. Especially those parts that are soft,
that contain fluid or air. He used the analogy of a balloon:
take the pressure off and the balloon goes bang. So, he
said, "you're talking about blood vessels, stomach, lungs,
possibly head, heart."

He also said that the chances of anyone remaining
conscious after decompression would be nil. This sounded
reassuring, but I'd made the mistake of reading accounts
by plane-crash survivors who described the smell of shit
and vomit in the plummeting plane, the sounds of groans
and retching. The eardrum-puncturing explosions. The
screaming, the gasping, the darkness, the tornado of
debris, the shriek of tearing metal, the fireballs streaking
down the aisle, the bodies flying from their seats. The
dense, acrid smoke that sears your lungs and poisons
your blood, flooring you in seconds flat. The unbelievable
violence of impact.

"Impact's like, it's like a giant hand grabbing you
and slamming you," one pilot said. "Mashing you into

the controls." A flight attendant described the experience of crash-landing on a highway as like being in a
big cardboard box tumbling down the stairs. She also
described a passenger staggering from the wreckage with
all his clothes burned off, except for two strips of elastic
around his ankles where his socks had been. Another pilot
described how a whirlwind of dirt and rivets had hit him in
the face, briefly blinding him. "When I got my eyes open
again all I saw was red lights," he said. "Everything was
lit up like a Christmas tree, and my face just felt like raw
hamburger."

I'd become obsessed, over time, with trying to imagine
what, if anything, Eleanor would have felt, would have suffered, during her last few moments of consciousness. Flight
770, I'd read, had taken a minute and a half to drop into
the sea. Ninety seconds. Ninety seconds—think of waiting
for the microwave or the elevator, think of holding your
breath—can be a long time. An extremely long time. Ninety
capacious seconds for Eleanor to think . . . what?

Nothing, I told myself, she would have thought nothing.
Sudden depressurization pops the brain. She would have
felt nothing, known nothing, feared nothing. I tried to
convince myself of this, tried to conjure for her a peaceful
end. A sudden, blissful blackout. A merciful inferno. And
then, from a plume of white smoke, the silvery aluminum
rain spiraling down, catching in graceful twists the last
glints of the sun.

I'd read about a Japan Airlines crash in which, as the
plane zigzagged like a leaf to the earth, passengers had time
to write farewell notes to their families. Somehow, this idea
comforted me: I pictured, implausibly, a serene planeload

of people engaged in contemplation and calligraphy. But I was also haunted by something a young Coast Guard diver had said on national TV: of the corpses he'd recovered from FIN, he said, "A lot died with screams across their faces."

I fantasized shooting him through the TV screen, shooting him right across his callow, rosy face.

I'd ordered eight books from amazon.com on plane crashes—on aircraft safety, cockpit voice recordings, pilot error, anything remotely connected—and had spent most of the past few days lying on the sofa with Absolut bottle at hand ploughing through them. I made notes and lists, wrote down words I didn't understand, copied diagrams. When I wasn't doing that, I was on the Internet, checking out every flying-related site I could find, especially chat rooms for the phobic, for people who were terrified of flying, who, if they flew at all, had to board in a wheelchair under sedation, who knew in their hearts that a jumbo jet was too big to stay in the air, who vividly imagined that a wing might drop off, that turbulence would tear the hull apart, that they'd be sucked through the toilet into space. The statistics said you had a one in seven million chance of dying on a domestic jet flight in the US, that if you flew every day you'd have to wait 19,000 years to cop it. The statistics hadn't saved Eleanor.

Lauren had called, wanting to come over on Saturday, take me out for a walk in the park or a bite of brunch; I'd told her I didn't want to go anywhere at the moment, thanks. I was engaged in "reflection," I told her, meditation, I needed to be alone.

"Um," she said, "I'm not so sure that's the best . . .

Don't you think it would do you good to get out, get some air? Weather's great . . ."

"There's plenty of air in my apartment," I said. "There's Ella, there's air. I'm fine, really. I just need some time alone right now. I'll give you a ring if I change my mind, okay?"

"Okay," she said, worriedly. "Are you still talking to that . . . that therapist or whatever she is, from FIN?"

"Oh, yes," I lied. I had told Christina Barnes that I was spending the weekend at a friend's house. She'd applauded my efforts, told me to take it easy, listen to my feelings, get plenty of rest.

What I didn't tell either of them was that I hadn't left the house in almost four days, except for late-night trips to the liquor store. The world, I was reluctant to admit, had become a loud and dangerous place, a kind of threshing machine for the senses. So many lights, so many cars, such a buzz and hum and blast of traffic, so many buildings, so many people living like rats in their holes, so many bodies scurrying toward and around each other, so many smells, the bad breath of the city in summer, smells from garbage bins and pretzel carts and dog turds, from steam vents and asphalt and exhaust fumes, from people dying alone in their apartments with their starving pets, so many sirens, so many alarms, so many emergencies, so many indecipherable sounds in the night, the sustained assault of New York on the nerves.

The night before, as I'd stepped off the curb to cross 79th Street, I'd been stricken, without warning, by panic: a car could come barreling around the corner and mash me into the ground, a truck could lose its brakes and flatten me. Someone could step up to me at the traffic light and poke a gun into my ribs. A crazy person could pound a chunk of concrete into my skull—it had happened just last week to a woman in Chelsea. Scaffolding could collapse, a bomb could go off, the liquor store could be robbed while I was there and I'd be left hogtied and butchered in the basement.

The liquor store delivered, I discovered. And I also discovered that half a Valium—from a depleted and past-dated vial pressed into my hand by Deborah from work, with a murmured "Just in case"—would blunt the edge for an hour or two, tame the violent, churning fear. But nothing could have calmed me the moment that, stepping away from the newsstand with my weekly haul, I thought I saw Eleanor. She was walking toward me in the late-summer dusk, wearing her navy-blue suit, her string of pearls, face averted as she searched for something in her open purse. My blood roared, my heart slammed against my chest, a siren blared through my head, I wanted, at the same time, to run away, to stay rooted, to run toward her. As she approached, she extricated a tissue from her bag and blotted her brow, then, with a final dab, discarded it and looked, at last, my way. Every volt of emotion drained instantly out of me. She had a long thin nose and papery skin, her lips were too pink and her curls too tight; she was, in other words, someone else's mother.

One morning, waking around three from the gnawed-at scraps of oblivion that passed for sleep these days, I was seized by the conviction that Eleanor was in the apartment, that she'd been in the kitchen making herself a cup of tea. I felt this so strongly that I got up to look for her. The place was, of course, empty, bathed with sickly yellow light from the streetlamp outside. I touched the kettle to see if it was warm, I opened the front door to see if she was disappearing down the hall. I still couldn't shake the feeling that she'd been there. Alcohol and diazepam, not good for the brain.

When I couldn't sleep, which was most of the time, I watched TV. Or surfed the Web. Or studied, obsessively, the color photos in the newsweeklies, searching for clues. The magazines all ran variants of the same images: the totemic piece of tail sticking out of the water like a shark's fin, with the airline logo at a seventy-degree angle, going under; the orphaned shoes—a white Mary Jane in *Time*, a man's black oxford in *Newsweek*—floating, ripple-ringed, on the surface of the sea; a pile of battered luggage. The penciled list that had been found inside a camera bag, gifts for a girl to bring home: *Marcia, light pink, size M. Ruth: hunter green. Roxanne: sky blue.*

I also, to calm myself, began to make lists. The names of things, missiles and robots and rescue craft—the Stinger, the Redeye, the Mistral, the Gremlin, the Grouse, the Gimlet, the Magnum, the Pirouette, the Aegis, the Deep Drone—and, when I'd exhausted those, the names of passengers on the plane. Next, the sizes of things. The 747 was so big that the entire first flight of the Wright brothers could have taken place inside it. The burning oil slick from the crash was the size of two football fields. The plane's fuel tank was the size of a double garage. The forward cargo hold was large enough to hold a car parked sideways. The camera-equipped undersea robot had a field of vision the size of a king-sized bed. The plane's hydraulic control unit was the size of two loaves of bread. The bomb that blew up Pan Am 123 over Lockerbie was no bigger than a coffee cup. And the crucial piece of evidence had been a scrap of plastic, fingernail-sized.

How big, I wondered unwarily, were the bits of Eleanor's body now, now that the crab and bluefish had been at her? Where was my mother's body? And where had it been all this time? One hundred and twenty-six bodies had been located on the ocean floor, sixty-seven, as of that morning, escorted up. I needed, desperately, a piece of her. I'd been told that scallop dredges would soon be dredging the crash site for any last scraps. I didn't like that word, *scraps*. Or any of the others: *fragments, remains.*

I'd seen an Aircraft Incident Report from an earlier crash, with a chart, Chart 4.7, entitled "Body Fragmentation." This was where experts interpreted the patterns of injury to the victims' bodies, constructing, from these traces, their narratives of damage. Thinking about that, I felt as if my own body might blow apart, burst into fragments from the pressure in my chest. I chipped a Valium with the kitchen knife and reached for the phone.

"Kim honey!" Bernice said. "I was going to call you myself, later. I was just waiting for a decent time—"

I glanced at the clock. It was 6:42. I assumed a.m.

"Sorry," I said. "I wasn't . . ."

"It's okay. I haven't been sleeping either."

"Any . . . ?"

"Nothing. And you?"

"The same."

"We're coming into Manhattan today," Bernice said. "I cannot spend another second in this Ramada. They're

having a Little Miss and Little Mister Universe pageant
here at the moment, can you believe it, all these excited
little kids running around." She stopped. She seemed
about to cry.

"Horrendous," I said. "Absolutely horrendous. How
could—"

"And Harold has to go into town anyway, he's part of a
delegation from the Families, meeting with some guy who,
well, who allegedly stole some piece of fabric from one of
the seats. At the hangar, you know? There's some kind of
residue, he says. I don't really know what it's all about,
all very hush-hush."

"Good," I said, ignoring the part about the residue,
"you need to get out of there. Get back out into the world
a bit." I could see what was coming next.

"And you?" she asked. "What are your plans for today,
honey?"

"No plans," I said. "I . . ."

"Well then, why don't we . . ."

"I don't know," I said. "I—I'm not feeling so hot."

She hesitated. "Love to see you, though, Kim. Not so
hot myself, either, but, well, you know, you have to keep
going."

I wanted, on the one hand, to see Bernice, to soak in
her warmth, the balm of her presence, like a hot bath, but,
on the other hand, dreaded all the effort it would take to
actually wash and dress and go out into the teeming streets.
Though, I thought, something could equally well happen to
me here in my own apartment—fire, rape, heart attack,
gas leak, earthquake, stroke, electrocution, overdose. A
tractor trailer could smash into my building, bringing it

down. A plane could explode and fall flaming on to my block, as the Concorde did on a Paris hotel, as Pan Am 123 did on to Rosebank Crescent, wedging corpses into chimneys and strewing its cargo of sewing needles to lodge, like thorns, in the rescue dogs' paws. A meteor could . . .

Turning my attention, with difficulty, back to Bernice, I suggested that we meet at a café around the corner from me, Café Simone, but it turned out that walking wasn't easy for her just then, her balance was fickle. Under stress, her MS tended to relapse; she was, as she put it, a little shaky on her pins.

"Frankly, honey," she said, "it would be easier if Harold could just drop me off at your place in the car, pick me up there again. So we could visit in peace—just quietly, you know."

I looked, weakly, around the apartment, at the litter and debris, at the empty bottles, the scribbled notes, the dead flowers, the unopened mail, the scrim of cat hair on everything. I decided not to care.

"Okay," I said. "Let's do that then, if you don't mind a bit of a mess. I could probably come up with a cup of coffee, cup of tea." I gave her the address, we agreed on a time—2 p.m.—and we said our goodbyes.

Now what? It was only seven. I thought, out of habit, of calling Anna but then remembered I couldn't. She hadn't called me back; I wasn't, sure as hell, going to call her. I felt a little flare of anger even at the thought. Staring at the phone, wondering what to do next, it occurred to me, vaguely, that I was acting like Eleanor, keeping alive—in my stubbornness, in my rage—the parts of her

I hated the most. As if I had no choice. As if, I thought, I'd fled so far from her that I'd circled the globe and found myself, without realizing it, heading back, right to the spot she'd once occupied. Right into the chalk outline of her absent body.

I tried to think about this, tried to feel something, but, thanks perhaps to the Valium, felt only apathetic regret. Regret, that is, that I couldn't feel more. On a bulletin board on the Internet—crashtalk.com—people had been speculating, still, about a bomb. Perhaps the bomb hadn't been in the cargo hold after all. Perhaps it had been placed even deeper inside the plane, in an empty, hard-to-reach compartment called the dry bay. This space, in front of the center fuel tank, had once held water that could be injected into the engines to increase thrust. But now that technology was obsolete. So the dry bay remained empty, rarely used.

I thought about Anna again, about how close we'd once been. How, as girls, we'd listened to Springbok Radio in the dark, wearing out the batteries of the small transistor on the bookcase between our twin beds. Reception was erratic—the radio had been dropped in the bathtub more than once, its aerial was held on by a paper clip—but the sprightly, faltering voices poured out and filled the space between us. Anna loved *Lux Radio Theater*, soapy melodramas about mistaken identity and cruel twists of fate; I preferred *The Creaking Door*, which gave me delicious horripilation and a squirmy feeling in my stomach, though Anna found it too scary and begged me to turn it off; we both liked *The Men from the Ministry*, laughing uproariously, goading each other to further bouts

of hilarity, though, in retrospect, I don't think we had a
clue what it was about (it was a British import, a farce
about bureaucrats, which, for all the relevance it had
to us—living under apartheid, where bureaucrats were
more apt to be butchers than silly buggers—might have
been beamed from Mars).

I thought of those nights, of the giggling and the fidgeting
and the repeated parental calls from downstairs for us to
go to sleep. Of our conspiratorial whispers, our shared
fantasy world like a shared dream hovering in the dark
between us. I'll never be that close to anyone again, I
thought, and the thought filled me with a dull, Valium-
muted despair.

When Bernice rang the buzzer, I was in a thin, scratchy
doze on the sofa, dreaming, I think, that Ella was hurt,
that her eye was torn and bleeding. The sound of the
buzzer shocked me awake, and I mistook it, in my blurry
state, for the smoke alarm, ran, in panic, for the door.
By the time I'd realized what the noise was, and had
regained enough presence of mind to use the intercom,
Bernice had buzzed twice more. I felt irritated, confused:
I hadn't planned to sleep: I'd planned to shower, or at
least wash my face, before she came, put on a clean
T-shirt, straighten up the house. Before I even had a
chance to comb my hair, I heard the elevator ping, then
Bernice's walker shuffling down the hall.

I greeted her at the open door, leaned in around her
walker for a hug. She was a little out of breath and, I
noticed as I stepped back, thinner, frailer-looking, her
wrists knobbly, her neck not doing such a good job of
supporting her head. Her smile faded as she looked at

me, and I tried to imagine what she might see: I knew I
didn't look good—kind of pale and greasy, puffy-faced,
was my guess—but I wasn't sure how bad. Touching my
face, I realized I still had the sofa's pile imprinted on my
cheek. I hadn't done any laundry since the crash. I wasn't
sure when I'd last brushed my teeth.

"So good to see you, Kim. Thanks so much for . . ." she
said, maneuvering her walker over the threshold, watching
her step. Then, once all four rubber feet were in, she
looked up, looked around, and her face grew stern.

"Honey," she said, "you need to clean up in here."

"I know, I . . . I just haven't . . ."

"No," she said, "I mean, you *really* need to clean up
in here."

I shrugged, limply.

"This isn't right," she said. "This isn't any way to live."

I looked around. I suddenly saw that the room was
filthy and squalid, with newspapers and magazines stacked
everywhere, with congregations of sticky glasses, a couple
of dried-up patches of cat puke. (Ella tended to lose her
lunch when there was tension in the air.) It didn't just look
messy; it looked like the habitation of a disturbed person,
someone well on the way to big-time decompensation. That
person must be me.

"And," Bernice continued, "looks like you've been
having a few drinks. A few cocktails, is that right?"

I shrugged again.

"Oh, honey," she said. She looked exhausted.

"Come," I said, heading for the sofa and swatting
vaguely at the loose cushions, as if to plump them up,
"let's sit down."

"Chair'll probably be easier to get out of," she said, lowering herself gingerly into it. I offered her tea, coffee, hoping I had some.

"Just water'd be great," she said. "With ice, if you've got."

When I'd poured us both some water and we were sitting face to face across the coffee table, I tried to redirect the conversation. I didn't want to talk about the apartment, about Eleanor or Louise. I wanted, I realized, to put my head on Bernice's lap and go to sleep. "So what's this meeting that Harold's going to," I asked, with some effort. "This seat cushion thing, or whatever it is?"

She shook her head. "Darned if I know. Top secret, they won't even know till they get there, meet with this guy. Best I can gather, he's someone who works out there at the hangar, thinks there's a coverup going on, thinks there's some, I don't know, some kind of residue on the seats. So I think he actually stole something, piece of fabric or foam or something."

"Residue from what?"

"Missile, I think. Missile fuel? Could that be right?"

"Oh. So we're back to that." I felt nothing but weariness at the thought of another theory, another explanation, another version of the story. I didn't care if this one turned out to be true or not; I was worn out, enervated, by the never-ending search for answers. Perhaps, I thought, sometimes there's just no explanation. Or the explanation is so complex, dependent on so many concatenated causes—*load factor, exceedances, event cascade*—that there was no point trying to untangle them. After the last NTSB briefing at the Ramada, I'd overheard a baffled family member, a young man with a scraggly new beard, turning to his companion and saying, "Planes don't just blow up, okay, I got that. The guy keeps saying planes don't just blow up. But sometimes, you know, maybe they do."

"Looks like it," Bernice said. "I told Harold, Forget the seat cover. Forget all of that. Right now, the only thing that matters is taking Louise home with us."

"Yes," I said. There was silence. I don't know what she was thinking. I was thinking again of body fragmentation, multiple anatomical separations, I couldn't help it, I was picturing, it was grotesque, a piece of Louise going home in the car with Harold and Bernice.

"Odd that they're both taking so long, isn't it," Bernice said suddenly.

"So long—?"

"To be found."

"I don't know . . ." I said.

"No, but think about it," she said. "One hundred and seventy-something, seventy-one, I think, identified. There were 230 people on that plane. Those lucky hundred and seventy-something families have taken their loved ones, gone home. And we're still waiting, both of us. Don't you think that's strange?"

I tried, fuzzily, to do the math. "I don't know. There's a one in five, one in four chance, something like that."

"No," Bernice said firmly. "I think it was meant to happen. That we were meant to meet."

"Maybe," I said, shrugging. Then, not wanting to seem too dismissive, I added, "Anyway, I'm glad we did."

"And," she continued, "you know what else? I think

they were meant to meet, Louise and your mom. Maybe they even sat next to each other on that plane—switched seats at the last minute and ended up next to each other on that plane."

The thought obviously gave her comfort. It came, at that moment, close to breaking my heart.

I pictured how Eleanor, settling into her seat, burrowing in, making a little nest for herself with pillow and blanket and neck support, would have reacted if Louise had sat down next to her, how, at the sight of a young black woman, her whole body would have tensed and contracted, tried to take up less space. How she would have turned her face away, shielded it with her magazine, her *Good Housekeeping*, her *Country Living*. How, if Louise had offered a friendly comment, a casual question, Eleanor would have responded with pinched civility, every line of her face betraying the strain. And I thought about how—though who really knew?—during that ninety-second plunge, Eleanor would have perished alone and uncomforted rather than clasp a black hand.

"Perhaps," I said, and tears came, stinging, from somewhere. Bernice, too, had tears in her eyes.

She shook her head firmly, as if to shake the tears away, shake those thoughts right out of her head, then took a sip of water. I took a sip of mine. We sat for a while, staring at the coffee table between us. It was coated, I saw, with dust, with the fine urban soot that blew in during the summer months. Bernice breathed deeply and looked around the room again.

"Nice big apartment," she said, "lots of light. You're lucky."

"I am," I said. "In this city."

"But, honey," she went on, shaking her head again, "if I had my strength, I'd be hauling the vacuum cleaner out right now, setting you to work on some dusting. Some dishwashing. We'd have this place right in no time."

"I'm sorry," I said. "I just haven't been feeling . . ."

"No, no, you don't need to apologize. It's not for me. It's for you. You can't just let everything go like this, it doesn't help."

"I don't know what helps and what doesn't any more."

"Well, I'll tell you one thing that doesn't help, if you don't mind me saying so, and that's the drinking." She looked into my eyes, held my gaze firmly. I looked away, gave the ghost of a shrug.

"Think of your mom," she continued, "how she would feel if she could see you like this."

"My mother wouldn't care," I blurted. "She never cared about me. She hated me." I had no idea where that came from. I had no idea that that was what I was going to say.

Bernice looked shocked, as if I had blasphemed. "Oh, that's nonsense, Kim honey. How can you even say such a thing? You sound like a child, sweetheart—you know that's not true."

"It's true, Bernice. She hated me. From the minute I was born. It was almost as if, I don't know, her body just rejected my body. Like a transplant that doesn't take."

"No," Bernice said, gravely. "You're just upset, you're not thinking right. You don't know what you're talking about."

"I'm talking about . . . that she hated me—"

"That's crazy, Kim, it's not possible. I know you're upset, but—"

"What do you mean, it's not possible? How can you even . . ."

"I know," she said. "I'm a mother. I know it's not possible, not possible for a mother to hate something that came out of her own body like that. It just doesn't work like that."

"Oh, Bernice," I said, helplessly. "You didn't know her."

"I didn't have to. This is one thing I know for sure, Kim. Whatever problems you might have had with her, however hard things might have been between you, there is no way a mother hates her own daughter." She looked ill at the thought. "No way. It just doesn't work like that."

Maybe not where you come from, Bernice, I thought, on Planet Civilized. But what about Planet Savage, where I come from, where it's just one body ripping into another, each one fighting, in a dark cramped space, for psychic survival? What if there just always happen to be, in that cramped space, the right conditions for an explosion—the heat, the bad mix of air to fuel, the pressure, the ignition source? What then? Perhaps, I thought, one body just has to blast free, eject itself to another place, another continent, another stretch of the sky.

I realized then that I was sobbing, sobbing bitterly, sobbing, as they say, like a baby. And the phone, I understood, had been ringing for quite some time. Bernice placed her hand on my arm, I took a deep, shuddering breath, and we listened. A man's voice began speaking hesitantly to the machine, not Harold's, as I'd first thought, but Paul's. "I just wanted you to know," he said, "that we, that I return to Paris tomorrow. We have made an identification. Some bone fragments, Kim, and part of a skull."

14

Friday, August 4

At the end of that week, they found the cockpit. It was in Debris Field #2, a second area of wreckage that had been identified two days before, closer to the airport than the original, extravagant spill. An unmistakable shape had appeared on the videotape, the nose of the plane, and when divers went down, they found the body of the pilot, Captain Kearney, still strapped into his seat. Nearby, on the ocean floor, was the flight engineer, Stan Matsuda, buckled into the jump seat. I imagined the seat tipped over, with its occupant face down, as if navigating a course along the bottom of the world.

Somehow, the discovery of these corpses gave me hope. They had piloted Eleanor into the deep, traced a trajectory for her through the twilight in flames, and now, if they'd been found, perhaps she would be too, strapped obediently into her seat. Waiting patiently, as she never did in life.

Sitting on the sofa with Ella on my lap, I watched, in real time, the cockpit being hoisted from the Atlantic. The Families' website had tipped me off to watch the coverage at noon. I'd expected something streamlined and sleek to rise from the sea, a sliced-off capsule like the head of a fish, but instead, what came dripping out was a terrible crumpled mess, an exorbitantly snarled and tangled skein of wires. I couldn't believe that a human body had been found in there, intact. Intact being a relative term, after a fortnight in the brine.

Now, with the cockpit located, investigators felt they could plot the sequence of the crash. The chief of the NTSB went on television with a chart, a cloven dotted line with, at crucial points, orange puffballs representing fire. The dotted line, he said, was the Boeing 747 "in various stages of crippled flight."

"We think we know what happened," he began. "What we still don't know is why."

The explosion, he said, tore a hole in the fuselage, causing, within seconds, the front section of the plane—cockpit and first class—to peel away and plummet to the ocean floor. This sudden loss of mass caused the rest of the plane to pitch sharply up, climb 3,000 feet, bank, stall, and then drop into a spiraling dive, at five times the normal rate of descent. The fuselage disintegrated as it fell, a wing broke off, releasing a fiery cascade of fuel.

Most of this I knew already. What I didn't know, though, was that, as the front of the plane fell away, the passengers nearest the fracture spilled into the air, like nuts out of a can. Eleanor, I'd established, had been in seat 33B. I went online and looked at a seating chart for the 747. At least, I thought, she'd been spared that.

The glass covers on most of the cockpit gauges were unbroken, the NTSB official said, the controls largely intact. I couldn't reconcile that with the mangled bird's

nest I'd seen dredged from the sea. I tried to imagine what
Kearney and Matsuda's last few minutes of life had been
like. "Power's set," from Matsuda, had been the last words
on the cockpit voice recorder. Then the whirring sound of
his seat moving on its electric track, then nothing.

I'd been reading transcripts of black-box recordings from
fatal crashes, grim, taciturn encounters with death. Mostly
what you heard was the cacophony of warning signals,
the relentless robotic voices repeating: "Sink rate! Don't
sink! Don't sink!" or "Terrain! Terrain! Terrain!" You
heard people trying to do their job, keep the machine
aloft, in the face of unimaginable, unintelligible circumstances:

COPILOT: Really . . . we don't have any control.
PILOT: We don't have control, not even the basics . . .
COPILOT: We keep going up. We are flying without speed.
   It can't be . . .

People piloting a malfunctioning plane are busy, don't have
time for oratory, often don't even have time, as requested
by air traffic control, to say their "souls on board." But
every now and then there'll be an exchange that's simple
and tragic, almost Shakespearean:

CAPTAIN: Hydro pressure is lost.
COPILOT: All lost?
CAPTAIN: All lost.

No such exchange between Kearney and Matsuda before
the power died, not even a Mayday, not even a shout.

I scratched Ella under her chin, on top of her head, along her spine. She undulated like a Slinky, shedding a smattering of piebald hairs on my newly vacuumed couch. I felt, like her, enlivened. The cockpit had been found. A new debris field had been located. The *Grapple* had, the day before, raised a sixty-foot section of fuselage with seats attached, part of the galley, even a rack of wine glasses, unscathed. It couldn't be long now. Why should Eleanor stay missing while others were found?

I thought of Paul, how jubilant he'd sounded when I'd called him back. Odd to think that a fragment of bone could bring such release.

"I can go home now," he'd said. "Michel can go home now. My parents will have at last some, something to bury."

By coincidence, in *The Times* that day, there'd been an interview with a peasant woman whose son was one of the "disappeared" in Guatemala. He'd been missing for a long time. She had one simple request: "If my son is dead," she said, "I want, at least, his little bones." I'd wept when I read that, as I wept, now, at all tidings of the missing and the dead, even, taped to a lamppost on the corner, a poster for a lost cat (*Sebastian, grey, very friendly, only half an ear*).

"Paul," I'd said, "I'm very happy for you. I hope this brings some, I don't know, some kind of peace." I envied him, envied him that scrap of his brother's skull.

"There will never be peace until we find out who did this," he said. He sounded utterly depleted, used up. "But for now, you know, this is enough. To be able to bring him home."

"I know . . ." I said.

"And, Kim," he went on, hurriedly, "I don't know how to say this, but . . ."

"I know," I said. "It's okay."

"It is okay?"

"Yes," I said, "perfectly okay." I discovered, as I said this, that it was true.

We exchanged addresses, phone numbers, e-mail information. We promised to stay in touch. I realized I knew almost nothing about his life in Paris, just as, I realized, he knew nothing about mine in New York, beyond these weird, fevered two weeks. I had a feeling I'd never hear from him again, that he'd want to forget this hiatus in time as quickly as possible, but I wasn't sure.

Before he hung up, he reverted, briefly, to type, recommending I read a long article on electromagnetic interference that had been posted on the Web by a Caltech professor. "It's very interesting," he said, "it raises the possibility that . . ." All right, I said, I'd read it.

He was leaving that night on Air France. Michel was traveling in the cargo hold, in a metal box. I asked Paul if he was afraid to fly.

"To tell you the truth, Kim," he said, hesitantly, "I think, I know this is a terrible thing to say but I think, I think I will be very angry when the plane lands, how do you say, in one part? In one piece?"

Noticing that the live coverage was over—the cockpit had been hoisted and hidden under a tarp, there was nothing more to see—I stood up, gently dislodging Ella from my lap. I had no interest in watching motocross races or cooking shows, documentaries on the life cycle of the newt. With Paul in mind, I decided to turn on the computer, check the body count for the day, check the latest arguments for extraterrestrials or friendly fire—the much heralded residue had proved a bust, just fabric glue, apparently, gone rust-colored with age—perhaps also hunt down the posting he'd described, on electromagnetism, animal magnetism, whatever it was.

First, though, I picked the cat hairs off my jeans, folded the newspaper, set the remote control neatly on top of the TV. The day after Bernice's visit, I'd called Rent-a-Maid and cowered around the corner in Café Simone for three hours, multiple cappuccinos making my heart pound, while some poor West Indian woman dealt with my filth. Now I was trying to maintain the order she'd created, keep bedlam at bay. It gave me, I found, something to do. I was also, except for very late at night, doing the Valium without the booze. Or the booze without the pills, but not, usually, both.

Bernice had been angry with me when she'd left, shaken and grave and very, very tired. In retrospect, I understood that, in some boozy and regressive way, I'd hoped she might comfort me, might hold me as I wept, had even perhaps allowed myself the luxury of losing it with that fantasy in mind. But she'd seemed oppressed, enervated by my tears, as if she had nothing to give, no comfort for anyone, and just wanted me to stop. As if she didn't want to hear any more of my perplexing confessions, as if my grief were an affront to her own. As if, if she'd had the strength, she'd have been weeping too, so would I please just be quiet?

She'd laid her hand on my arm as we listened to Paul's message, and I'd stopped sobbing then, both of us seized by a numb, dull shock. She'd seemed provoked by his news, resentful, almost petulant—why him and not her? She was angry, too, she told me, at the grief counselor who'd barked questions at her about Louise, her hobbies and so on, and then suggested, at the end of the hour, that Bernice adopt a child. Angry at FIN, who wouldn't give Louise's boyfriend, Ted, a discounted fare to visit the site. Angry at Harold, who was wearing himself out, neglecting her, in his crazed quest for information. And angry at me for wallowing, like a pig, in dirt and drink, bad-mouthing my dead mother.

"Time to get yourself together, girl," she'd said, when Harold had buzzed downstairs to fetch her. I'd watched her pick her way, painfully, to the car, felt relief at being left alone again—who did she think she was, anyway, telling me what to do?—but, at the same time, a faint sorrow, an anticipatory regret, as if something were over.

Nothing new on the Families' site, I saw as I logged on, nothing new from FIN. Ullman from the FBI was quoted as saying that the cockpit section was a key piece of the investigation, that analysts were now exploring a whole range of "failure and malfunction scenarios."

"But," he added, "on the basis of the physical evidence found thus far, that plane should still be flying."

It should be, I thought, but it isn't. That's what needs to be explained. What if, for all your failure and malfunction scenarios, it never is explained? I thought of Paul again, his dogged belief that someone, somewhere, was responsible. I thought of him taking his brother's bones home in a metal box.

I thought of all the near misses I'd read about, all the people who were scheduled to be on Flight 770 but hadn't been, or vice versa. The teenage girl from Greenwich, CT, who was saved because her parents offered her the choice of a Jeep or a trip to Europe, and she chose the Jeep. The ninety-five connecting passengers from Chicago whose flight to JFK was delayed by mechanical problems—they must, at the time, have been so irked. The three Greek men, like characters from some classic drama, who'd missed their connecting flight to Athens and had been rebooked, reluctantly, on to 770; FIN's only other direct flight to Athens that night was full. At the very last minute, right as they were boarding the ill-fated plane, a few seats opened up on the direct flight. Indecision, hesitation—what about their luggage? too late to get it back, major inconvenience. But to avoid changing planes at Heathrow . . . they galloped, just in time, to the other gate.

Then there were those who should have been spared but, for some reason, weren't. One of the flight attendants hadn't been assigned to work that flight but had switched her schedule the day before, wanting to see her ten-year-old son in the school play. A businessman had been booked on another flight altogether, out of Newark, but missed it because his driver got lost (highway repairs, detours, a single wrong turn). Rebooked on to Flight 770, the passenger made a mad dash across the Hudson, and the driver, this time, found his way. And, ghoulishly, two flight attendants employed by FIN had similar names—Linda Martin, Linda Martin Folle—so the wrong husband received the condolences. His wife was safely in Rome, but seeing her name in the paper had shaken him up, he said, given him a glimpse of an alternative, branching reality. Another existence that, but for chance, might have been his.

I'd dreamed, too, that Eleanor had missed the plane, that I was driving her to catch her flight but we got lost on dark, forsaken streets, had no ticket when we got there, went to the wrong counter, South African Airways, couldn't find her passport, which had mysteriously disappeared, and then, finally, couldn't find the plane, which was parked in a distant, oily, unlighted corner of the airport, already full. She was panicking, and so was I, racked with anxiety, even when I woke. My dreams since the crash had become like another, exhausting life, vivid and wrenching, messy and desolate, the foul rag-and-bone shop, I knew, of the heart.

I stared at the screen of my Mac, with its soothing screensaver of clouds. I felt unanchored, adrift; I felt that, if I wasn't careful, I might float away. I thought about how, flying into a cloud or in the dark—flying blind—a pilot is worse than lost: his body and brain conspire to misinform him, providing him with the illusory sensation of level flight. Instinct, in this situation, is worse than useless: it's a liar, a provider, via the fluids in the inner ear, of contradictory sensations, sensations that refer to the body's immediate past, while the pilot and the plane are already occupying the future. A future in which, unless the pilot disciplines himself to disbelieve his own body and attend to his instruments, to the true tilt of the artificial horizon, the plane is already rolling, irrecoverably, to one side.

I felt in my own body a blind, spiraling vertigo, the nausea of no fixed point of reference. I stared at my computer screen as if it were an instrument panel and tried to think of some immediate action to take. I thought about calling Lauren but I knew she'd be in class. I thought about ordering some more books on line, an *Aeronautical Chart User's Guide*, for one: I didn't understand why there were three norths, why navigation so often entailed charting a route off course, an imaginary route leading somewhere else. I thought, fleetingly, about pouring myself a drink. Then I remembered there was something I wanted to look up.

The paper on electromagnetic interference turned out to be fifteen dense pages, with tables and graphs; I had nothing better to do, so I printed it out. On the night of the crash, the professor claimed, there'd been at least ten military planes and ships in the vicinity of Flight 770. This meant, she said, that the environment was "electromagnetically severe." It was conceivable, therefore, that electromagnetic interference (EMI)—a sudden pulsing or spiking, a rapidly changing radio environment—might have caused the 747's electrical systems to go haywire. To flip out, act up, all at once. This would explain why transmissions from the cockpit stopped at the same moment as signals from the transponder in the plane's belly—at the very same moment, too, that the black box cut out.

A pulse, I gathered, is an event in which the intensity of a signal increases for a brief moment, then subsides. I still wasn't sure what a spike was. I didn't know what a transponder was, so I looked it up: A transponder (transmitter + responder) is a device that, when a certain signal is transmitted, automatically responds with a self-identifying signal.

The professor had various hypotheses (I, II, and III) about the probable "pathway of electromagnetic insult."

But, she concluded, let us not underestimate the difficulty of calculating the electromagnetic interaction between two electronic systems. "As one goes to the interior and encounters thousands of wires going to numerous black boxes, antennae, etc., through various cavities and other strange structures, the calculation problem gets quickly intractable."

A by now all too familiar weariness came over me. All right, then, this was possible, electromagnetic interference, possible but intractable. The missile was possible, too, the bomb, the exploding dry bay. So, I knew, were other eventualities: the sliver of metal on the runway, the mechanic who neglected to remove a piece of tape. The chemical fire in the cargo hold. Wind shear, wake vortex, the freak occurrence: the swan sucked into the engine at high speed, the vulture bursting through the windshield. The instruments that lie, convincing the pilot he's at 10,000 feet when he's about to hit the ground. The death ray, the asteroid, the meteor, the green egg. Any or all of the above. Why not? Why search for explanations? Why seek to blame? Accident investigators talk about tightly coupled systems, about event cascades, concatenation, when what they really mean is that they don't know, can't explain. The causes are too numerous, too complex, too trivial, too intertwined to plot. The disaster has occurred, the body is missing. That's all I know for sure, all the explanation I'm likely to get. There's no one to accuse, I thought, nothing to do. Nothing, in the end, but to reclaim the bones, if any are found—sign the papers acknowledging them as mine, take them home, and bury them.

I picked up the phone and, before I could second-guess myself, speed-dialed Anna's number. I'd sent her an e-mail or two over the week, curt and functional, but my last live contact with her had been to scream "Fuck you."

Angus seemed surprised to hear my voice, said Anna was making supper but he'd call her, just a wee second, love. I heard, or imagined I heard, a muffled consultation, then the sound of footsteps carrying the phone away. Then Anna's voice came on, tremulous, scared.

"Oh God, Kim," she said, "is it . . . ? Have they . . . ?"

Of course she would have leapt to that conclusion. I hadn't, in my haste, considered that.

"No, no," I said. "No, I'm sorry, no, not yet. No news about that. Yet."

"Oh," she said. Her tone changed, hardened. "Well then, what—"

"They found the cockpit, did you see that?"

"I didn't watch it but Angus did. Said it was a real mess."

"It really can't be long now, Anna."

"What are the figures for today, d'you know? I haven't looked yet, we had a meeting at school." She spoke cautiously, non-committally, like someone at a dinner party, feeling out the guest on her left.

"One hundred and ninety-three recovered, 191 autopsied, 189 ID'd, 188 families notified, 181 released." I had the numbers up on my computer screen, from the New York State Emergency Management Office. I performed magical thinking on them every day, various additions and subtractions, a private numerology designed to prove, somehow, that Eleanor would be next. That, in fact, she might already be there, implicit in the array of figures, in the interstices between 193 and 191, between, why not, 188 and 189.

Anna said nothing. I wondered how, over 8,000 miles of space, over the curved and centrifugal surface of the earth, over some unimaginable circuitry of satellites and fiber optics and microwaves, to say what I meant. To acknowledge, in the face of Anna's neutral, constrained tone, that something savage had happened between us last time we spoke. That it was true, it was real, but it wasn't, somehow, the point.

"Anna," I began.

"Angus went down . . ." she said, at the same moment.

I stopped, she carried on. "Angus went down to City Hall this week, Department of Records. Usually it takes six months to get copies of anything, you know, any document. But as soon as they heard FIN 770, they fell all over themselves trying to help. Oh, what a tragedy, it is true that there was a bomb, blah-de-blah-de-blah. So anyway, the upshot is he'll have it next week."

"Have what?"

"The birth certificate, Kim. I told you . . ."

"Oh yes, okay. Great." I had completely forgotten about the birth certificate, couldn't believe Anna was still harping on it, couldn't believe the FBI or anyone else would care if they ever saw it. I assumed that Anna, like me, needed something to do.

"Great," I repeated. "Thanks."

"Anything else new?" she asked. "At that end?"

"No," I said, "unfortunately not."

If this were a dinner party she would have turned,

congenially, at this point to the person on her right, Left
Guest not really rising to the occasion.

"Anna," I repeated, "look, I'm sorry."

She said nothing. I could hear her breathing.

"I was . . . well, you know how it is, the stress. The
waiting. The nightmares."

"Yes," she said.

"And I was, um, I don't know, maybe drinking too
much?"

"Well, that's not good."

"No," I agreed. "I—"

"But you know," she blurted, in a sudden burst, "it was
just so damn unfair, Kim."

"I know," I said, "I'm sorry." I said this reflexively but
then realized I didn't really think I'd been unfair. Mean,
yes, cruel, maybe, but not unfair.

"I mean, think about it, you were the one who got away,
who just buggered off. You were the one sitting in New York,
doing whatever you wanted, coming home maybe every year
or two, showering gifts on everybody, while I had to deal
with her day in and day out. Every day, you know, every
day it was something."

"I thought that's what you wanted," I said. "I thought
you liked that. To be close." I felt a pang even uttering the
word, imagining an embrace.

"Liked that! Kim, you know what she was like. Nothing
was ever right. Nothing I ever did was right—the way I was
raising my kids, my job, what I was wearing, what I was
earning, Oh your hair looks funny like that, Oh you're
letting yourself go. If I went out, or I didn't go out, if I disciplined the girls, or didn't, nothing. Nothing was ever right."

"But then why . . ."

"And Angus! The way she treated him, the things she said. Alcoholic, child abuser, all this stuff, I don't even know where she got half of it. On and on to me, sometimes to his face, poor Ang. Most men wouldn't have put up with it, I just thank God I found a lovely patient man. But even he was at the end of his rope with her, you know, just getting to the end of his rope."

"But then why . . . Why did you put up with it? Why didn't you, I don't know, establish some boundaries?" I sounded, to my own ears, like Christina Barnes. "Why didn't you just move away?"

"How could I have?" she asked.

I knew there was no answer.

"Especially after Dad died," she added. "She needed someone, she was afraid to go out. Everything had changed here . . . And with you sitting in New York—" she repeated, as if sitting were my actual occupation, my job description.

"I had to get away, you know that."

"Yeah, well, someone had to stay."

An image came to me of passengers hurtling down an evacuation slide, shoving each other, pushing and jostling, while the unlucky ones, the ones who'd turned toward the wrong exit or stopped to look for their bags, the ones burdened by babies, were left behind. I didn't like to picture myself as one of the jostlers, so quick to jump ship they got burns from their clothes.

"But," I said, "just last week you were telling me that, you know, that it was all me, that the problem was me. Now you're saying . . . something else."

"Well," she said, hesitantly, "it's both. It's confusing . . .

Things aren't that simple, Kim." I waited for her to continue, without, for once, a retort rising to my tongue.

"And you know," she said, in another burst (I'd never heard her so passionate), "most of the time it was okay, it wasn't always so bad. Not the way it was with you, the way you two just set each other off. You two just really pushed each other's buttons, I don't know why. I knew how to deal with her, I knew she just couldn't take any stress, poor old thing."

"I'll say," I said.

"Yes, but I let a lot of it just roll off my back. I didn't let it get to me, like you did, I knew that was just the way she was. She *meant* well, most of the time, Kim. And she was so good to the kids, you know, she adored them. They adored her, that was for real."

"I know," I said.

"If only," she began.

"Yes," I said. I felt I knew what she wanted to say, all the "if onlys."

We were both silent for a while. I was thinking about Eleanor's life, how, in another time, another place, it might have been different, might have been full.

"I'd be scared to live anywhere else, anyway," Anna said suddenly, an apparent non sequitur. "Somewhere I didn't know, with people I didn't know. I'm not like you, Kim."

"I know," I said, then, attempting a joke, "luckily for you."

"We owe her money, too. Quite a lot. Owed, however that works—with the will and the insurance and everything, I can't deal with any of that right now. You need a death certificate, the guy told me."

"I have money," I said, then remembered I'd left my job. "Some money, anyway, if you need—"

"No, no," she said, hastily. "We're fine."

"Well, I'll bring her, bring the . . . back. To Johannesburg. Once, you know, she's found. I'll bring her."

"Yes," she said, as if this were self-evident.

"And we'll have some kind of, I don't know, ceremony."

"Well, of course," she said. She had no way of knowing I'd just decided that, chosen that. That it had not, until this moment, been self-evident at all.

As I hung up, I felt agitated, still angry somewhere deep and probably unreachable, but, at the same time, elated. I felt as if I'd had a near miss of some kind. I thought of a cockpit voice recording I'd read about, in a Chinese jet, with a Chinese-speaking crew. As they came in for landing, their descent was too steep, but the crew didn't notice this because of the fog. The ground-proximity alarms went off, repeating robotically, "Pull up! Pull up! Pull up!" Just before impact, one crew member turned to the other and asked, in Chinese, "What does 'pull up' mean?"

15

Monday, August 7

As soon as I heard Harold's voice on the phone, I knew
what it meant. There was only one reason he'd be calling
me at 7 a.m. I was grateful, surfacing into consciousness,
that I'd laid off the Valium the night before, that I was
foggy now only from the residue of a dream (searching for
Eleanor in a crowded place, airport or railway station,
where, in the swift tide of other people, the littered,
half-constructed hallways, the murk of a gathering dusk,
I began to understand that I'd never find her).

Harold's voice was thick, barely recognizable. He'd been
crying, I realized, which shocked me, the way it had
shocked me to hear my father weep, on the telephone, once.
Eleanor had been in intensive care after an emergency
hysterectomy; Roger was at home, alone, probably for the
first time in his adult life; calling to give me an update, he
was lonely and scared, as I'd never heard him before—as,
with his stiff upper lip and grim charm, he'd never allowed
me to glimpse him before. Sitting, shocked, in my office,
looking out over the restless greedy city as he spoke, I'd
realized for the first time how much he depended on her,

how, somehow, he needed her craziness, the craziness of their life together, how, for reasons I'd probably never understand, he'd been complicit all along.

"Harold?" I said. My voice didn't come out right. I was afraid to say more.

"Kim," he said, "I've got news." For a moment, I wondered, bizarrely, whether it might be news about Eleanor, whether somehow they'd notified him, to break it to me.

"Louise?" I half whispered.

"They called half an hour ago. From the medical examiner's office."

"Oh, Harold—"

"Positive ID, from DNA."

"Oh thank God—"

"It's just," and here he choked off, as if his throat were closing.

"It's just—?"

"A foot, Kim." I thought, at first, that he was referring to a unit of measurement, was trying to wrap my mind around that (a foot of what?). "Her right foot. Still in its Timberland boot." And then he wept, bleakly, flatly, like someone long out of practice.

I felt as if all the blood were draining out of me, to be replaced, slowly, by an icy nausea. I thought of the passport photo Bernice had shown me, the only picture I'd ever seen of Louise, the one that had run in the papers too—the buoyant hairdo, the buoyant smile. The artful scarf.

I had no words. My brain failed to supply any.

"Still intact," Harold said. I didn't know whether he

meant the foot or the boot. The word intact was beginning to seem meaningless to me, a grotesque joke against the dictionary.

"Oh, Harold," I managed, at last.

"She bought them just for the trip, you know. For hiking in Cornwall."

"Oh God." I thought about how, instead, the boot had hiked along the seabed. All by itself.

Neither of us spoke for a few seconds. I wondered whether I should say something like, I'm so happy for you. Something like, Well, at least you can go home now. I couldn't imagine getting the words out; they'd die in my mouth like a lie. Then Harold took a deep, shaky breath and said, "Well, we just wanted to let you know, honey. We'll be leaving today probably, no point in sticking around."

"Yes," I said. "Well, at least you have—" I couldn't say "her"—"something, now." What about the rest of her? I wondered—a question I could never ask. Didn't they feel they should wait for more, hope for more? What if another part of her washed up somewhere weeks from now?

"It's enough," he said. "It has to be. We need something to bury, that's all. And to bless."

I didn't ask how the, how Louise was getting home. To Utica, four hours by car or train. I didn't want to know.

"And Bernice?" I asked. "How's she doing? Could I have a word—"

"She's . . . Not right now, honey. She's—"

"No, of course," I said. "I understand. Please give her my love, my lots and lots of love."

"And you," he said, "you be strong now. It won't be long, I'm sure. And it'll bring such release, I don't know how to explain—"

"No," I said, assenting, somehow, to what he'd said. I couldn't think about Eleanor right then. The foot in the boot was much too real.

"Oh, and Harold?" I said, after a pause. "I know this is weird, but what size? I just somehow feel I need to know . . . to know, you know, what size. Just to be able to—"

"Eight," he said. He didn't sound surprised.

We said our awkward, halting goodbyes; we promised, fervently, to stay in touch; it was possible, I thought, hanging up, that we even might. I wanted to, and yet I felt ashamed, exposed before them, as if they'd seen too much of me. Who else would ever see me like that, a motherless child?

I lay back, limply, on the bed. My mind was a perfect, crystalline blank. I wanted it to be.

I felt abandoned, stranded, the last one left. I felt newly unprotected, as if there were nothing now between myself and death, as if death were an actual presence, which might, at any moment, walk through the door.

After some time, I got up, gingerly, wrapped my robe around me. Ella was mewling to be fed. I made myself a pot of tea, picked the newspaper off the doorstep. Every day I made a promise to myself that I wasn't going to read any more of the crash coverage, and every day I broke it.

On the front page was a human-interest story about a woman whose fiancé had died on the plane. She'd been going to join him in Paris later that week, where, it turned out, he was planning to present her with a 1.7-carat diamond ring. Incredibly, on the night of the crash, the tiny, blue velvet-lined jeweler's box with the ring inside had bobbed to the surface, among the smoldering fuel and chunks of debris, the oil slicks, the charred human flesh. A tiny piece of bubble wrap, tucked in for cushioning, had kept it afloat.

Stories like that made me sick. I didn't want to read about other people's good fortune. Which, relative to mine, it seemed to be. She, of course, took it as a sign.

I logged on and checked the medical examiner's figures for the day. One hundred and ninety-five recovered, 194 autopsied, 193 identified, 193 families notified, 190 bodies released. Bodies, or parts of bodies, such as a foot.

The phone shrilled suddenly, scaring me. It was not quite eight. Could this be it, then, the 194th call? My heart, as I picked up, was pounding.

"Anna! You frightened me."

"Sorry. Did I wake you? I know it's early."

"No, no. Someone called earlier. My friends Harold and Bernice. They got . . . their daughter back."

I heard, in her silence, her bad grace, the same as mine.

"I don't know how much longer this can go on," she said, when I'd rung her back. "I just don't know how much more I can take. Sally keeps asking me where she is, I just don't know what to say any more."

"You know," I said, "it's possible that they might never find her. We have to, I don't know, prepare for that. Somehow." This was the first time either of us had admitted this, put the idea into words.

"Of course they'll find her," Anna said, stubbornly. "They've found all these other people. She can't just have, you know, disappeared." Some passengers had done just that in the explosion over Lockerbie, I wanted to tell her: vanished, vaporized.

"No," I said.

"Anyway," she said, "I phoned to tell you something. Something strange."

As if, I thought, the conversation we were having wasn't strange enough already.

"We got the birth certificate," she continued. Not that again, I thought. What is my sister's obsession with that document?

"Good," I said. "Thanks. That's everything now, isn't it? That they want?" "They" meaning the FBI.

"And to get that," she went on, "Angus had to get the marriage certificate, Mom's parents."

"Uh-huh."

"And it turns out they got married in 1938, Leonard and Belle."

"Yeah?" I said. It sounded about right.

"No, Kim, you're not getting it. 1938. Mom was born in 1935, right? She's sixty-four now." I noticed how Anna had, without thinking, used the present tense.

"Hmm," I said, mildly surprised, as I did the subtraction. "So she was a love child, our mother." I said it in a deliberately absurd way, lurve chile. "Who'd 'a thought it? That bad old Grandma Belle . . ."

"Well, actually," she said, "it's a lot more complicated than that. I spoke to Larry . . ."

"You spoke to Larry? Uncle Larry?" Now I was genuinely

surprised. Larry was the eldest of Eleanor's brothers, a medical-supplies salesman in Durban. They hadn't been in touch for, oh, at least twenty years. All the brothers—Larry, Stephen, in Botswana, and Nigel, in Australia—had sent polite notes of condolence to Anna when the news came out. Why not me? I'd wondered jealously, then realized that nobody knew where I was.

"And it turns out he knows the whole story, they all did." The whole story turned out to be quite succinct: Leonard, in addition to being a Welshman, had been a Jew. Belle's parents, from staunch Voortrekker stock, wouldn't hear of her marrying him. So Belle, at eighteen, had left home, set up house with Leonard, borne her first two children out of wedlock, and married him the day she turned twenty-one.

Children know everything about their families, I thought, everything that matters; then they forget it and have to relearn it when they grow up. I felt that I knew this history somehow—that, although it was news, it wasn't a surprise.

"Wow," I said, "that's quite impressive." I thought of my Grandma Belle, how gutsy she must have been, how willful. I wished I remembered more of her from my childhood, before Eleanor stopped taking us to visit. I remembered her small, cluttered flat, with its pouffes and screens. I remembered the costume jewelry heaped on her vanity, big earrings and brooches like bunches of grapes. Her stinky, yappy little Pekinese, always underfoot. The book on yoga we found on her shelf, with photographs of people in loincloths, a great source of hilarity to Anna and myself. And the faint scent sometimes, after noon, of gin.

I wanted to know more. I'd do some research, I decided,

use those expensively acquired investigative skills. I felt proud, curious and proud, new sensations for me where family was concerned.

"Well," said Anna, primly, "I don't think Mom thought it was so impressive. Obviously not. Obviously she was ashamed."

"Ashamed? She should have been proud. That her mother had some guts. That she did what she wanted to, married for love. Especially, you know, in that bloody country. In the thirties, too, when the Afrikaners were supporting the Nazis."

"That's easy for you to say, Kim—sitting in New York, with all your liberal friends. Then it must have been, I don't know, a huge stigma. And, you know, the, uh, Jewish thing. That's a bit of a surprise. I'm not sure how I'm going to tell the girls about that, Bridget is getting confirmed this year."

"Oh, Anna, for God's sake, who gives a damn about any of this any more? It's not some horrible dark secret, you know—it's just . . . information. It's just who we are, where we come from."

"Well," she said. "I just wish I'd known."

"Why?" I asked. "What difference would it have made?"

"I don't know but—" She paused, groping for words. "It just would have."

"It doesn't really change anything, does it? It just clears away some of the lies, that's all. It's not, I don't know, bloody Rosebud."

"What are you talking about, Rosebud?"

"Take too long to explain," I said, with a shrug she couldn't see.

"Well, anyway," she said, with a familiar tinge of hurt in her voice, the one that crept in whenever I pulled intellectual rank on her, "I can see why Mom wouldn't have wanted us to know."

"I can too," I said, after a pause, "but it seems such a shame. Such a waste. The, how does it go, expense of spirit in a waste of shame." The words rose to the surface of my brain from long ago, from Roger's recitations in the car, on the way to school, in another world.

"Now what are you on about?" she asked, irritated.

"Shakespeare," I said.

As we hung up, I leaned back in my chair and stared out of the window, at the scrawny tree in the morning sun, suspending its shadow beneath it like a hang-glider. I wondered how I felt. Oddly exhilarated—I had a different story now, a different narrative of who I was—but then, as I thought of Eleanor, increasingly sad. I thought, again, of how afraid she must have been all her life, afraid of falling. And how trapped she must have felt, pregnant with me—no way out, short of a respectable marriage, whether she wanted it or not. My heart ached, my throat, the back of my eyes. Now she'd fallen, I thought, three miles through the air; now her cover was blown, her bones were picked clean.

I thought of all the secrets that must have come out in the crash, the secrets of 230 dead people, the sordid little things that didn't matter any more. Such a violation of privacy to die that way, with your body split open, your luggage gutted and strewn on the face of the sea, your bedraggled effects displayed in a moldy cardboard box. I thought of what might float to the surface: the pornography and the paraphernalia, the drugs, the works. And I thought of all the family myths that wouldn't survive the scrutiny, the fingerprinting and the X-rays and the DNA matching, the documentation of scars and injuries, the five hundred versions of Agent Garcia all over the globe, peering into every last scrap of paper from a person's life. Clues, all of them, but not necessarily to a crime.

One man in the crash had left a cross-dressed corpse— news to his wife back in Wapakoneta, Ohio. Another passenger, it turned out, had been gay, which his parents hadn't known and which his insurance company had seized upon as a pretext not to pay (AIDS risk, they'd argued, hence low life expectancy). And, after the passenger list was published, a Brooklyn man's landlord rang the FBI to announce that his tenant had been insane. When investigators searched the place, they found a filthy, trash-strewn apartment, fouled by a ravenous dog, with ancient newspapers taped over the windows and one-dollar books from the Strand stacked to the ceilings. There were rambling writings all over the walls, outlining a major conspiracy against him by the teachers' union, but nothing to suggest he planned to blow up a plane. He was over forty, the news reports said, but without family, an apparent "danger sign."

By that standard, I thought, they'd have suspected me. But I had family, I thought. I had the Families, I had Anna, and I had Grandma Belle. Maybe I'd even give Uncle Larry a call.

I stood up and, filling a jug from the kitchen, watered the African violets on the windowsill. The sun was strong and they looked parched, ashen, but I knew, from previous bouts of neglect, that they had considerable capacity to revive. I washed my face, put on a clean white T-shirt and jeans, brushed my teeth, made the bed. Then, not knowing what else to do, I went online and, out of habit, checked the Families site, FIN, the FBI, altexplanation.com and crashtalk.com. Crashtalk said, citing inside information, that the airframe had been stressed, that there were indications of an early overpressure event. People on altexplanation were discussing the dangers of the supercooled drizzle droplet. The FBI page said, as it had for nineteen days: *Information from the public is always critical to the ability of law enforcement to do its job. If you should have any information concerning this tragic incident, please contact the FBI at 1-888-245-4636. All calls will be kept in the strictest confidence.*

Very soon now, I felt, I would stop all this searching. I didn't even know what I was looking for any more.

A small faction on the Families site was holding out for the missile theory (coverup, friendly fire) but otherwise there seemed to be a growing consensus that static electricity was to blame. A consulting engineer explained that static charges are often suspected as the triggering event in fuel explosions that cannot otherwise be explained. A static charge—think of your nylon socks on the carpet, he said, think of petting the cat—is created by the friction of two dissimilar materials rubbing together. This kind of charge can create a risk of fire.

The center fuel tank of FIN 770 was primed for a

possible explosion since it held very little fuel and had been overheated, idling on the runway, to the point that there was a dangerous mix of vapor and air. There were two possible scenarios, apparently: the leak scenario and the dissipation malfunction scenario, but I didn't bother to read more about them. Or, alternatively, electricity from high-voltage lines might suddenly have jumped to low-voltage lines, such a leap being possible, in principle, anywhere the two lines are bundled together.

The problem with this theory, he said—or, perhaps, the beauty of it—is that it can never be proved. Static electricity leaves no trace, and the explosion of the fuel tank damaged or destroyed everything around it. So the evidence might itself have been consumed in the blast. Static, he concluded, is "a phantom."

That, I thought, is probably good enough for me. It wasn't an explanation, but it would do. I could live with the idea of the errant, elusive spark, the self-consuming cause. The friction of unlike substances. It made sense to me, gave me a kind of peace.

I turned off the computer, deleting, before I did, all the crash-related bookmarks. I called Maude, who said she had some photographs she wanted me to see. Old ones and new ones, Eleanor just before she left. Later in the week, I said, how about then? I called Lauren to see if she was free for lunch. She wasn't—office hours, she said, not that the lazy bums ever bothered to come—but tomorrow would be fine, Café Simone at one. I thought I might go to a movie that afternoon, but I'd have to pick one, I knew, with no violence, no blood, no death, no car crashes, no ambulances, no coffins, no people crying, no happy families, no unhappy families, no mothers, no babies, no partings, no reunions. I wasn't sure if such a movie existed.

16

Wednesday, December 19

I didn't recognize her when I first saw her, waving, anxiously, from behind the glass doors, which opened automatically to disgorge, in a miserly manner, one passenger at a time. I wore on my face, I imagined, the same expression as all the other new arrivals—beaming yet uncertain, some ancient fear of abandonment tensing our features until, ah! the familiar faces crystallized from the crowd. But Bridget looked unfamiliar at first, tall, with a strange shaggy haircut and a new, lip-distending set of braces. "Auntie Kim!" she called, nervous, high-pitched, and then I saw Sally beside her, also waving, and, behind them, looking, for some reason, in the wrong direction, Angus and Anna.

My sister's body felt strange as I hugged it, solid and fat across the back, the fabric of her dress damp with sweat. I couldn't remember when last we'd hugged like this, hard, as if we meant it. I felt sweaty too, overdressed, having been, as always, unable to believe, while packing in New York, that it really was brilliant summer somewhere else, that I'd soon be able to bare my arms. It always felt unnatural to me, perverse, to travel within a day from midwinter to midsummer, my body responding to the sudden warmth like a sluggish, squeamish creature roused from hibernation.

Angus hugged me next, his clothes reeking of cigarette smoke, his body bony and jittery to the touch. Then, gentlemanly, he commandeered my luggage cart, pointing it toward the exit. The girls succumbed politely to my embraces; Sally, small and sturdy, with a round face, still a child in her T-shirt and shorts; Bridget, in the hair shirt of adolescence, shifting and fidgeting, tugging at her ear, studying my clothes (what was I thinking, wearing black?).

Anna and I took a good look at each other, our eyes meeting over their heads. She looked older, more harried, baggier about the eyes. And I must look, I imagined, haggard and pale, some kind of spiny sea creature unused to the light.

"Well," Anna said. "Let's get you home. You must be exhausted."

"Not so bad, actually," I said. "I did get some sleep on the plane—" Which wasn't true, unless you defined sleep as a tense, prickly state of semiconsciousness, sustained, like a meditation, by the drone of the engines, devouring space.

"Plane full?" she asked. "It looked pretty full, all these people just streaming out of customs."

"Yep," I said. "Packed." I didn't tell her that I had surveyed my copassengers closely, not, as before, for their sex appeal, but in an attempt to predict which of them, should we crash, for instance, on a frozen peak in the Andes, would be the one to devise a way to make blankets out of seat covers and drinking water out of snow, and

which the one to trample, screaming for his mother, over
the gangrenous feet of his fellow survivors. And—a tough
call—which the one to propose eating the rest of us.

Nor did I tell her how, shortly after takeoff, a luggage
bin had popped open across the aisle and I had ducked,
reflexively, into the brace position, causing my neighbor, an
overpainted Afrikaner businesswoman, to roll her eyes.

"Shall we . . . ?" Anna asked, pointing with her chin
toward the "Exit" sign. "Got everything? Come on, girls,
stay close now."

As we maneuvered, en masse, through the crowds, I
was distracted by how, in my mind, the Johannesburg
airport had shrunk: how small and shabby it now seemed,
a teeming, inefficient operation, something from the third
world, as opposed to the glamorous and imposing space
I recollected from childhood, a futuristic edifice of which
only your best clothes were worthy. The days, I thought,
when air travel was still an elegant undertaking, like an
ocean voyage, rather than, as now, a matter of herding as
many bodies as possible into a tin can. Some of which —a
cost of doing business—never arrive.

"Watch your step, Kim," Angus warned, as we exited,
past an armed guard, into the day. The air hit my skin
like a hairdryer's blast. And then the familiar shock of the
light, always, anew, a surprise—so brilliant, so enormous,
so unsparing.

"Wow," I said, fishing in my handbag for my sunglasses,
"it's bright. I always forget how bright it is."

"Was it snowing in New York?" Sally asked, shyly.
"When you left?"

"No," I said. "We actually haven't had any snow yet

this winter, it's been pretty mild." They believed, I'd discovered, that I inhabited a perpetual blizzard. Snow, for them, was something that existed only on Christmas cards or television, and in the New York City of their imaginations, permanently aswirl with snowflakes. They sent me, as gifts, bulky hand-knitted socks, mohair lap-rugs, little afghans for Ella.

Reaching the curb, we waited while Angus went to fetch the car from the lot. Bridget positioned herself as a lookout, a few feet from us, scanning the stream of traffic, while Anna stood guard over my luggage. After the fifteen-hour flight, I felt glazed, pixilated, unreal. The cars that chugged by looked, to my eyes, diminutive, like toys. The air smelled of petrol and eucalyptus, plus something else, earth perhaps. And the vegetation on the center divider looked alien and oddly menacing, tall plants with spiky leaves and lurid orange blooms like the heads of birds. I couldn't remember what they were called.

The light roared down. I began to roll up my sleeves.

"Watch your bag, Kim," Anna warned, anxiously. "Sal, hold Auntie Kim's handbag while she does that. They'll snatch it right from under your nose."

"Here's Dad," Bridget announced. "I see him coming."

Anna insisted that I sit in the front seat, while she ensconced herself with the girls in the back, keeping up a constant stream of chatter all the way home, pointing out, along the route, landmarks which I no longer recognized, or the sites of now-vanished landmarks, which I no longer recalled. I said little, preoccupied as I was with fighting back panic every time the car turned a corner or crossed the stream of traffic, at which point I, accustomed to driving

on the right-hand side, would be seized by the nightmare
conviction that Angus had decided, for some reason, to
disregard the rules of the road and drive us headlong to
our deaths.

Their house was unfamiliar, too, an anonymous suburban bungalow with neat flowerbeds and a small swimming
pool. They'd moved since my last visit, four years earlier—
further out of town and, to my eyes, slightly downmarket.
As the electric gates swung open, I noticed a sign warning,
in three languages, of the dog (black icon with pointy teeth)
and another announcing, in just one, that this property
was protected NIGHT AND DAY by a GLADIATOR security
system.

"At last," Anna said, showing me into a painfully tidy
living room, magazines fanned out just so on the coffee
table. "Now you can just put your feet up, have a cup of
tea. But you probably need the loo first, don't you? Bridge,
show Aunt Kim where the cloakroom is."

I washed my face with cold water, dabbed it with the
embroidered guest towel. I brushed my teeth with the
throwaway toothbrush from the airline. Then I tried to
repair my makeup—lipstick, powder, concealer—but I still
looked unhealthy, undercooked. My hair needed washing.
My feet were swollen, my back ached. I longed for a hot
bath, for solitude, for sleep. But there was going to be tea
and chitchat, a special cake, I'd been told. I took a deep
breath, catching a whiff of pot-pourri. I looked into my own
blank eyes.

"All right," I told myself, "you're here."

*   *   *

ANNA HAD INSISTED, as the months went by and Eleanor remained missing, that we hold some kind of ceremony. "For the girls," she kept saying, though we both knew that wasn't necessarily why. I'd held out, for a long time: it was too soon, still too soon, always too soon, what if, God forbid, we had the ceremony and then . . . ? But Anna had become increasingly insistent, surprising me with what I felt to be a role reversal: surely I should have been the one pushing for a quick, if symbolic, end to the waiting, surely she should have been the one continuing to hold out hope, or, at the very least, some notion of the decent interval? "I just don't want to go into the new year like this," she began saying, somewhere around the end of October, and I realized that this boundary had become real to her, had acquired psychological solidity. And then I realized that I, too, didn't want to enter into another year, another cycle of the calendar, in the same suspended state. A state that had become, for me, a pretext not to reenter my own life, or, more to the point, reinvent it.

My three-month leave from Hite Consulting had become a six-month leave. They didn't want to lose me and I, still in limbo, couldn't quite bring myself to quit. I knew, however, that I wouldn't be back. They probably did too.

This had presented me, for the first time in my life, with the problem of what to do with myself all day, every day, from seven in the morning until eleven at night. The problem had seemed insoluble, at least without large doses of alcohol, for a month or so, and then, responding on impulse to a notice on the bulletin board of my gym, I had ended up volunteering to tutor third, fourth, and fifth graders at a school in the Lower East Side. I taught them reading, geography, and, when no one else was available, math. It gave me something to do, somewhere to go, a reason to get out of my pajamas five days a week. I couldn't say that I really enjoyed it—the children got on my nerves, nobody had ever taught them to sit still and pay attention—but something kept me going back. The time went by quickly. The children's lives were sad. And, eventually, I learned patience. Enough, anyway, for the task at hand.

The investigation of the crash continued; I followed it in a perfunctory way. By December, 214 victims had been recovered, 213 positively identified. The body of Eleanor Lilian Roth, seat 33B, was still missing. We had been warned, by FIN, the FBI, and the NYPD, that it would probably never be found. Anna and I each had a theory: I believed that Eleanor had been blown to bits, vaporized, in the explosion, that nothing of her remained. This was not, as Anna claimed, physically impossible. Anna preferred to think that her mother was resting, peacefully, on the bed of the sea, carried somehow—ocean current or blast wave— beyond the borders of the search. We both believed that she might still be found, and knew, at the same time, that she wouldn't be; believed that we might yet bury her and, at the same time, that her body would remain, as it perhaps had always been for me, an imaginary one.

Autopsies had shown that at least nineteen passengers had survived the explosion, the fire, and the fall: both smoke and water were found in their lungs, suggesting that they were still breathing, still gasping for air, as they went under. I didn't like to think about that. Nor had I accepted the airline's invitation to visit the hangar where the plane was being reconstructed, to view the giant, reeking wreck of the 747. Not when I found out that we Families were required, ahead of time, to sign a release saying we wouldn't sue the airline for "mental distress" arising from our visit.

My mind was quieter now, my days and nights too, except for a single, haunting dream. I'd had the dream about three months after the crash—"perfectly normal," a "sign of healing," according to Christina Barnes—and it had left me shaken, transformed, as if it had happened in my waking life—more real, even, than that.

I was in a little house somewhere, in the dark, an odd little house, ramshackle. Outside, nearby, was the ocean; I couldn't see it but could hear it, the muted slap and mutter of the waves. My mother walked into the living room with a magazine, sat down, and began to read. And my heart leapt with incredulous joy. So she wasn't dead after all, it'd been a mistake, she'd just been away for a while and now she was back.

"Mom," I began, excitedly, "I thought you were . . ." Then I stopped in mid-sentence, confused, unsure. I'd been going to tell her about the mistake, that I'd thought she was dead, but now I suddenly doubted myself, doubted whether the crash had happened or not. She looked up at me, indistinct in the violet light.

"Mom," I began again. But there she was, in front of me, so, with a new surge of elation, I changed my mind: the crash had happened after all, but she'd survived. She was here, wasn't she, in the flesh? She'd been in the hospital for a while, the burn unit, but now she was back. She was well.

"Mom," I began again, jubilantly, "I thought you . . ."

Again, I stopped, confused. I had been about to tell her, again, that I'd thought she'd died. But what if, I thought, she really is dead and she doesn't know it? How will she handle the news? I can't tell her that, I thought, and desolation sifted back into my heart.

"Where were you, Mom?" I asked her. "Where've you been?"

I moved closer to her chair. I could hardly see her in the dusk, I wasn't sure if I'd hear her if she spoke. The dream was fading, receding. But, as I awoke, I felt I knew what she was going to say: that, wherever it was, she'd been lonely there, she'd been going to pieces, she'd been unable to get back.

The dream had left me steeped in sadness, but at the same time grateful, as if, in fact, I'd had a visit. Not from some region beyond death—I didn't believe in that—but from the Eleanor who lived inside me, with whom, I believed, I might be beginning to reach some kind of accommodation. It was the first time I'd thought about her loneliness, her profound isolation, rather than my own. It was also, I think, the first time I understood that she was dead.

THE NEXT MORNING, we went—Anna, the girls, and I—to the church where Anna wanted to hold the ceremony, the same stone church where our parents had been married, where Roger had been buried, where Bridget and Sally had been christened. I had slept for almost twelve hours, a black and dreamless sleep, waking in Sally's narrow bed sweaty and, for a few seconds, afraid: a shelf of stuffed animals looming over me, brilliant shards of light piercing the broderie anglaise. It had taken me a whole, wild arpeggio of heartbeats to recall where I was. Now, still feeling discombobulated, even after a pot of strong tea, feeling like a peeled shrimp in the boiling light, I stared at a bald and raggedy patch of ground. This was, Anna informed me, part of the church's "memory garden." This was where she wanted to plant a tree.

"What's a memory garden?" I asked.

Bridget looked at me pityingly, as if I were feeble-minded. "It's like," she said, flipping her hands open, fingers splayed, "when people are cremated, or whatever, and they don't have, like, a grave, so you put a plaque or whatever for them. A stone, or something."

"Or," Anna added, "if people don't want to have a religious ceremony when they die, but their families still want a way, you know, a place, to remember them. Then they put a plaque or they plant something. Look—" and she gestured to the little plots around us, lushly planted, mostly with pansies or chrysanthemums, and with a fragrant mauve flower that looked something like Queen Anne's lace but whose name, from my childhood, I couldn't recall.

"So you don't have to have a, you know, a church ceremony?" I asked, cautiously.

"You don't *have* to," Anna replied, equally warily, "but that's what we were thinking of."

We looked at each other over the unplanted earth.

"I just think—" I began.

"Well, that's all up for—" she said, at the same time. We both stopped, then she continued. "All up for discussion."

"I think," I said, "it would be nicer, realer, you know, not to bring religion into it. Especially . . ."

"Yeah, I know," she said, hastily. "Though, technically, that's all through the mother, isn't it?" I understood that she was alluding, in the only way she could, to Eleanor's Jewish heritage, to the embarrassing problem of Leonard.

"Well, you know," I said, and was surprised to discover that I meant it, "whatever you like. It's really for you, for the girls. For her, too, what she would have wanted."

"No," Anna said gently, touching my arm, "it's for you too. Mainly for you, really, because you're so far away. We can come anytime, water the tree." Tears stung, suddenly, in my eyes. I was grateful for my sunglasses, grateful for the blinding light.

"I don't know," I said. "Maybe we could all just say something, out here. As we plant the tree. Each say, you know, what we want to say." Whatever, I thought, that might be. I didn't think I'd know until the moment I opened my mouth to speak.

"We could do that," she said. "Sal could write a poem, she writes beautiful poems. Wouldn't you like to write a poem for Nana, Sal?" Sally shrugged, shyly, squirmed a little. "I might read a psalm, though." Anna looked at me, anticipating objection. I nodded. She relaxed.

"What tree were you thinking of?" I asked, after a pause. "And anyway, how do you get to plant a whole tree, when everyone else just gets enough room for a few pansies?"

"Because of the, you know, the circumstances," she said, glancing at Sally, who was making, with precise, repeated motions, an elaborate arabesque from the toeprints of her sandals in the dust. The dust, the earth there, as I had forgotten, was red. The color of rust, the color of dried blood.

"But what tree?" I repeated.

"We were thinking of a mimosa. Mom loved the big mimosa tree in our old garden, you remember, how she would come in sometimes with all those sticky little yellow blossoms in her hair, say how much she loved the smell?" To my shame, I did not.

I tried to think of other trees I could remember: jacaranda, blooming in a purple haze; plum tree, heavy with bees in the spring; mulberry, with the heart-shaped leaves, thorn tree, which you had to watch out for. Eleanor had taught me the names of all the flowers—mesembryanthemum, agapanthus, protea, salvia, Barberton daisy—but not, for some reason, the trees. Strelitzia! I thought, suddenly: that's the flower with the birdlike head.

"Mimosa?" I asked. "Don't they get huge, though?"

"Not really," said Anna, with a shrug, as if the distant future didn't concern her anyway. We stared again at the shabby patch of soil. Bridget, losing interest, wandered off. Anna looked as if she might be growing tearful. No sunglasses. I wanted to warn her about UV damage, cataracts, all the things that could happen to one's body if one didn't protect it.

"Come on, girls," Anna said, grasping Sal in a warm, one-armed hug, "let's go and have a nice rich tea somewhere."

We drove to the shopping mall, because it was safer—armed guard to watch the car, armed guards at the entrances—and sat at a little café, outside, which was really inside, with a green-and-white striped umbrella to shade us from the fluorescence. Anna ordered tea and scones, Bridget iced coffee, NO whipped cream, Sally orange juice and *melktert*, and I, without thinking, a Coke float. Anna looked at me skeptically.

"Coke float?" she asked. "That what you drink in New York?"

"Just feel like one," I said, sheepishly. "My body doesn't know what time it is."

That Saturday, Anna told me that she had arranged a small party for me to meet some of her and Angus's friends, friends who'd been, as she put it, "sterling" throughout her ordeal.

"Great," I said, pausing in my efforts to decipher the local newspaper. There were endless reports of crime and violence (carjackings, knifings, infanticide, rape), interspersed with cheesy pinups, home-grown beauties in thongs. Everything seemed faintly alarming, faintly dire. Even the supermarket ads alarmed me: things cost, thanks to inflation, about five times what I expected them to. I thought of Weimar Germany, pictured taking a sack of rands to the chemist's shop to buy Pears soap. "What time?"

"About four?" she said.

"Four? What kind of party is this?"

"A tea party, silly. It's easier for people who have kids . . . and, you know, people don't really like to be on the roads at night any more."

"A tea party? That's so civilized. We don't have tea parties in New York, no one has time. And no one drinks tea. But I was kind of hoping it would be, like a, a drinks party, you know."

"Don't worry," she said, with a wry glance, "we hit the sherry at five."

Anna, I had discovered—or rediscovered—had a slight

edge to her, a dry, witty manner that we'd both acquired, I realized, from Roger. For some reason, I always forgot this quality of hers as soon as we parted: from a distance of 8,000 miles, she devolved unfailingly in my mind to a fat, dull housewife, bovine, inert. This was not, nor had it ever been, the case; I wondered why I'd needed so badly to believe it was. I wondered if I'd be able to hold on to my sense of her, this time—whether I'd be able to retire the dumb housewife, that tired old thing. At the moment I was enjoying Anna's sharpish tongue, the way she wielded it, in a kindly, grumbling way, on Angus and the girls, Angus having been dispatched earlier with a shopping list. I was also enjoying watching, from my sunny spot at the breakfast table, long since cleared, the humming, efficient manner in which she multitasked in the kitchen, icing a chocolate cake, feeding the dog, and rinsing some lettuce while checking, periodically, on the progress of a batch of cheese puffs. If I'd been expecting twelve guests in a few hours' time, I would have been running around in a perfectionistic frenzy, micromanaging my world with lists, cleaning supplies, and monomaniacal quests for the perfect cocktail napkins.

"Need some help?" I asked, halfheartedly.

She looked up from the sink, arched one eyebrow. "Uh, no," she said, knowingly, "you just stay right where you are. Relax a bit. Read the paper."

"I've finished the paper," I said. "Bloody depressing."

"I know," she said, drying her hands. "You get so used to it, though . . . So what do you feel like doing? Want to have a swim? Or do you feel ready to tackle the garage?" The garage was where Eleanor's documents were stored, as well as Belle's. I was planning to do some poking around.

"Not yet," I said, "but soon. Tomorrow, maybe, or Monday." I stood up, looked through the window bars at the small, neat, sparkling pool. "Where are those girls, anyway? Why aren't they outside on a day like this?"

"Kim," Anna said, indulgently, "it's always a day like this, remember? Sal's in her room, probably, reading. Kid reads all the time. Or drawing—she's doing this weird kind of cartoon strip, a whole planet of dragons, it's quite amazing really."

"That one's going to be the artist in the family," I said. She reminded me, obliquely, of myself at ten.

"I hope so," Anna replied.

"Or the unhappy one."

"Or both——"

"And Bridge?" I asked. "Where's she?"

"Listen," Anna said. "Can't you tell?" From somewhere down the hall, from behind a closed door, came the unmistakable strains of Ricky Martin. "She's got a couple of school friends over today, Marion and Thandi. God knows what they're up to in there . . ."

"Thandi?" I said. "Eleanor must be spinning in her grave . . ."

"Or she would be, if she had one," Anna added, and, after a split second of hesitation, we both burst out in laughter, barking out in relief, release, in the sheer violation of taboo, laughing and laughing, laughing helplessly, laughing at the spectacle of the other laughing, Anna clutching a dish towel to her midriff as she leaned over the sink, as if in pain, I with my head in my hands, laughing and laughing, tears, surprisingly wet, surprisingly salty tears, an inexhaustible supply of them, running down my face.

AT THAT MOMENT there was one thing I wanted to tell Anna—it almost spilled out, in a rush—but I didn't and probably never would. I was afraid she wouldn't understand, that she might even be appalled.

In the weeks and months after the crash, I'd discovered that I didn't want to see the plane, had no interest in inspecting the wreckage in the hangar or the large, spiral-bound books containing photograph after photograph of orphaned possessions. I had no interest in taking a trip out with the Coast Guard to some arbitrary spot on the ocean's face, the coordinates of the crash, and trying to summon an appropriate response. But I did want to know—shamefully and secretly—what it might feel like to fall.

This obsession grew in me, covert, stubborn as a cyst. So one Sunday morning, acting on blind impulse, I went online to find a place within a two-hour radius of New York where I could take skydiving lessons—not at some future date but right then, that very day. Without giving myself time to think, I took a cab to Grand Central and got the next train, staring out, my mind a perfect blank, at the bright blue sky, the dense, fleshy clouds, the first vivid intimations of autumn on the trees.

The skydiving school was crowded, chaotic, more like a mob of people clamoring for a ride at Disney World than the serious, disciplined corps of risk-takers I had imagined. I was told I'd have to wait an hour or two for a slot, which I was content to do, reckoning that it would give me time to observe the goings-on, to get a sense of what would be expected of me, to prepare myself mentally. But then, within ten minutes, the man with the clipboard was back, saying that someone had dropped out (odd turn of phrase at a skydiving school) and I could go with the next group, right then.

"But," I asked, "don't I get any training . . . ? Any practice . . . ?" I had pictured doing dives and rolls into the dirt, military-style, from a wooden tower.

"The instructor will tell you everything while you're putting on your suit."

The instructor, a small, wiry man, made sexist jokes with a colleague—about who always got the cute ones and the physiological effects thereof—while he brusquely buttoned and belted me into the jumpsuit and harness. The legs and sleeves of the suit needed to be rolled up; everything felt entirely too big and bulky, as if I were a child. He told me that he would strap himself to me, when the time came, and that I should just follow his movements, nothing to it. As we walked to the plane—strong, restless breeze on the runway, a feeling of being, out there, somewhere illicit, exposed—he demonstrated the position I should assume during free fall (feet down, which at the time seemed obvious) and reminded me to bend my knees on landing. This was the sum total of my instruction. He also asked me if I wanted to pull the cord myself, or whether I wanted to leave it to him. Leave it to him, I said. He showed me how.

"Yes, but you do it," I said. "I don't trust myself."

The plane was cold and bare inside, hollow, metallic, and

we sat in two long rows, facing each other, as soldiers do (a configuration known to be safer, but not as cost-efficient as the nose-to-tail orientation of passengers on commercial flights). There were, perhaps, some twenty of us, neophytes and instructors, some engaging in loud braggadocio, most silent. I didn't look at anyone, nor did I look out of the window. I concentrated on not thinking about anything, on being aware only of the loud, rattling roar of the engine and the cold metal against my rear. I concentrated particularly on not thinking about what, in a few minutes, I was about to do.

Then, suddenly, in a rush of wind, the door was open. We all stood up, crouching under the low ceiling, and shuffled forward single file like a chain gang, the instructors now strapped umbilically to their charges. It felt odd to be so close to someone I didn't know, his pelvis against my buttocks as if we were lovers spooning together, and I concentrated instead on trying to shuffle in step with him, down the long, inexorable aisle to the door. Pairs of divers were dropping out, methodically, one pair at a time: nobody balked or screamed. And then I was next, one step away from the impossibly loud, cold, turbulent threshold; I felt a subtle pressure from behind, I shut my eyes, knowing I'd never do it if I didn't, stepped forward, and jumped.

Free fall is a misnomer, implying, as it does, the body dropping like a stone through space. Instead— the first, great shock—the air is like a sea, a rough sea, with huge waves seizing and buffeting you, manhandling you, roughhousing with you, so that you literally don't know which end is up. We live, after all, in a vast

ocean of air: most of the time, clinging to the earth
like bottom-feeders, we forget that fact. I found myself
gasping and crying out, flailing like a drowning person,
struggling to straighten myself into a vertical, feet-
down position, but not having a clue, in the brutal shock
of such force, where down was or where, for that matter,
my feet were. I could feel the instructor struggling
against me, pulling me in another direction, counteract-
ing all my instincts, which had now become useless,
obsolete. I could hear myself gasping—loud, urgent gasps
for air.

And then, just in time—a powerful yank upward, the
slow-motion unfolding of the chute, and the sudden, blissful
arrest: the body instantly regains its orientation, your
eyes—which you didn't know had been closed—open, and
there beneath you, in its heartbreaking, variegated beauty,
is the earth.

In those endless, ecstatic minutes, as you float closer
and closer to the ground, you are calm, you are raptur-
ous, you are more alive than you have ever been. Like
the slowest imaginable zoom lens, you take everything in,
you see everything, not just the dollhouse scale of our
human life—our tiny patches of turf, the timid parallels
we paint on parking lots—but every leaf, every stone,
every dapple of light, every detail of this inexplicable,
profligate planet: why have you never noticed this before,
why has it escaped your attention, the miraculous beauty
of the world?

You coast softly, sweetly, to the earth. You land gently,
on bended knee. You have not thought of Eleanor once,
of plane crashes, of death. You are thinking, instead,

about being alive. You are triumphantly, ecstatically alive. And your most intense desire, at that moment, is to go right back up there and do it again. But this time, alone.

ACKNOWLEDGMENTS

I would like to acknowledge my indebtedness to the following works, which helped inform my imagination during its long free fall: "There Are Survivors," by Carolyn Ellis, *The Fall of Pan Am 103* by Steven Emerson and Brian Duffy, *Black Box* by Nicholas Faith, *Takeoff* by Daniele del Guidice, *Hijack: The Survivors' Story* by Katie Hayes and Lizzie Anders, *Lockerbie* by David Johnston, *Inside the Sky* by William Langewiesche, *The Black Box* edited by Malcolm MacPherson, *In the Blink of an Eye* by Pat Milton, *Deadly Departure* by Christine Negroni, *Am I Alive?* by Sandy Purl, *The Downing of TWA Flight 800* by James Sanders and *Prehospital Emergency Care & Crisis Intervention* (Prentice Hall).

I would also like to thank the Bogliasco Foundation, the Tyrone Guthrie Centre, and Hunter College for their support. For research assistance, I would like to thank Kris Cheppaikode and Cheryl Friedman. For shelter and sustenance of various kinds, I'm grateful to Larry Bender and Martine Guyot-Bender, Simon Byers, Alan Rowlin, Maurice Isserman, and Marcia Williams. Heartfelt thanks, too, to Michele Berdy, Kim Witherspoon, Maria Massie, and my editor, Geoffrey Mulligan.